The
Uninvited

By Cat Winters

The Uninvited

Young Adult
The Cure for Dreaming
In the Shadow of Blackbirds

The Uninvited

CAT WINTERS

WILLIAM MORROW

An Imprint of HarperCollins*Publishers*

THE UNINVITED. Copyright © 2015 by Catherine Karp. All rights reserved. Printed in the United States of America. No part of this book may be used or reproduced in any manner whatsoever without written permission except in the case of brief quotations embodied in critical articles and reviews. For information address HarperCollins Publishers, 195 Broadway, New York, NY 10007.

HarperCollins books may be purchased for educational, business, or sales promotional use. For information please e-mail the Special Markets Department at SPsales@harpercollins.com.

FIRST EDITION

Designed by Diahann Sturge

Library of Congress Cataloging-in-Publication Data has been applied for.

ISBN 978-0-06-234733-6

15 16 17 18 19   OV/RRD   10 9 8 7 6 5 4 3 2 1

For my parents, who filled my childhood with books and love

If I can stop one heart from breaking,
I shall not live in vain;
If I can ease one life the aching,
Or cool one pain,
Or help one fainting robin
Unto his nest again,
I shall not live in vain.

—EMILY DICKINSON

The
Uninvited

The Buchanan branch of the American Protective League, better known as the APL, continues to urge residents to report all suspicious activity to the group's headquarters at the Chamber of Commerce on Willow Street. As a reminder, typical enemy behavior includes the following tendencies: food hoarding; interference with the draft; slackers who refuse to enlist for military duty; refusal to purchase Liberty Bonds; possession of books, sheet music, and phonograph albums celebrating German culture; speaking a language other than English; the use of hyphenated nationalities when describing one's self (e.g., "German-American," "Polish-American," etc.); anti-war sentiments; the production of Socialist pamphlets and newspapers; and the discussion of unionization among factory workers. The APL states that this country's best defense against espionage and other war-related crimes involves everyday Americans monitoring the loyalty of their neighbors. "We encourage each Buchanan citizen to do his part in chasing the dangerous specter of Germany out of Illinois," said local APL chief Charles Williams. "We commend every single individual who takes it upon himself to cleanse the country of the enemy."

—*Buchanan Sentinel*, October 4, 1918

Chapter 1

I admit, I had seen a ghost or two.

The childhood night my mother's father died, when silver moonlight graced the floorboards and the antique furniture in our front room, I came upon my granny Letty—gone one year and a month—rocking in my mother's chair, next to the upright piano.

Uncle Bert—gone since 1896—stood on our front porch at sundown on Independence Day 1912. The bitter smoke of his fat cigar stole through the metal screen of our front door, spoiling the aroma of Mama's cherry pie. A half hour after he left, we received a telephone call from my cousin, saying my aunt Eliza had died of appendicitis.

Uncle Bert again smoked on our porch the day my brother Billy was shot in the Battle of Saint-Mihiel in September 1918.

I likely don't need to mention that these Uninvited Guests

were not welcome sights. My mother saw them, too, and she agreed that such visits always signaled loss. Their presence suggested that the wall dividing the living and the dead had opened a crack, and one day that crack might steal us away to the other side.

Granny Letty paid another call to our house October 4, 1918. I saw her but a moment, standing in the yellow haze of twilight near the lace curtains of my bedroom, just an hour before my father and brother killed a man.

OUR FRONT DOOR BLEW OPEN and whacked the wall. The dogs barked. Someone groaned in pain. Mama's bare soles hurried down the staircase.

"What on earth happened?" she asked, her voice coming as a muffled shriek beyond the walls of my upstairs bedroom.

I rubbed at my forehead, finding my skin covered in sticky sweat. Spurred on by the panic surging through the house, I managed to climb out of bed after three days spent on my back with the flu. My legs buckled. I grabbed hold of my bedside table and knocked copies of *Motion Picture* magazine and Emily Dickinson's *Poems* to the floor with thumps and smacks and the wild fluttering of pages. The stripes of my brown and yellow wallpaper blurred and rippled before my eyes.

"What happened?" shouted Mama again from down below.

I pushed myself upright, fetched my robe from the back of my door, and eased my way down the staircase on the legs of a feeble old woman, not feeling at all like a twenty-five-year-old young lady used to farm work and activity. To keep my balance, I clung to the rail with both hands, as if clutching the helm of a sinking ship.

Down in the front room, my father guided my seventeen-year-old brother, Peter, toward the kitchen by half-dragging the boy beneath his armpits. Peter's right fist swelled and purpled and no longer looked like a human hand. Something dark lined the crevices in his knuckles and stained Father's overalls. The two of them resembled each other with such chilling similarity at the moment—wheat-blond hair, stocky Illinois builds, large blue eyes, dazed by booze and some unknown horror. The house reeked of whiskey because of them.

Mama hounded the men into the kitchen. I clasped my temples to keep my head from swaying off my neck and rolling to the ground—which it seemed inclined to do—and followed after everyone.

"What did you do?" Mama grabbed Peter by the wrist and pumped cold water from the sink over those ballooning fingers. Peter hollered with the same unholy racket he had made when he knocked out two teeth jumping off a fence at the age of five.

Father, his face bright red, perspiration dripping off his nose, braced himself against the kitchen table. "The Krauts killed our Billy," he said in a voice that was slurred and gravelly, "and they dumped this damned flu into our country. I read it in the paper. They turned the germs loose in an American theater."

"What did you do?" asked Mama again. "Whose blood is this?"

Father lowered his head toward the table and swayed. "The damned Kraut went and died."

I pulled my robe around my chest.

Mama turned off the water and gaped at my father.

"What are you talking about, Frank? What German went and died?"

Peter leaned over the sink and vomited. Father just stood there at the table and rocked from the alcohol and the aftermath of whatever violence they had just wreaked upon some poor soul.

"Those Krauts who own that furniture store—the last store in town owned by German immigrant bastards . . ." Father cleared his throat with a grinding ruckus that reminded me of our old tractor sputtering its last breaths. "One of them got himself killed."

Mama gasped. Before she could utter a word, Father added, "The police know. Everything will be fine. We don't want another Collinsville case, like that Prager lynching. No national attention."

He said all of this with his face hanging down toward the uneven grain that ran in scraggly lines across the table's blond wood.

Mama paled. "Are you saying that you and Peter killed a man tonight?"

"No." Father shook his head. "That wasn't a man. He was a German."

I turned and staggered out of the room.

I was done.

Our oak staircase seemed to stretch four stories high above me, but I grabbed the handrail and forced myself to ascend the steps, my breathing labored, the muscles in my back and legs quivering and threatening to send me toppling back down to the ground floor. My parents' shouts and cries down below roused me out of the delusion that this was all just the hallucination of a fever dream.

"Stop yelling at me, Alice!" said Father from the kitchen, his voice volleying across the dark-wood walls around me. "It was just a German. A goddamned German. You should be proud of your boy and me. You should be proud."

I shook all over and panted for air. Upstairs, the stripes on my bedroom walls continued to wiggle and blur, but I somehow changed into a skirt and a blouse and packed two canvas bags full of clothing, toiletries, Emily Dickinson's poems, and Peter's old copy of J. M. Barrie's *Peter and Wendy,* which I read to him when he was no more than ten. I also grabbed Billy's letters from the war, including my favorite one: an optimistic note that included Billy's caricature of one of my piano students—prim little Ruby Rogers—putting Kaiser Wilhelm to sleep by boring him with a sonata. Kaiser Willie snoozed on our settee and rested his feet on one of the hounds, while Ruby plunked on the keys of our piano.

I buttoned up my green wool coat and fitted my knit cloche over my hair, which I didn't even bother taking the time to pin up. With both suitcases and my purse in hand, I turned my back on the lace and ruffled bedroom that had housed me from infancy to womanhood, and I shut the door behind me.

Mama sat at the bottom of the staircase and cried into a handkerchief monogrammed with a gold *R* for our surname: Rowan. She looked hunched and small and old in the black dress she wore to mourn Billy. Her neck straightened when I brushed past her with my bags. Her damp brown eyes peered up at me with almost childlike astonishment.

"I need to go, Mama." I rested my luggage on the floor and wrapped my hand over her shoulder, which drooped from her stooped-over posture. "It'll likely take me a while to fully recover from this illness, but I can't stay here another minute."

She nodded with her lips pursed and grabbed hold of my fingers, her hand as cold as winter. "You should have left years ago, Ivy. You're twenty-five, for goodness sake. You wasted so much of your youth hiding away in this—"

"Don't." I squeezed her shoulder. "Don't make me feel like an old maid again. You know quite well I stayed because of—"

"I know." She nodded, her eyes moist and bloodshot. "Billy always called you 'Wendy Darling' because of how much you watched over him and Peter, didn't he?"

"That's what happens"—I peeked over my shoulder, toward the sound of Father clanking the neck of a whiskey bottle against an empty glass in the kitchen—"when one lives with Captain Hook."

"You should have gotten yourself married to Wyatt Pettyjohn after school."

"I've always been too choosy. You know that."

"Life's too short to be that choosy."

"For some people it is. But for others"—I swallowed and turned away from her white-streaked hair and red-rimmed eyes—"life's far too long to not be selective."

She removed her hand from mine.

I bent forward and kissed her cheek, tasting salt and the burn of her sorrow. "I'm not going far," I said, my voice low, my lips shaking. "Probably just to town for now."

"I can't even remember the last time you went to town."

"Helen dragged me out to a Douglas Fairbanks picture the afternoon before she left. Remember?"

"That was way back in July."

"I know." I stood up straight, my hand still upon her. "Come stay with me if you feel like leaving, too. I know the farm is doing well right now, but all that prosperity isn't worth"—I glanced back toward the kitchen again—"this."

"Yes." She wiped her eyes. "I will, darling. I'll join you if I need to."

I let her go, and a connection snapped. A binding stronger than the cord that had once tethered me to her womb frayed and split in two, and my stomach ached. The pain hit me again when I opened the front door and walked out on the commotion of Peter blubbering in the kitchen and Father choking on his drink. Despite my discomfort, I ducked my head out from under the black cloud that would now haunt my family worse than my Uninvited Guests, and I left that troubled white farmhouse.

Chapter 2

My westward journey led me close to a mile down a country lane to Willow Street, once called Werner Street, before the war made us cleanse the country of everything German. A train whistle pealed through the clear night air, and I heard the steady *click-clack, click-clack, click-clack* of the endless line of freight cars that would take a good fifteen minutes or more to traverse the heart of the town. My legs gained strength, and without a shred of regret, I passed the other farms in our pancake-flat Illinois terrain, toward the town I hadn't visited in three months, out of fear of brain-cleaving migraines and a paralyzing terror that the house would crumble to pieces if I dared to step away for a spell. Both brothers no longer belonged to me. Wendy Darling had failed her boys. Time to move onward.

Another mile ahead shone a constellation of streetlights in downtown Buchanan, where most of the businesses slept for the night. To my left, past the southbound bend of the Minter River, rose the mills and the factories that seemed almost a separate city of their own. The black outlines of smokestacks and rooftops as flat as the land bled into the darkness of the nighttime sky, and I almost believed I imagined their towering silhouettes. Our city made itself known for its textile industry and railcar manufacturing—plus we boasted the county seat—so we were somewhere, compared to hundreds of other towns speckled across the vast Midwest. Some of our buildings, including City Hall, even stood over three stories high, and most were built of brick and a fine Illinois limestone.

A quarter mile or so from the first downtown establishments, before I crossed the old covered bridge that spanned the river, a sign painted red on white rose up in the dark:

INFLUENZA!
DO NOT ENTER!

My feet stopped on the road, and a cold October breeze shook through my dress and my bones. The sign seemed primitive—medieval—like a warning for European travelers about to stumble upon the Black Death. It defied logic. Buchanan had been fighting influenza strains since it first existed in the 1860s, but no one had ever been stopped from entering the town because of it.

I kept plodding forward along Willow-not-Werner Street with my bags banging against the sides of my calves, and enter

11

the town I did. Another sign, a hospitable black-and-white one, greeted me as I came upon the business district.

WELCOME TO BUCHANAN, ILLINOIS!
FRIENDLIEST CITY IN AMERICA
POPULATION 12,500

I passed the barbershop, the *Buchanan Sentinel* headquarters, and the Moonbeam Theater, the latter in which Billy had spent his days and nights as the projectionist after he left home at the age of seventeen. A poster for a Mary Pickford film called *Johanna Enlists* caught my eye, and I remembered how much my chest had once fluttered with anticipation whenever I spotted new motion-picture advertisements. When we all still went to school, Billy, Helen Fay, Sigrid Landvik, Wyatt Pettyjohn, and I would sit on wooden folding chairs inside the darkened theater and watch marvelous flickering fairy tales, projected onto a bed sheet used as a screen—back when downtown Buchanan possessed magic. When Saturday afternoons tasted of heaven.

Ford delivery trucks rested alongside the curbs in front of several storefronts, the black paint gleaming beneath electric streetlamps with bright, bulbous casings. In front of other businesses awaited wooden wagons that would be drawn by horses in the morning. Telephone and electricity wires dangled overhead, strapped to ugly utility poles, and streetcar tracks ran the length of Willow Street, tying the business district to the Westside neighborhoods, where the nonfarming middle class dwelled. I saw rows of white awnings and autumn-kissed maples that hadn't yet shaken free of their leaves.

Up ahead another block, to my right, lay Liberty Brothers Furniture, which had been called some other name like Schreiner or Schumacher Furniture before the war. Unless I veered down a side street, I would be required to pass the store's front door and its prominent display windows on my way to my destination: the town's hotel. Furthermore, I *needed* to pass the store, to see—to witness with my own eyes—whatever grisly aftermath might await inside. Part of me hoped Father and Peter were simply telling a terrible tall tale, offering empty, drunken boasts about conquering the town's last remaining German business owners.

The light of the streetlamp in front of the store twinkled across a sidewalk littered with shattered fragments of glass. Someone had smashed the front windows and the pane of the door with a blunt and powerful object, perhaps Peter's baseball bat. Long streaks of yellow paint dribbled down the bricks and the black trim of the outer walls and formed soupy puddles on the cement. Spots of blood trailed out from the front door and disappeared behind me, toward our home. The entire scene made stories of the American Protective League's raids on German families and union headquarters sound tidy and civil in comparison.

I dared to tread a few steps closer to peek inside, and the soles of my shoes crunched across the sparkling shards. My mind conjured images of the Germans I'd seen on the propaganda posters—fleshy men in spiked helmets with hate raging in their animalistic eyes. *Huns,* we called them. *Boches. Krauts.* Like the lecherous Mr. Weiss, whom the citizens of Buchanan had kicked out of town for failing to buy Liberty Bonds. They smelled of sauerkraut, and they spat as they spoke. They loved beer and war and indulged in rape and torture the same way we enjoyed baseball and summer picnics.

Only one person stood inside the store amid the damaged furniture. It was a man, a young one near my age, also in his mid-twenties, if I had to wager. He had short brown hair with a soft hint of curl and broad shoulders that hunched as if in either pain or sorrow. Or both. He stood there in the middle of the mess my family had hurled upon the business, his hands stuffed in the pockets of his tan trousers, his face directed toward a dark stain that marred the floorboards. He wore a tweed vest and white shirtsleeves and looked to be a gentleman, not a brute.

Perhaps this wasn't one of the family members.

He raised his head, as if my gaze had formed a cold mark on the side of his neck, and he turned his face my way, revealing blue eyes and lips drawn in a taut line.

The dead man's brother.

I had seen him in the store once before when passing by on my way to purchase sheet music down the way, but I hadn't paid him much heed. I didn't even know either of the men's names. They were just "those Germans who sold tables and chairs."

I slipped back into shadow and continued onward with my bags. My shoes ground across more piles of glass before I reached the stone bank building next door and met with smoother sidewalk.

I would wait to make amends the next day, when the hurt wasn't so fresh and the sun softened the viciousness of night.

LIKE WERNER STREET ITSELF, the Werner Street Hotel had boiled, bleached, and scrubbed its German name clean at the start of the war a year and a half earlier. Therefore, it was the Hotel America that I entered with my bags weighing down my arms and my family's sins burning a hole through the center of my stomach. In the far corner, next to the sheer curtains covering one of the lobby windows, stood an American flag with a wilted, wrinkled air, as if it had tired of everything expected of it. Wicker chairs sat in welcoming angles in front of an unlit fireplace that smelled of ash, and blurry photographs of Buchanan's dirt-covered streets from the late 1800s hung on burgundy walls. Potted ferns attempted to lend a resort-style ambience.

Behind the front desk sat a fellow with red hair parted smack-dab down the middle of his skull—Mr. Greene, if I remembered his name correctly from Buchanan's second-most-notorious adultery story, as told to me by my friend Helen Fay. He lounged in a chair with his big brown shoes propped upon the wooden countertop. His face hid behind the October issue of *Blue Book*, my brothers' favorite fiction magazine because of the Edgar Rice Burroughs stories. His feet wiggled a little, and he seemed content, despite the rumors that his wife had left town with a handsome young anti-Prohibitionist only five months earlier.

"Good evening." I plunked my bags on the floorboards. "Do you have any rooms left tonight?"

Mr. Greene lowered the magazine to his lap and squinted at me through round wire spectacles. He possessed the type of aging-gentleman complexion that looked wrinkled and craggy and doughy white, with fuzzy little pipe-cleaner eyebrows that matched his strawberry hair.

"It's a little late for a lady to be traveling at night, don't you think?" he asked.

"Well, I . . . um . . ." I brushed the sweat from my palms on the sides of my skirt. "It's just . . . I was ill this past week, and now that I'm a little better I want a . . ." I swallowed down the quaver in my voice. "A respite from the house."

He nodded. "I had that same illness myself. Knocked me clear off my feet right here at the front desk."

"Oh. I'm sorry to hear that."

He waved away my concern. "Aw, no need to feel sorry for me. I'm still here. Unlike some . . ." He swung his feet off the counter and dropped his soles to the floor with a dull thud. "I keep hearing this particular strain of the flu is killing horrific amounts of people, especially down in the foreigner part of town."

"Oh?" I stiffened with my arms straight by my sides. "I . . . I didn't realize the flu had turned quite so serious. I saw the sign warning travelers not to enter Buchanan, but—"

"The germs spread at that Liberty Loan parade on the last day of September."

"I was already sick and missed the parade."

"Well"—he shook his head and knitted those pipe-cleaner eyebrows—"it's pretty bad. People are saying it's taking younger adults mainly. Healthy ones." He lifted his copy of *Blue Book* with all the pulpy newsprint pages flapping about. "If you want to know the truth, it reminds me more of a science fiction story than a regular old flu. There's something unnatural about it."

I pressed my hand against my right temple to stave off a bout of dizziness. "I'm sorry to hear it's that serious."

He opened a drawer and stuffed the magazine inside. "You know, I'm the one who should be sorry. Influenza isn't a very hospitable subject matter for a hotel looking to sell a good night's sleep, is it? Let me start over again." He folded his hands on the counter and sat up straight. "We do have vacant rooms if you'd care to stay for the night."

"Yes, I would. Thank you. Sh-should I . . ." I stepped toward the hotel's open register, smelling old pipe smoke and perfumes embedded in the fibers of the pages. "Should I fill out my name in here?"

"The fountain pen's not working." Mr. Greene cupped his right hand around his mouth and lowered his voice. "There's an APL fella who checked in a little while earlier." He gestured with his thumb toward a staircase upholstered in worn red velvet. "I think he broke the pen on purpose when he was snooping around in the register. Probably trying to run me out of business."

I glanced toward the stairs and dropped my voice to a whisper. "How do you know he's in the American Protective League?"

"He pretended to be from the gas company last month. Asked to inspect my pipes. I think he's spying on me."

"Why would he do that?"

"Because he's got nothing better to do. I'm one hundred percent American, though—don't worry about that." He nodded toward the wilted flag in the corner. "He won't find anything German here."

"Well, my own family would fall under the category of 'super-patriots,' so there's no need to worry about me either. Ooph." A hot flame of pain flared between my eyes. I winced and rubbed the bridge of my nose and thought of the German brother standing amid blood and battered furniture at Liberty Brothers. "I'm sorry. I'm still recovering from the illness. If you need to know my name, in spite of the broken pen, it's Ivy Rowan."

"Oh! Frank's daughter."

The pain deepened, planting spiked heels in my sinuses, splintering my bones with a steel pickax. "Yes. I'm his daughter."

"I went to school with him. I still see him at the saloon now and then."

"Yes, well . . ." I swallowed. "That's the only time you're likely to find him in town. The farm demands so much work these days. Our crops are helping to feed Europe."

Mr. Greene leaned forward on his elbows and peeked toward the staircase. "Say that last part a little louder," he said in another whisper. "Please."

"I said"—I raised my voice—"our crops are helping to feed Europe. The government pays us well, but the pressure is high."

He scowled and shook his head.

"But it's a good pressure," I added, allowing my words to echo across the burgundy walls for the APL informant to hear. "We're happy to grow our wheat for the starving overseas." I sighed, exhausted, my shoulders slumping. "I'm sorry, but I just really need that room."

"Sure, sure. I'll get you settled."

Mr. Greene stood and turned toward a grid of keys that hung on tiny golden wall hooks. With the soft clink of metal tapping wood, he fetched a silver one that dangled under the number twenty-two. "I'll help you with your bags." He pivoted back around on his heel. "I hope I haven't frightened you with all this talk of disease and death and"—another whisper—"*spies* before bedtime."

"No, it's all right." I forced a smile. "I've already survived the illness, and I hope my mother is strong enough to continue to avoid it. Hopefully, this is just a short scare that will pass swiftly."

"Let's hope. They're not panicking in Chicago yet, which is always a good sign."

"Yes, that's true."

I followed Mr. Greene and my swinging bags upstairs to the empty room, but I didn't dare admit that it wasn't the flu that pricked at the nape of my neck and drove me to glance over my shoulder every few seconds, as if a dead man stood there, waiting for me to apologize on hands and knees.

MY HOTEL BED CREAKED and wheezed worse than my bones and my lungs had during my bout with the fevers. If I stayed perfectly still, the creaking stopped, but then an awful silence gripped the hotel. I feared that the APL man stood on the other side of my wall, listening through a water glass to hear if I'd confess in my sleep my repulsion toward the German's murder. No floorboards whined from his footsteps, though. He didn't cough or belch or produce other bodily sounds made by men when they think ladies aren't listening.

For the past twenty-five years, I had fallen asleep to the clamor of Father and Mama bickering downstairs and the snores that ceaselessly rumbled from the boys' room next door to mine. The dogs were always barking out in the yard, and feet pattered nonstop through the house. Breezes rattled through the cracks between the windows and doors. The chimney whistled. Our home possessed a heartbeat, a pulse, and a steady breath that perpetually assured me that I never wanted for company. The noises told me that everyone remained alive and well despite the anger simmering and bubbling like molten lava beneath the foundation.

Nighttime silence, therefore, struck me as unnatural and wrong.

I curled onto my side with a low groan of bedsprings, and I hummed "Down in the Valley" to fill the room with some sort of sound. Eventually, my eyelids thickened and fluttered shut. I fought to block out visions of the shock of blood on Father's overalls, and over and over I imagined myself walking through the doors of that shattered and butchered German furniture store. I envisioned telling the murdered man's brother, *I'm sorry. It was my father and brother who killed him. I'm sorry. What can I*

*do to help? How can you purge me of this guilt that's now wedged
like a razor blade in my belly?*

My stomach burned for hours, moaning and complaining
and undulating with waves of shame-fueled pain—roiling, claw-
ing pain. Eventually, well past midnight, my brain succumbed
to a restless version of sleep, and I dreamed of a fall morning
ten years earlier, when I was fifteen and Billy twelve. Peter, just
seven, played somewhere off in the fields, chasing bugs or the
dogs, his blond hair blending in with the rustling stalks of corn.
Billy and I worked in the stable, raking the stalls, stirring up the
sweet scent of hay that epitomized the smell of our childhood.
He and I were the same height by then, and we shared the same
hair color—a blend of hues that people called everything from
dark blond to brown, and even red, depending on the light and
the beholder. We were known for our golden-brown eyes, freckled cheeks, and prominent cheekbones, supposedly inherited
from an Iroquois great-grandmother whom no one ever talked
about. People called us both "handsome," but that word always
made me feel like a boy.

In my dream, as in real life, Father walked in on us just as Billy
started flinging hay at me and chuckling with his rich belly laugh.
I froze when I saw Father standing at the stable's entrance—half
in shadow, half in sunlight. His thick arms, covered by the blue
sleeves of his work shirt, hung by his sides, and he narrowed his
eyes beneath his hat. His jaw tightened.

My heart leapt into my throat, for Father was always hollering
at Billy and tanning his hide for one thing or another.

Don't play the piano like your sister. That's a girl's instrument. Stop reading so much and get your damn head out of the clouds. Stand up straight, boy. You look like a half-wit.

"You think your chores are a joke, boy?" he asked in a low growl that turned my blood cold. "You know what I ought to do when you disrespect our farm and your pa like this?"

Billy stood there with the rake still poised in the air, frozen in the act of sending golden strands of hay flying off the rusted teeth.

"I ought to whack you on the side of the head," said Father, "and knock out all those lazy, pompous thoughts of yours."

Billy stood up straight, and with a boldness and defiance I'd never seen in him before, he tossed his rake into a pile of horse dung. "Is that why *you're* so stupid, Pops?" he asked, and my chest tightened. "Someone knocked out all of your intelligent thoughts by whacking you in the head?"

Father grabbed a shovel and ran at my brother. Before I knew what was coming, he raised the blade and struck Billy in the side of the head with the sickening thud of metal hitting bone. I screamed and felt my own brain crack wide open just from the sound alone. Billy dropped to the ground but didn't lose consciousness. He vomited during the rest of the day, and Dr. Lowsley came to visit. We had to say one of Billy's friends threw a baseball bat that accidentally smacked him in the head. We all lied for Father and prayed for Billy. Dr. Lowsley instructed us to wake Billy up throughout the night and check to make sure he stirred, but Mama's footsteps didn't whisper across the floor-boards to my brothers' room often enough.

Around midnight, I planted myself on the edge of Billy's bed, and I watched him for the rest of the night—just as I would watch over everyone in that house for the rest of my years within those walls.

My brain would split wide open again if I ever didn't keep the household intact.

MUSIC STIRRED ME AWAKE in the Hotel America. I opened my eyes and stared at the hulking black outline of a chest of drawers across the room, and for a good thirty seconds, all I could hear were my own ragged breaths.

There it was again—music.

Jazz music.

The faint syncopated rhythm of horns and drums and a lusty piano slipped through the window along with a draft and settled inside my soul. The sounds relaxed my shoulders, soothed my lungs, and erased the sharp aftertaste of the German's death and my dream about Billy and the shovel. Somewhere beyond the hotel's thick brick and mortar walls, people found the strength to pick up instruments and continue on with their lives, despite the strange influenza, despite the war, despite the murder that had knocked me sideways and thrust me out of my own home.

My toes bobbed to the beat of the percussion. Deep breaths

assuaged some of the burning in my stomach. I lay back down on the warm sheet and shut my eyes, and when I fell back to sleep, I dreamed I danced on a mahogany table, dressed in a giant pair of bright-blue butterfly wings . . . wearing absolutely nothing else but my naked skin.

Chapter 3

I opened the door of my hotel room and found a short, dark-haired man in a charcoal-gray suit loitering at the far end of the hallway. He leaned his right hand against the wine-colored wallpaper at the top of the stairs and seemed to be listening in on someone who whistled "For Me and My Gal" down in the lobby.

I dragged my bags out to the hall, doing my best to look my most American—if such a feat is at all possible when one is closing up a hotel room while wracked with guilt over a death.

The man turned my way, and I spotted a familiar young face with a stubby nose and thick, round glasses that magnified the eyes behind them into enormous brown orbs.

The orbs blinked at me.

"Ivy?"

"Oh. Lucas." I picked up my bags and wandered down the

hall toward the fellow, who happened to be one of Billy's closest pals. "What are you doing here?"

"Shh." He touched an index finger to his lips. "Never mind me. How's Billy over in France?"

I set my bags down again. "He's . . . umm . . ." I blinked back tears and rubbed my neck. My throat stung too much to speak.

"Oh, God." Lucas stood up from the wall. "Is he—?"

I nodded, my chin quivering.

"I'm so sorry. I didn't know."

"Thank you. We just found out last week."

"Jesus." Lucas turned his face back to the staircase. "I should have been over there with him. I should be with all of them. The draft board turned me down because of my danged eyesight."

"I'm sorry."

"I'm doing what I can here at home, though." He glanced at me out of the corners of his astronomical eyes and peeled back the lapel of his coat. A silver badge with the emblem of an eagle flashed at me from his vest. The words AMERICAN PROTECTIVE LEAGUE spanned the perimeter of the thing, surrounding the phrase SECRET SERVICE.

I shuddered in spite of myself.

"Well . . . I see" was all I could think to say.

Lucas closed his coat and folded his arms over his chest. "As a matter of fact, I think I'm about to catch a slacker."

"Oh?" I lifted my bags.

"Mr. Greene's son, Charlie, down there is eighteen, but he's not enlisting. The draft age just got dropped from twenty-one, and he's eligible to go."

"Well, I should actually be off . . ."

"Say, how old is your other brother, Peter?"

I stiffened with my elbows locked. "He's not eighteen until December, Lucas. We just lost Billy, for heaven's sake."

"He could still get in, though. Several boys write the number eighteen on the bottoms of their shoes. When the draft board asks, 'Are you over eighteen?,' the boys technically aren't lying when they say yes."

I stood there and gaped at this baby-faced buddy of Billy's who used to set up model trains with my brother in our basement and once ate a worm on a dare in Mama's vegetable garden. Lucas's brown eyes peered back at me through those bottle-cap lenses, and the edge of his silver badge poked out from beneath his gray coat.

"I'm sure Peter will enlist as soon as he's able," I said, and I maneuvered past him with my bags and headed down the stairs. "Good bye, Lucas."

He didn't respond, but I could feel the weight of those probing eyes of his on the nape of my neck. All the hairs back there bristled. An awful chill sliced down my spine.

Down in the lobby, in the morning's hazy yellow sunlight, a young redheaded fellow—Charlie, the "slacker," presumably— swept lint and coins from beneath the whicker chairs. He whistled to himself, clanked the change into his pockets, and paid no attention to me, so I waddled with my suitcases over to Mr. Greene at the front desk.

"Pleasant stay?" asked Mr. Greene, sliding *Blue Book* back into its drawer again.

"Yes, thank you."

"No problems from—?" He gestured with his head in the direction of the staircase and Lucas.

"No. Thank you." I unhooked the gold clasp of my handbag and fetched three crisp dollar bills from my cache of piano-lesson earnings. "Do you happen to know of anyone who's renting rooms nearby?"

"Well . . ." Mr. Greene slid my payment toward himself across the glossy countertop. "I'm sure any one of the women on Widow Street would be happy to take in a boarder."

"Did you say *Widow* Street?"

"Um, that's what . . ." He cleared his throat and averted his eyes from mine. "That's what we townies call Willow Street these days. Far too many young wives are losing husbands overseas, I'm afraid."

"So I've read in the newspaper." I swallowed and snapped the clasp shut. "Unfortunately, many of the widows—and their husbands—were my classmates."

"Yes, I suppose you might be that age."

"Men in their twenties are a dying breed, or so it seems."

"Well . . ." He scratched behind his right ear. "I reckon you should have no trouble finding a room with one of those nice young ladies, if you know them."

I bit my lip. "I haven't been very good about keeping in touch with everyone since school. I've been teaching piano lessons out at our farmhouse, you see, and . . . well . . ."

"You know what I just remembered?" Mr. Greene leaned forward with a hush to his voice and focused his eyes back upon the staircase. "I've seen a sign for a room in the window of the Dover house."

"E-Eddie Dover's house, you mean?"

"That's the one." Mr. Greene's cheeks flushed pink. "He has that fine-looking widow. A Chicago girl. I remember seeing the young missus watering geraniums on the front porch when the weather was warmer."

"And you don't think she's found a boarder yet?"

He shrugged. "I'm not sure. She lives"—his voice dropped to an almost inaudible whisper—"on the corner of Willow and Plum. A red mailbox sits out front. Go ask her."

"Is the APL worried about her? Is that why you're whispering again?"

"I just don't want that fella following you around. Frank Rowan's an upstanding man, and I wouldn't want any harm coming to his daughter."

"Oh." I shrank back, and my elbows dropped off the countertop. "Thank you. I appreciate your help."

I picked up my bags and moved to leave, but before I reached the exit, Dale Cotton—one of Peter's classmates, a tall, beefy boy—threw open the front door and blew into the lobby, his brown hair tousled and shiny with perspiration. He wore a white work apron from his father's flower shop, and bits of soil sprinkled the floor below the hem, as if he sweated dirt.

"Jesus Christ!" He bent forward and fought to catch his breath, his cheeks bright red.

"What's going on?" asked Charlie. "What are you all worked up about?"

"There's been a murder—a violent one—just down the goddamned street."

I squeezed my hands around the handles of my bags.

Charlie stopped sweeping. "Where?"

"That *Boche* furniture store," said Dale. "Two vagrants came through town last night. Demolished the place. Beat a German to death with their bare hands."

The redhead winced, and I lowered my eyes toward the faded gold spirals of the rug beneath my feet, which blurred and writhed like coiled snakes.

"You gotta come see." Dale lunged toward the door, the soles of his shoes slipping and squeaking. "The place is surrounded by reporters, police, the APL, and even the goddamned mayor. There's more excitement than when the train crashed into those Southsiders."

"Jesus Christ!"

Charlie let the broom fall to the floor with a splat, and both boys tore out of the building and down the street, as if the sight of blood carried more weight than gold. Without glancing back at Mr. Greene to catch his reaction to the killing—or at the staircase to check for Lucas—I used my right shoulder to shove open the door and exited the Hotel America.

Out in the glaring daylight, on both sides of the street, rows of American flags snapped in a breeze from beneath the white awnings in front of each store. Model Ts driven by regular middle-class folk puttered past me, motoring off in the direction of Liberty Brothers Furniture. Three boys on bicycles rode by in streaks of brown overalls and caps, and I heard the word "murder" stream from their lips.

With my thick heels clapping across the sidewalk, I trekked westward on Willow, away from the hotel and the furniture store, away from the reporters and police and even the "god-damned mayor."

I HAD SEEN EDDIE'S WIDOW, May Belmont Dover, the year before, at the 1917 Fourth of July picnic—one of the few Buchanan functions I'd attended since my high school graduation in 1911. Billy always did his best to lure me out to the town, tempting me to the Moonbeam Theater by buying me copies of *Motion Picture* magazine, promising to introduce me to the parents of potential piano students if I attended Buchanan's Independence Day festivities.

I remembered what May looked like. She could have waltzed straight out of a Hollywood motion picture, even in her plain cotton dress and floppy straw hat that hid her dark ringlets. Billy referred to her as "Buchanan's Vamp." Father and Peter couldn't keep their eyes off her and the *V*-shaped dip in her flimsy white bodice, as I recalled from the picnic. "Eddie's jazzy new wife was a souvenir from his last big weekend in Chicago before enlisting," my friend Helen had said when she joined me at the picnic, twirling her finger around a red curl with a hint of jealousy, for she had once kissed Eddie at a dance. Eddie sat beside May on a blue gingham blanket and gazed at his wife as if she were a chocolate sundae topped with a voluptuous crimson cherry. As if he wanted to lick her all over until she melted in a flood of vanilla and red lipstick.

The Dovers' tapioca-colored home rose up ahead, beyond two trees ablaze with autumn leaves. I spotted the red mailbox out by the street, as Mr. Greene instructed, and noticed Eddie's family name painted on the side of the box in flowery white handwriting. A weather vane topped with a galloping silver horse pointed to the west, above an upstairs dormer window.

I climbed the steps to the wide front porch and reminded myself, *This is the start of your new life, Ivy. No more worrying. No headaches. Just living.*

I knocked on the door, and I waited.

Childish voices and laughter chirped from the backyard in the neighboring house to the right. The weather vane above me squeaked a little from a nudge of the breeze.

I knocked a second time and then turned to leave, discouraged, when footsteps approached from the other side of the door. The latch clicked. The door opened. There she stood.

Mrs. Eddie Dover.

The Vamp.

She blinked her eyes like she'd just woken up from a long and luxurious nap, and her fingers lazily buttoned up her midnight-black blouse, as if she'd just slipped out of bed and gotten herself dressed. Thick ringlets the color of velvety ink spilled down her shoulders to the famous May Belmont Dover breasts that Peter spoke of often, when he didn't think I could hear him. The buttonholes of her shirt strained to keep those mountainous curves inside.

"Can I help you?" she asked in a drowsy voice.

"Yes, hello. Umm . . ." I readjusted my bags in my hands. "I'm looking to rent a room. Mr. Greene at the Hotel America said you used to have a sign advertising space for a boarder."

"He did?" She peeked out the door in the direction of Mr. Greene and his business, even though the hotel stood three blocks away, beyond other houses and trees. "I haven't had that sign hanging up since summer."

"Well, he brought up your name, and—"

"Didn't I meet you once? You look familiar."

"Yes, we met at last year's Fourth of July picnic. I knew your husband in school."

She rolled her eyes. "*Every* girl in Buchanan knew Eddie in school."

"I didn't know him well. You've probably never even heard of me. My name's Ivy."

"Ohh . . ." She tilted her head and nodded with little dips

of her delicate chin. "Oh, yes. I think I might remember you now. Eddie said he hadn't seen you since you finished high school together. He said you never left your house. Called you a recluse."

"Well . . . I . . ."

"Are you running away from home or something?"

My hands sweated on the handles of my luggage. "I-I-I beg your pardon?"

"You have that desperate look about you." She crossed her arms and peered down the street again. "Is an irate husband about to show up and cause a scene?"

"A . . . what?"

"Or are you a war widow, too?"

The muscles in my arms ached and shook to the point where I had to plunk down the bags on her porch. "No, I'm not a widow. One of my brothers just lost his life in France, though, and my family is . . . um . . ." I braced my hands on my hips. "Well, we're not doing well. I've decided to head out into the world and live my own life now. Sort of"—I forced a smile to my face—"burst out of my cocoon, so to speak."

May merely blinked in response at first, but then she arched a dark eyebrow and said, "You picked one hell of a time to spread your wings, little butterfly."

"Yes, I suppose I—"

"Have you heard about this wicked flu?"

"I already had it, just this past week. How about you?"

She leaned her right hip against the doorjamb. "I had a terrible headache the other day. I thought I might be getting sick, but then I sat down for a spell and recovered." She picked at the little nail of her left pinky. "Which was a shame."

"What?" I leaned forward. "How on earth is recovering a shame?"

"I thought God might have sent this flu to help all us Widow Street girls join our darling husbands. That would've been kind of Him."

I swallowed and debated how to respond to a statement such as that.

"Do you have an income that would allow you to pay rent?" she asked.

"Yes. I've been teaching piano lessons to children out at my family's house for the past seven years."

" 'Tickling the Ivories with Ivy'?"

"Yes." I blushed. "That's the slogan I use on my card."

"I've seen your card in the music store window. How did you put it there if you're a recluse?"

"I don't actually . . ." I cleared my throat and leaned forward on my toes. "I don't personally call myself a recluse. But my brother Billy hung that up for me. He helped me find students before he . . . before . . ." I gestured with my thumb to the east. Toward France.

She nodded in understanding.

"Do you play an instrument?" I asked. "Is that why you were in the music store?"

"No." She toyed with another nail—the one at the tip of her

left ring finger, on which she still wore a gold wedding band, I noticed. "The store's just next to the beauty parlor where I get my hair done."

"Ah." I grabbed up my bags. "Well, I'm really sorry to have troubled you this morning."

"Hey." She cocked her head again. "Even if you are a recluse—"

"I told you, I don't call myself—"

"Even if you're a tad on the shy side, don't you have any other old school friends who'd take you in, besides handsome Eddie's widow?"

I backed down the porch steps and debated if I should mention a word about Helen, a principal player in Buchanan's first-most-notorious adultery story. Or Sigrid Landvik, who ended up marrying Wyatt Pettyjohn, an old beau of mine of sorts. "My closest friend moved out of town just this past summer," I decided to say, and it was the truth. Helen left town with Buchanan's exiled German, Mr. Weiss.

"You've never married, then?" asked May, shading her eyes from the morning sun with her left hand, the light glinting off her gold band.

"No, I'm an old twenty-five-year-old spinster, I'm afraid." I offered a thin smile and turned to leave.

"Not any more, you're not."

I stopped. "I beg your pardon?"

May pushed her door farther open with the tips of her fingers. "You're not just an old spinster anymore. You're now the distinguished first-ever boarder at Dover's Home for Women of Independent Means."

"But—"

"You said you have an income, right?"

"Yes."

"And I have the spare room. I lost interest in the idea of a boarder when Eddie got killed, but maybe I should talk to someone else besides myself and ghosts."

"Ghosts?"

"It's just a manner of speaking." She nodded toward the house's interior. "Come inside. I'll show you the room."

"Th-thank you. Oh my goodness, thank you." I hoisted up my luggage and ran back up to the porch with my square heels clomping all over the place.

May led me inside to a small front room with pale yellow walls covered in paintings of furniture and fruit and women bathing in lakes in dresses that hugged their hips and bosoms. A green sofa and an armchair inhabited the center of the room, and a black Singer sewing machine, along with a naked dress form and a large basket of fabric, took up the leftmost side. The air carried feminine fragrances similar to the ones I remembered from my aunt Eliza's house. Roses and lavender. Toilet waters and potpourri.

A framed photograph of Eddie sat upon a table at the back of the room, and its presence seemed the only speck of evidence that a man had ever dwelled in the place. He wore his U.S. Air Service uniform in the photo, and he looked nothing like a fellow about to die. My eyes lingered too long on his fair hair and broad shoulders.

"Who is the artist of all of these watercolors?" I asked, turning my attention to one of the bathing ladies.

"I am."

"You paint?"

"Mm hmm." May nodded and straightened the image closest to her.

"They're beautiful." I leaned closer to better observe the details of the rippling reflection of the woman on the water. "I used to wish I could draw well, but music's always been my calling. My escape. Along with poetry."

"You should write songs, then, like George M. Cohan."

I laughed. "Maybe."

"So . . . this is the main room." She held out her arms and swiveled toward a doorway in the back-left corner. "And that's the kitchen back there. Nothing too fancy, but it has everything you'll need. The room over there belongs to Eddie and me."

She spun on her heel toward a door to my right and didn't correct herself for speaking of Eddie in the present tense.

"And up here"—she headed over to a staircase that started next to the bedroom door—"is one big attic room, which can be yours, if the place suits you all right."

I followed her up a turned staircase with a small landing in the middle, and I noticed the steps made mere whispers of sound compared to the squeaks and hollers of our rickety stairs back home. The silence made me worry the Dovers' house, like the Hotel America, might sit too still for proper sleep.

Upstairs, we reached an open room with a bed smothered in white ruffles and a ceiling pitched like the roof. Everything that couldn't fit into the rest of the house—crates, rugs, lamps, a toaster, two copper washboards, a chest of drawers, a doll's crib, Eddie's Buchanan High School football uniform—appeared to have found a home on the attic floor.

"So"—May placed her hands on her hips—"what do you think?"

"It's nice." I rested my bags in an empty square of flooring next to the bed. "Plenty of room. Good amount of sunshine."

"I'll bring up my spare key after I head back downstairs." She traced a finger through dust on an old credenza parked near the top of the stairs. "It has been lonely here, I do admit. I should have probably left that ROOM FOR RENT sign up longer."

"I'm sure you've still been adjusting"—I eyed Eddie's football jersey—"to life."

She nodded with her lips pursed, and her eyes, which also strayed to Eddie's clothing, moistened.

I suddenly worried I'd see Eddie up there, standing in the shadows amid his belongings.

I don't know why we females of the family see them—these Guests, Mama had said to me after I'd witnessed my first one when just a child. *We just do. Granny Letty saw them as well. They always arrive before someone dies, as if to warn us to steel ourselves against grief.*

I rubbed at a chill that breezed across my arms. "Have you heard anything about the . . ." I licked my lips. "The *incident* that occurred down the street last night?"

May furrowed her brow. "What incident?"

"Did you ever meet those two German brothers who own a furniture store at the other end of Willow?"

"Sure, that's where we bought our sofa when we first moved into the house, but"—she lifted her hands—"that was a whole month before Uncle Sam declared war on Germany."

I took hold of a round brass post at the foot of the bed. "Some people killed one of the brothers last night."

"Oh, Lord." She cringed. "I wish I could say I'm surprised, but after that story about the Robert Prager lynching—"

"It wasn't a mob lynching." I pressed the bed knob against my stomach and felt words tumble from my mouth. "It was a man and his son. They were drunk and furious about the loss of a family member and killed the Kraut with their own bare hands."

May leaned the small of her back against the credenza. "Which of the German brothers was it?"

"I'm not sure. Why?"

"The older one has been living in Buchanan for quite a while—since 1912 or so. Hardly even has an accent anymore. But that younger one . . ." She crossed her arms over her chest. "People say he didn't leave Germany until after the war broke out in Europe."

"Do they think he's like Mr. Weiss?"

May shrugged. "There are rumors he's a traitor and a spy. My neighbor somehow knows whose phones are being wiretapped in town, and she said the Schendels have been the main targets of the APL's investigations, mainly because of the younger brother. Their sofa is comfortable. That's the most I can say about them." Her eyes flitted toward the square window behind me. "Do they know precisely who killed him?"

My heart thumped with such guilt and terror, I feared she heard the organ hammering against the wall of my chest. "I . . . I beg your pardon?"

"I don't like the idea of murderers lurking nearby. Do they know who the killers were? Was it the APL?"

"I—" My lips and chin both shook so much that May must have seen my face twitching and quivering like a frightened rabbit's.

"Ivy?" She stepped forward. "Are you all right?"

My entire head vibrated, and the room blurred and rattled until May looked as though someone were shaking her up like a bottle of ketchup.

"Ivy? Do you need me to—?"

"My father and brother—they beat the German to death," I said, and the next thing I knew, my skull hit the floor.

Chapter 4

*E*ven though the words of German writers should have been banned from my brain, I remembered that Goethe once said of honesty, "Truth is a torch, but a terrific one; therefore we all try to reach it with closed eyes, lest we should be scorched."

Oh, boy, was he right.

Spitting out the truth about my family in front of May Dover—pushing out all that ugliness in one blunt go with my eyes open wide—burned, blinded, stunned, and crippled me for the better part of the day. May revived me with smelling salts and dragged me onto the foamy sea of white ruffles on the attic's bed, which clogged my nose with tickling dust. She even went so far as to remove my shoes and prop my feet up on a satin pillow. Despite such fineries, I remained a mute and useless slug of a tenant, unable to sit up and apologize for the crime I'd just confessed.

"Feeling better?" she asked at dusk, when sunlight stopped boring a fiery hole into my brain and shadows yawned across the attic floor. The homey aroma of vegetable soup—a scent that reminded me of my mother—entered the room along with May's footsteps, and I opened my eyes to the sight of her carrying a tray with a spoon, a glass of water, and a steaming bowl of a dark broth. She bent her legs into a slow and graceful lunge and set the small supper on a leather traveling trunk beside the bed. A gold key shimmered beside the tray.

I shifted onto my side, toward her and the soup. "Didn't you hear what I said before I collapsed on your floor?"

May perched herself on the edge of the bed and smoothed out her dark skirt. "Yes. I heard."

"About my father and brother?"

"Yes. You said they were the ones who killed the German." She looked me in the eye with an expression I couldn't decipher.

I swallowed. "Do you want me to gather my bags and leave?"

"I've already unpacked your bags into that chest of drawers."

"You have?"

She nodded. "My own father served a prison term for assaulting and robbing our landlady back when I was a young child. I haven't seen him since I was seven years old."

"Oh, good heavens." I sank back against the ruffles. "I'm sorry."

"I'm not telling you that information for you to feel sorry for me. I'm simply saying that if I had to go around taking blame for his sins, I would have killed myself long ago." She sat up straight and folded her slender hands in her lap. "You are not your father and brother, Ivy. If you didn't take part in that murder, you're not guilty of their crime."

"I know." I nodded. "I've been trying to tell myself the same thing, but the guilt's still there. It's stuck"—I pushed my fist against my middle—"deep in my stomach."

"Well, there's no need for it to be there."

"The police are concealing what happened, though. They're telling the town that two vagrants came through Buchanan and killed the German. They're worried that this part of Illinois will turn into another Collinsville."

"Unfortunately"—May heaved a loud sigh—"I think many people would be proud to have Buchanan called another Collinsville. If you want to know the truth, my mother is Italian, and my father was born in Dublin, but I've never dared admit that I'm not one hundred percent American to anyone in this town besides Eddie."

I squeezed my eyes shut and breathed through a cramp that resembled a knife blade scraping away at my gut.

"Hey," said May with a nudge. "You're not going to faint again, are you? I'm not running off to the police to tell them what you said. You don't have to worry about me."

"I need to talk to the slain German's brother."

"And say what?"

"Apologize. Help clean up his store. Make him feel better." I rolled onto my back and stared up at the sharp peak of the ceiling above. Little bits of gray and feathery spiderwebs dangled overhead. "Even if the surviving brother is the suspected traitor and spy, he's likely hurting just as much as I did the day I learned about our Billy's death."

"He's probably turning tail and sailing back to Germany."

"Maybe. But if not"—I curled forward and lifted my upper back off the sheets, panting through another flare-up of pain—"I have to set things right. Especially if this flu is taking lives. He could be next. I've got to help him. Something tells me I absolutely must go to his store."

I PULLED MY WOOL COAT TIGHT around my middle and wandered past the darkened windows of Weiss's Bakery, one block west and across the street from Liberty Brothers Furniture. Dried yellow paint stuck to the bakery windows, undoubtedly left over from the July raid on the store. I glanced inside the storefront and saw the cream-colored walls and the empty glass display counters where Helen, Sigrid, and I would sometimes treat ourselves to after-school cookies. We picked out our future wedding cakes and breathed in the scents of frosting and cinnamon until our heads went dizzy from the sweetness. We had no idea that Helen would one day involve herself with the green-eyed man with the thick accent who worked with his American wife behind the counter. Or that Buchanan residents would eventually want to murder people like him.

An unseen cord tugged me onward down the street in the darkness. *You must see that surviving German brother,* I told myself. *You must talk to him before anything else terrible happens.*

*That pain in your stomach? Than gnawing agony? It will grow far
worse than your migraines if you don't hurry up and set everything
right.*

I crossed Willow Street in the dark and traveled another block
east before meeting up with the CLOSED sign posted on the front
door of the furniture store. The black letters gleamed in the glow
of the streetlamp behind me. The paint my father and brother
had splattered across the red bricks had dried into dirty yellow
veins that branched down the wall to the ground. Someone had
taken the time to sweep away the broken glass from the sidewalk,
and they had nailed sturdy planks over the damage to the door
and the windows. Yet the paint lingered. Ugly scars running
across the store's protective skin.

Electric lights shone inside the business. I peeked through a
slip of exposed window and spied the brown-haired young man
again. He crouched on his hands and knees on the floor and
scrubbed at the bloodstains while wearing his tweed vest and
tan trousers.

I pulled back from the window and steadied my breath, which
fluttered like moth wings in the base of my throat.

Truth is a torch, but a terrific one . . .

It took just a gentle nudge of my right knuckle to make the
door swing open. An obnoxious bell above my head jangled
in response, and the German peered up from his scrubbing
with startled blue eyes. Down on all fours like that, despite the

gentlemanly clothing, he resembled an animal caught with his foot in a snare—feral, defensive, ready to lash out with teeth and fists.

"Who are you?" he asked in an accent that somehow made both a harsh and a singsong sound. "I saw you last night with your bags."

"I'm sorry."

"Sorry for what?"

"Just . . ." I drew a deep breath and tried to ignore the odd way he formed words in the back of his throat—and how his head seemed the ideal rounded shape for a spiked German army helmet. "I heard about your brother's death. My own brother died recently, too, and I wanted you to know . . . I'm . . ." I pressed my teeth together in a way that made my molars rattle against one another. I accidentally bit the right edge of my tongue and tasted blood. "I'm sorry you're experiencing the same pain."

He eased his grip on the scrub brush and sank back on his heels. "What is your name?"

I sealed my lips shut. My name belonged too much to my family.

The German set the brush aside and got to his feet. He stood taller than me by at least a half foot, and his build looked to be slender yet sturdy. His arms and shoulders belonged to a fellow who hoisted around tables and bureaus and wide wooden beds.

He put his hands on his hips and cocked his head at me. "What happened to you?"

"What do you mean?"

"Why were you traveling though the dark with your luggage last night?"

"I told you"—I gulped so loudly he must have heard the sound—"my brother died. I've been sick since I learned that news, and now I'm trying to recuperate. I just . . ."

He stepped toward me across the floorboards—boards still blotchy with pink stains of blood.

I backed away. "Don't . . . I-I just—"

"Ach. Sie hat Angst vor Deutschen."

My back banged against the door, and my shoulder blades smarted. "W-what did you just say?"

He came to a stop no more than four feet away. "I said, 'Ah, she is afraid of Germans.' Go away if you're so scared. I don't understand why you came in here if—"

"I'm not afraid of Germans."

"Then why are you shaking like I'm pointing a Kaiser-issued rifle at your head, Fräulein? I bet you call me 'Hun' and 'Kraut' behind my back."

"I'm just here to see if you need any help cleaning up your store."

He relaxed his shoulders a breadth of an inch and lifted his chin. His eyes held mine in a stare that didn't entail a single blink. "What did you say your name was?"

"I didn't say, but it's Ivy."

"Ivy what?"

"It doesn't matter. I'm the only Ivy I know around here." I

pushed my back off the boarded-up door and stood up straight. "What is your name?"

"Daniel." He swallowed as if cramming anger down his throat. "And I have a terrifying Kraut surname, so if that makes you feel like you need to call in the American Protective League, then you had better—"

"What was your brother's name?"

He was the one who shrank back that time around. He turned his eyes to the floor and shoved his hands in his pockets. "Albrecht. Albrecht Schendel."

"Did Albrecht have a wife?"

"He did, back home. She died six years ago, though. There's a sweetheart, one town over. An American woman."

"I'm sorry."

The German's hands remained stuffed inside his pockets.

"I really do want to help you clean up the damage," I said. "I want to prove you'll find kindness here, despite what happened last night, and what happened to Robert Prager down in Collinsville back in April."

He lifted his face. "You don't understand, do you?"

"I . . . no, I can't say I understand what life is like for an immigrant treated as the enemy, but—"

"That's not what I'm talking about." He clamped his lips together and stared without blinking again. "You are—how do you say it over here—'naïve'? Is that a word in English?"

"Yes." I frowned. "It's a word."

"You can do nothing to make me feel better about what happened."

I balled my hands into fists to curb the ache in my gut. "Do you have someone else who will help you with the damage, then? Other family members? A wife?"

"I don't need anyone else. My life here is over."

"I doubt your brother would want you thinking that."

"You don't know anything about what my brother would want." He backed way. "You know nothing about what it feels like to have your life ripped apart and—"

"I'm sorry."

He turned and kicked the scrub brush across the room, where it clattered against the rockers of a chair lying on its side, like a dead deer in a road.

I jumped.

He ran his hands through his hair, grabbed his scalp, and trembled with a wave of some sort of merciless emotion that stopped him from breathing and turned his face a troubling purplish red. His entire body shook as if gripped in the throes of a seizure.

I trembled as well. "Are you all right?"

No answer. No breathing.

"Mr. Schendel?"

He exhaled a burst of air that could have been a groan or a sob. "Oh, *Gott*," he said. "Oh, *Gott. Was soll ich tun?*"

I grabbed the doorknob but couldn't make myself leave.

He kept speaking German—"*Was soll ich tun? Hilf mir,*

bitte"—still clutching his scalp, still standing over those faded pink stains.

Music erupted outside the boarded-up windows with such force that I gasped, and my shoulders jerked. Brass and winds and drums and a piano—that jazz band again, playing closer than when I had tried to sleep in the Hotel America.

"Do you hear that?" I asked.

Daniel panted. "What?"

"Do you hear that music?"

"Of course. I'm German, not deaf."

"Where is it coming from?"

He turned his upper body toward the boarded-up windows and lowered his hands from his head. "It's just a jazz band that plays upstairs in the Masonic Lodge across the street."

"Every night?"

"I don't know. They didn't used to." He exhaled more ragged breaths and rubbed at his neck with a pained grimace. "It's 'Jelly Roll Blues.' "

"By Ferd Morton?"

He nodded. "You know it?"

"I almost bought the sheet music once, but I had to purchase Chopin for one of my students instead. I've been teaching piano lessons out at our farm—"

I cut myself short, for the music loudened, as if telling me to shut my trap, stop bothering this stranger about my miniscule little life, and just listen. We both stood there, motionless, mute, absorbing the song into our bodies as if receiving anesthetizing shots of laudanum to kill off the pain. Daniel closed his eyes, and the hardness eased from his jaw. The red heat drained from his cheeks. He let his hands hang by his sides and breathed in a gentler rhythm. Soft sips of air glided through his nose.

I closed my eyes, too, and let the melody slide through my blood until my heart *thump-thump-thumped* with jazz and strength and an unexpected surge of hope.

The last note died away, and the room fell silent.

I raised my eyelids and found Daniel watching me over his shoulder.

"You can start on the bloodstains . . . if that's what you truly want." He walked over to the bristly wooden brush he had kicked across the floor and picked it up.

I shook off the music's spell—literally wiggling my arms and hands to bring my brain back into focus—and ventured over to him on legs gone wobbly and rubbery. My fingers managed to pluck the cleaning tool out of his hand without actually touching his skin.

"I'll have the stains gone before the night's over," I said. "My father cut himself all the time when he was working on our farm, and I learned how to clean up the mess."

"Well, bully for his clumsiness, then."

Daniel wandered away before I could check his eyes for any signs of his knowing the identity of that clumsy father of mine.

I SCOURED THE DARK FLOORBOARDS with a solution of vinegar and water that made my nostrils sting until I thought they'd bleed. Across the room, Daniel fitted a new wooden backing onto a lacquered maple cabinet that Peter and Father must have knocked over during their attack.

My mind did a terrible thing: it strained to envision how my family members actually managed to destroy both the furniture and Albrecht in the very room in which I knelt. My nostrils burned all the more, and my stomach knotted and groaned, but I couldn't stop seeing them in there, beating a man to death, violating his property, spilling the blood that sullied the wood below my knees.

At one point Daniel dropped the new piece of wood and swore under his breath in German—or at least the words he spat out sounded like swearing. I kept my face directed toward the fading pink splotches and scrubbed and scrubbed and scrubbed and scrubbed.

My father and brother murdered your brother, I wanted to confess from across the store as the bristles ground against the floor. The words perched on my lips and buzzed across the edges of my mouth, but the poisonous admission refused to leave my body. *I'm sorry. They were drunk. The telegram about Billy came last week. They must have been drinking in the saloon and got riled up from all the sympathetic shouts and the anti-German slurs. It was my father and brother who beat him with their own bare hands.*

Daniel looked up at me, and I worried that he had somehow heard my confessions in my mind. I lowered my head and kept on scrubbing.

He returned to his hammering and asked over the din, "How old was your brother?"

"Twenty-two," I called back. "How old was yours?"

"One month shy of his twenty-ninth birthday."

"Does that make you the older or the younger brother?" I asked with my heart pounding to the beat of his hammering.

"The younger."

Oh, Christ.

The potential traitor and spy.

I poured another wash of vinegar over the floor and dwelled on a brand-new fear: Herr Daniel Schendel might rush over with that metal hammer of his and strike me in the head. An eye-for-an-eye act of revenge. One Rowan sister in exchange for one Schendel brother. The scenario seemed awfully Shakespearean, but before April of that same year, I never would have imagined a mob of Illinois citizens stringing up a German by the neck either.

Daniel rested his hammer on the floor with a gentle clank and ran the tips of his fingers over his work.

Another jazz song shimmied through the boarded-up windows.

I glanced up. "What's that one called?"

"I beg your pardon?" he asked.

"You knew the name of that other song. I figured you might know this one, too."

He kept his back toward me, but I could tell by the way he held his neck straight and still that he was listening.

"That's too easy," he said. " 'Livery Stable Blues' by the Original Dixieland Jass Band."

I lifted the bristles off the ground. "Are you a musician?"

"I play guitar."

"Really?"

"Yes." His shoulder blades stiffened beneath his tweed vest. "Really."

"Maybe you should go over there and play with them sometime."

He glanced back at me with a scowl. "Maybe you should mind your own business."

"I just—"

"You seem like a person who's 'always just' something or other. I'm not going to go play with a band who wouldn't want me with them. They're probably also . . ." He stopped and pinched his lips together.

"Probably also what?" I asked.

He just sat there, half turned toward me.

I sat up tall. "What were you going to say?"

He stood and knocked his knee against the cabinet with a thud that must have hurt. "I think it's time for you to go."

"What did I say?"

He marched toward me. "Go fix up somebody else's messes instead of mine."

I pushed myself to my feet. "I'm not done with the—"

He hooked his hand under my elbow and yanked me toward the door, pinching my skin.

"Wait! I want to finish the job."

He pushed me against the door and shoved his blue German eyes and hot breath in my face. "I know who you are, Ivy. Scrubbing away all those bloodstains will never, *ever* erase what they did."

The boarded-up entrance fell open behind me, and I was out in the cold, dark air with the door slamming shut two inches from my nose.

Chapter 5

I stopped and leaned against the cold bricks of an unlit corner to catch my breath. My stomach clenched. Pain shot down my legs and burned through my feet, and my skull cracked into two separate pieces, like Emily Dickinson once described in a poem.

> *I felt a cleaving in my mind*
> *As if my brain had split . . .*

He knew who I was.

Oh, God. He knew.

Two blocks behind me, the jazz band played on as if nothing were amiss, the beat of the drums a distant pulse, the cornet a faraway wail. The furniture store tugged me back toward it—my legs thrummed with the urge to turn back around and return. To make amends. Yet I forced myself to move again, away from him. Away from the blood.

A car motor rumbled from somewhere nearby, and a stab of fear shot through me. Maybe someone had seen me enter his store. Maybe Billy's friend Lucas had been observing my actions ever since that morning—spying, listening, watching with his magnified eyes.

Headlights rounded the bend two blocks down. Words written in frosted block letters jumped out from the storefront window beside me: BUCHANAN CHAMBER OF COMMERCE.

"Oh no! Damn!" I muttered aloud.

I had just helped out the prime target of the local American Protective League's scrutiny, and there I stood, next to their headquarters.

I dashed around the corner, pressed my back against a wall in the shadows, and prayed the driver would continue heading eastward on Willow. The car growled closer—I could feel the engine humming across the bottoms of my feet. I smelled gasoline and oil and hoped the driver hadn't seen me. Perhaps he was simply a regular person traveling home for regular reasons.

The engine *pop-pop-popped* to a stop around the bend, and I heard someone pull the automobile's clutch lever all the way back to set the rear parking brake. I sucked in my breath and held the air in my lungs, willing my body and my clothing to blend into the wall. Doors opened and shut. Male laughter bulldozed over the cornet and the piano down the way.

I calculated how quickly and quietly I could run down to the next corner and disappear into the blackness of night. Before I could even think to move, however, one of the men from the automobile uttered the name "Schendel."

I froze.

"What do you think we should do about the brother?" asked a fellow with the rasp of a smoker, all rocks and sandpaper.

"He's not going to be around much longer," said a man with a voice so smooth, I bet he grinned every time he talked, no matter how viperous the words coming out of his mouth. "He's going to need a loan if he wants to repair that store, and we've already made sure none of the banks lend the *Boche* any money at this point. Where the hell is Harry? He's late."

"Do we even know who killed the other brother yet?" asked a third voice, a jumpy one.

"We have a good idea," said Mr. Smooth. "It had nothing to do with any of our volunteers, so make sure no one goes around taking credit for it. The mayor isn't happy. He doesn't want the word 'vigilante' showing up in the paper."

"Let's just go ahead and ship the surviving brother to Fort Oglethorpe," said Mr. Smoker from down in the rockiest depths of his throat. "Be done with it."

"Damn that Harry for always running late." Mr. Smooth must have pulled out a set of keys just then, for I heard them jangle. "I want to do this fucking walk through town before the night gets any colder. My family jewels are already starting to freeze."

The other two fellows chuckled, but their coughs and laughter and terrible language disappeared inside the building before

I could hear anything more about shipping Daniel to wherever they wanted to send him.

My legs longed to run back to the furniture store again.

Should I warn him? I wondered. *Should I park myself in front of his door and protect him through the night?*

I wavered. I tapped my fingers against the chalky bricks of the wall beside me and envisioned myself standing guard in front of Daniel's store with my arms crossed over my chest and no weapons to speak of.

Ridiculous.

Resigning myself to my uselessness, knowing Daniel didn't even want to see me again, I slipped down the side street in an attempt to slink back to May's house on less visible roads.

The back of my neck prickled when I rounded the corner down the way, and I feared that if I turned my head, I'd find the shine of Lucas's spectacles in the lamplight. Or the face of the deceased Albrecht Schendel.

TWO BLOCKS LATER, around the corner from Halloran's Dry Goods, a new disturbance erupted across town: the sputtering coughs of an automobile engine fighting to spark to life. I recognized the desperate sound from my early days of learning how to turn the starter crank on the family's Model T truck.

"Oh, God." I puffed a sigh. "What now?"

I picked up my pace, and when the choking ruckus grew louder and shrieks of distress joined in with the struggle, I tore around the bend to Lincoln Street, forgetting my own worries.

Another block south, an olive-green truck sat on the railroad tracks—an ambulance. *Stalled.* A Red Cross emblem marked the wooden enclosure on the back. Patients likely lay inside. Flu patients. Children maybe.

A train whistled down the way.

"Oh, God!" I ran toward the vehicle with my feet clapping across the asphalt. "Do you need help? Oh, God!"

Again and again some unseen person down in front of the vehicle's grille turned the starter crank, but the ambulance sputtered and rattled and refused to budge from the tracks.

"Put it into neutral and just push it off the tracks!" I yelled. "Get out of the way so we can push it!"

The fuzzy glow of a train's lantern came into sight through a patch of fog down the way. Another whistle keened through the night, this time closer and with an urgency that pierced my heart and quickened my feet. The ambulance stayed stock still, and the person in front of the truck kept cranking and fighting that poor grinding engine.

"Move!" With the strength of a quarterback, I knocked aside the person at the crank—a blond woman in gray—until she lay in the road, safely away from both the ambulance and the tracks. I shoved the crank into place, gave it a firm upward twist, and jumped into the driver's seat with the engine rumbling awake. My pulse beat in my ears, and the locomotive roared my way, the whistle blaring, lights shining. I pushed the hand lever forward, released the clutch pedal, and, after a quick adjustment of the spark advance and the throttle, the truck careered off those tracks with a squeal of rubber. The train thundered behind me, its wheels churning, wind whipping across the open driving compartment, and the whistle hollered through the night with the ear-shattering wails of an Irish banshee.

I brought the ambulance to a stop and, with a groan, collapsed across the steering wheel, in shock that I remained alive and in one piece.

Beside me, a pair of hands gripped the dashboard. Erratic panting filled the truck while the train whistled farther and farther into the vast and distant void of the eastern farmlands.

"Are you all right?" I asked whoever sat with me, but my voice—raw and deep—didn't sound like my own. It hardly even sounded like a voice.

The passenger didn't answer. I lifted my head and, in the light of a streetlamp shining through the windshield, I saw a skinny black girl, no older than seventeen, wearing a white surgical mask over the bottom half of her face. She was dressed in a dark necktie and a Red Cross coat, skirt, and hat—all made of gray wool—and her arms and shoulders trembled. She stared at me in that hazy light, her brown eyes wide and damp.

"What happened to Nela?" she asked with a squeak in her throat.

"Who?"

"Nela. The woman at the crank. Where is she? We're supposed to be doing this together."

"I'll go . . ." I peeled my fingers off the steering wheel, one by one, the muscles so stuck in a crooked position that my hands curled like claws. "I'll make sure she's all right."

I slid out of the driver's seat and landed too hard on my feet, jarring my neck, and then I staggered over to the supine blond woman lying in the road near the tracks. She also wore the gray Red Cross uniform, and like the girl in the front seat, her mouth and nose hid beneath a gauze mask, the blue eyes above it wide and unblinking. Her chest rose and fell with shallow contractions that didn't make a sound.

I bent down beside her, my knees digging into the sharp gravel below my skirt, and I touched the wool-covered arm above her right elbow. "Are you all right? Can you hear me?"

"They said . . ." She still didn't blink, and her voice emerged from her larynx as a breathy murmur. "They said . . . we could help the Southside families at night." Her accent—what I could hear of it—sounded Polish. Maybe Russian, or Czech. "But we had to drive ourselves. I do not know how to drive. *She* does not know how to drive."

"Neither of you ?" I furrowed my brow. "You mean to say that the Red Cross sent two nondrivers out to helm these vehicles at night? Don't they know how dangerous these railroad tracks are—and how badly a person can break her arm if she doesn't know how to turn the crank?"

The woman finally blinked, her blond eyelashes fluttering. "One of our own volunteers, another Polish woman, is lying in the back of the ambulance with a fever. She was to be our driver. Liliana."

A pair of feet crunched across the crumbled flakes of asphalt in the road behind me. I peeked over my shoulder and found the young black volunteer walking toward us with her arms wrapped around her waist. "We have to deliver everyone in Southside," she said, "the Poles, the Russians, the Romanians, the blacks—*everyone*—to Polish Hall."

My jaw dropped. "The hospital isn't treating Southside residents?"

Both women shook their heads.

"It's too full," said the blonde. "No room."

"Here, can you sit up?" My hands hovered over the woman's shoulders. I feared I'd fracture one of her bones if I touched her with even the gentlest of movements. "Does anything feel broken or numb?"

"No." She wiggled herself up to her elbows. "I was just stunned. I didn't expect anyone to fly at me in the dark, and that train . . ."

I slid my arm around her back and helped to raise her up to a seated position while the other girl crouched down beside us. The three of us sat in the street, not more than five feet down from the still-humming tracks. If the APL brought their nighttime walking patrol to that part of town and spotted us huddled together on the ground like that, so close to an ambulance, I wondered if they'd even bother to ask if we needed help.

"How many patients are lying in Polish Hall right now?" I asked.

"Over a hundred," said the blonde. "Maybe two hundred, with five to seven deaths a day."

"Five to seven?"

"Will you help drive us, ma'am?" asked the younger girl. "You somehow seem to know a thing or two about trucks. I've never seen such a useful white woman in all my life."

I looked between the two of them. Both women peered at me with those damp and pleading eyes that poured the weight of the world upon my shoulders.

"Well . . ." I swallowed. A flock of excuses flapped around inside my brain. *It's too late, and I'm tired . . . I'm too busy worrying about the brother of a murdered man . . . The APL are prowling the streets tonight . . . My heart is still pounding over that escape from the train . . . My father always told me Southside was a breeding ground for diseases, and I should never, ever think of going near it . . .*

"I suppose . . . all right." I nodded. "I can help for a bit, but I can't guarantee I'll feel well enough to drive for long tonight. Just . . . tell me how to get to the social hall, and we'll start by getting your patient delivered. My name is Ivy, by the way."

"Thank you, thank you, lovely Ivy," said the blonde, grabbing hold of my elbow. "God bless you. I am Nela, and this is Addie. And, as I said, Liliana lies in back."

"It's nice to meet you." I helped Nela to her feet by holding her arm and the back of her waist. "I'm just sorry I had to meet you this way."

DOWN ON THE SOUTH SIDE OF THE TRACKS, the monstrous shadows of the textile mills and railcar factories rose up along the river like smokestack-covered watchmen. We drove past endless rows of immigrant housing with webs of clotheslines crisscrossing alleyways and yards, and the air smelled of industry and pollution. Soot and refuse. Progress and poverty. The darkness seemed a living thing down there, its fluid weight settling over the homes and the factories and the treeless strips of weeds for yards. The entire region exhausted me. Everything seemed to sleep and wither and drown in blackness.

"There it is," said Nela, pointing across the steering wheel toward the left-hand side of the street. "Polish Hall."

I peeked through the windshield and spied a two-story brick building attached to a small Polish grocery store. Electric lights illuminated every window despite the late hour and the lack of life in the rest of Southside. I pulled the ambulance alongside the curb.

Before I even set the emergency brake, both of my passengers leapt off the seat and disappeared toward the back compartment. I followed after them and found them lifting a canvas stretcher that held a pale young brunette woman, also dressed in a gray Red Cross uniform. Her eyes were closed, and the movements of the stretcher jostled her small shoulders and her long legs.

"Hurry!" Nela hoisted up the front end of the stretcher and led the way to the brick steps of the hall. She said something to her patient in Polish, but all I understood was the woman's name—*Liliana*.

"*Nie!*" Liliana's eyes flew open, and she grabbed hold of Nela's hand. "Do not take me here! *Nie! Nie!*"

"What can I do to help?" I asked, and I hurried past them so I could at least open the front door for them.

"Stay with us so you can drive us," said Addie, maneuvering the stretcher up the steps from the back. She had to duck her head to avoid Liliana's feet kicking her in the head with those thick Red Cross boots.

I pushed open a weighty paneled door, and the stench of vomit and whiskey socked me in the face with such a blow that I stepped back and held my breath. In the main front room, beneath beautiful golden-wood walls and stained-glass windows, a shivering mass of coughing and wheezing bodies huddled beneath blankets, both on the floor and on cots. To my utter horror, blood flowed inside that hall—nosebleeds mainly. Horrific scarlet rivers that drenched clothing, cots, blankets, people, and even the walls. I swear upon a stack of Bibles: people bled from their noses with such force and velocity that the blood from their nostrils *shot across the room and hit the walls*. They resembled victims of heinous knife attacks, or people wounded in the face by bullets. Not sufferers from influenza.

Not more than five feet away from me, a woman leaned over the side of her cot and vomited a black fluid that resembled tar, her lips blue, her face a purplish brown. A mahogany-colored body with wide-open eyes lay on a pile of blankets not more than five feet from where I stood, clutching the door, my legs shaking.

Nela and Addie lugged Liliana to the back of the room and

turned to the left, through an open doorway. I covered my mouth to stifle the smells and attempted to follow after them—to do something besides gaping at the horror. My feet slipped in a dark puddle. I gasped, righted myself, and kept walking.

A young black man buried beneath a pile of blankets grabbed hold of my leg and forced me to a stop.

"Get me outa here, miss," he said from down on the floor, his fingers tight on my shin, hurting the bone. "I gotta go. Please, get me outa here."

"No, it's for the best if you stay." I peeled his hand off my leg and lowered his head back down to the scuffed floorboards. "There are doctors who can help you here."

"How many doctors do you see here, miss? How many?" He nodded across the room toward a gray-haired physician in a white coat who forced a man down to a cot as the man shouted, "I want to kill myself! I don't want to die like this. I want to take a knife to myself and my family."

A Girl Scout in a khaki dress and hat stood behind the physician with a bottle of whiskey at the ready.

Another Girl Scout dashed toward the back staircase with a bedpan.

"Oh, God." My eyes bulged at the sight of children cleaning up bodily fluids and tending to the sick—including, I noticed, my piano student Ruby Rogers, who mopped the floor on the far side of the room. Her chestnut-brown braids poked out from beneath a gauze mask, and blood stained the skirt of her uniform. "Girl Scouts are helping? Little Ruby Rogers is helping? Ruby!"

"There aren't enough nurses or doctors, miss," said the young man, and his grip grew fierce. "They're all at the regular hospital. Get me outa here. I'm not sick anymore—I swear to God, I'm not."

"What is your name?"

"Benjie," he said, his brown eyes glossy with tears.

I squeezed his shoulder. "How old are you?"

"Nineteen, and I want to live to see twenty. I sure as hell won't if I'm stuck in this godforsaken place."

Someone called my name behind me, and I peeked up to find Addie and Nela rushing my way with the stretcher, which still held Liliana.

"There's no room," said Nela. "We can't leave her here. I'm taking her to my house."

"Let's try the regular hospital again," I offered. "Maybe—"

"It's full!" Nela continued backing Liliana toward the door. "If we show up, they'll send us away and glare at us, as if we're covered in Southside germs."

"All right. I'll be right there." I let go of Benjie. "I'm sorry. I need to go."

"Take me with you!" Benjie pressed his fingers deep into the flesh above my elbow. "Please, for the love of God and all that's holy, take me with you. Please!"

"Can we take him, too?" I asked Nela.

She swung the front door open by hooking her ankle around the bottommost edge. "The house isn't large."

"He's my neighbor," said Addie from the foot of the stretcher.

"Hey, Benjie. Can you walk yourself out of here on your own? Are you able?"

Benjie scooted himself up to his elbows. "I think so."

"We should take him." Addie readjusted her hold on the handles. "His daddy's a doctor helping a Negro regiment overseas. Benjie could probably be of use once he's up and about."

"Fine." Nela tugged the stretcher and Liliana toward her, out the door. "But he's got to swear he'll help when he gets better. We're going to be busy."

I helped Benjie to his feet and, with my arm braced around his bony upper back, I guided him toward the exit.

"You're going to be just fine," I murmured in an attempt to comfort myself as much as him. "No need to panic. This is just a passing illness. They're not panicking yet in Chicago, which is a good sign."

Before we reached the last row of cots, I witnessed a little boy bleeding from his ears, as well as his nose, and he cried tears of red.

NELA LED ME DOWN A DARK ROAD just south of the mills, along the edge of the river. I kept the throttle pulled all the way down to keep the ambulance running smooth and steady for our patients in the back. We puttered past Foursquare houses and little Queen Annes almost as nice as the family residences in the northern section of town.

"There's the house right there." Nela pointed toward one of the Foursquares, a boxy brick two-story with a dormer attic window that resembled May's. It sat at the end of the street, right before the neighborhood ended and a long stretch of darkness that looked to be a soybean field began.

"Is there anyone in there who might get exposed to the germs?" I asked.

"No. My Fred—an American—married me right before his number came up for the draft. He set me up here, but I'm staying with Mother and the rest of my family while he's gone."

I adjusted the throttle, pushed down on the brake pedal, and eased the vehicle to a vibrating stop in front of her house. Nela and Addie sidled out of the passenger side and flew off to fetch our transports from the back.

Once inside, we lit oil lamps, set the kettle boiling for tea, tucked Liliana into Nela's bed upstairs, and made Benjie comfortable on a yellow sofa in the living room. Nela bent down and struck matches to light a fire in the hearth, below a wedding photograph of her and a young man with hair so blond it looked almost white. Addie and I covered Benjie with a blanket crocheted in red and ivory yarn.

A woman near my mother's age, dressed in a polka-dot Mother Hubbard dress and a ruffled nightcap, poked her round face inside the front door, and a gust of cold air blew inside the house.

"I saw the lights and heard that ambulance rumble up to the curb," she said in an Irish brogue. "What the devil is happening in here?"

"We're fetching flu patients, Mrs. O'Conner," said Nela, coaxing a small and sizzling flame to life on one of the logs. "If you're not already busy with your family, we could certainly use some spare blankets."

"Half my house is sick with this unholy plague. God help us all." Mrs. O'Conner made the sign of the cross over her chest, her wide sleeve rustling with the movement. "I can bring spare blankets if you come over to check on my grandbabies. You're a trained Red Cross nurse, aren't you, Nela?"

Nela nodded and struck another match. "I am."

"We should fetch more of the sick," said Addie, straightening her mask over her nose. "Soon."

Nela pushed herself to her feet. "Bring your blankets, Mrs. O'Conner, and I'll be over when I can. Ivy"—Nela's blue eyes darted toward me—"you'll keep driving us, yes?"

I pursed my lips, and a hundred more excuses to flee this current situation squawked inside my head.

"Yes," I said, despite the trepidations and the aches in my head and my stomach. "I'll help."

WE DROVE THROUGH A NEIGHBORHOOD of squished-together houses with peeling paint and no front yards whatsoever—cheap and rapidly assembled structures built for Buchanan's flood of mill and railcar workers toward the end of the past century. We peered through the dark for large white signs with the word IN-FLUENZA written in red letters, nailed to front doors. I smelled chimney smoke and something akin to the scents of rot and decay.

"Most folks hate having those signs on their front doors," said

Addie with a shift of her weight on the seat beside Nela. "They make them feel dirty. And punished. Whites are always saying my people carry more diseases as it is."

"But"—Nela braced her hands against the dashboard and craned her long neck forward to better see the doorways through the windshield—"those signs are the only way we can tell if people need treatment. They own no telephones. They can't call anyone for help."

I gripped the steering wheel and squinted through the nighttime streets for quarantined homes, and all I could think about was the amount of time Dr. Lowsley spent paying me personal house calls during my recent bout with the same strain of the flu. He had fussed with aspirin and cold presses and thermometers and made sure Mama served me tea and warm soup. No one needed to hang up a sign to flag down ambulances in the dark or put me in a hospital swarming with people vomiting black tar. Even Father—a man who had never paid me much mind once I started looking more woman than girl—meandered into my bedroom one night and held my hand beside my bed for at least an hour. I never would have possessed the time to die under such watchful care.

One block down from the tracks that divided South Buchanan from the rest of the town, not far from the spot where I'd just saved the women's lives, we found a house marked with one of the red and white influenza signs. Addie and Nela scrambled to fetch the stretcher, and I followed behind them to a plain wooden door with an iron handle. Nela knocked and called out something in Polish, and when no one answered, she turned the knob and pushed the door open.

"Do you know the people who live in here?" I asked.

"No, but I feel in my heart that they need us." She stepped inside, and Addie and I sauntered in after her, with Addie holding the back end of the stretcher.

A pair of older women wearing dark scarves over their heads' spoke in hushed tones around a table in the front room. They were dressed in long black clothing from another world, another century, and when they lifted their faces to us, they wrinkled their brows and frowned.

Nela said something to them in Polish. The women nodded and, with bony white fingers, pointed toward the staircase behind us.

We clopped up the steps while the tan stretcher swayed in the space separating Nela and Addie's hands. The entire place stank of booze.

"People are drinking hard to fight the germs," said Nela over her shoulder, as if she worried I might think less of the residents for the odor—not knowing about my own father and brother's whiskey-fueled atrocities. "That's why the emergency hospital smells like liquor, too. The doctors administer whiskey."

"Well, then," I muttered under my breath, "I certainly don't need to worry about certain members of my family getting this disease."

Upstairs, in a narrow hallway unlit by a single lamp, we passed two bedrooms in which families slept like passengers piled into crowded railroad cars, with two to four people per bed.

"*Grypa?*" called Nela through the dim hallway. "*Grypa?*"

"*Pomocy!*" said a female voice from down the hall.

"Down here. Someone's calling for help." Nela steered the stretcher toward the sound of the voice, in the rightmost section of the house, and Addie followed behind with the bouncing empty stretcher jerking her elbows.

We came upon a room housing a man, a woman, and three children, including the girl who had called out to us, a pretty young thing with almond-shaped eyes who looked to be fifteen or sixteen. Her honey-blond hair, damp with fever, stuck to the sides of her face and trailed across a pair of cracked white lips, and she shuddered beneath a mountain of patchwork quilts, nuzzled between another girl and a boy.

Nela lowered the stretcher to the ground and spoke with the girl in Polish, rubbing the child's shoulder and nodding the whole time. She then turned to us and said, "She's the first one sick in the house and wants to leave before the others get it. Help me lift her, Addie."

Addie took hold of the girl's feet and assisted Nela in lifting her over her sister and onto the stretcher. The girl shivered and drew her scrawny knees to her chest, but I gave her my coat and helped the others get her laid out flat on her back to better distribute her weight.

We carried our transport down the flight of stairs and slid her into the back of the truck, behind the wooden covering marked with the large Red Cross emblem that stood out like a blood-colored beacon in the dark. After leaping back into the driving compartment, we journeyed into the night—off to the warmth of Nela's house—before setting right back out again.

The Buchanan Committee of Public Safety reports a continuing rise in the number of influenza cases within the city limits and in the surrounding farmlands. The disease, commonly referred to as "Spanish influenza," resembles a highly contagious "cold" involving pain, fever, and an intense feeling of sickness. Most patients recover after three or four days; however, doctors state that some patients develop severe complications, such as pneumonia or meningitis, resulting in death.

"Under these current circumstances, sneezing, spitting, and coughing have turned as dangerous as German poison gas," said Buchanan Health Commissioner Elmer Tomlinson. "We are taking public hygiene highly seriously." Mr. Tomlinson asked Buchanan police officers to stop and scold all coughers and sneezers who fail to use handkerchiefs. Furthermore, he instructed local businesses to monitor the use of handkerchiefs by customers and patrons within their establishments. Any owners who fail to comply with this regulation will find their businesses shut down.

Schools, theaters, motion picture houses, restaurants, churches, and chapels remain open at present. Any ensuing quarantines will be noted in the Sentinel.

—BUCHANAN SENTINEL, October 6, 1918

Chapter 6

I arrived at May's front path just as daybreak awakened in a blaze of bright-orange streaks in the eastern sky. A light drizzle cooled my flushed skin. I lifted my face to the tangerine clouds and bathed in the lush sprinkles for a moment of respite, before ducking beneath the covering of the Dovers' front porch.

In addition to Liliana and Benjie, the Red Cross volunteers and I had transported six influenza patients to Nela's house throughout the night. Mrs. O'Conner kept the fireplace and the tea piping hot, and a bounty of blankets warmed the cold.

Back inside the comfort of May's house, I sank myself down on her stiff parlor armchair and leaned my head against its cushioned backing. The stench of death and sickness clung to the fibers of my hair, the same way Billy's cigarette smoke always embedded itself inside my clothes and my hair after he took up the habit.

"I don't know what I'd do without these little coffin nails right now," he had told me out on our front porch, the night before he would board a train and leave us for good. He blew a smoke ring into the air like Alice's caterpillar friend and added, "Pops turns to drink when he's anxious, and that's all fine and well, as long as his temper's at bay. But I prefer my good pal tobacco."

"Cigarettes are called coffin nails for a reason, Billy Boy," I remembered telling him. "Be careful with those things. You're risking your life."

As I recalled, he turned his face toward mine in the moonlight, and he didn't even need to say one word for me to understand the ignorance of my comment, considering where he'd be traveling in the coming weeks.

A WARM HAND TOOK HOLD of my wrist and shook me awake.

"Ivy," said May in a soft coo. "Wake up."

My eyes blinked open to the sight of the first light of dawn shining against May's smooth face and brightening the watercolors on the wall behind her.

"I stayed up late and waited for you." She stood up straight and tightened the sash of the red silk robe she wore. "You had me worried after trekking off into the night to see that German. I thought the first-ever boarder at Dover's Home for Women of Independent Means either eloped with the enemy or got shanghaied into the German armed forces."

"I'm sorry." I winced at a sour taste in my mouth and scooted upright in the chair. "I didn't actually speak with the German for long."

"Did you tell him who you are?"

"He already knew. He threw me out of his store."

"Oh. I'm sorry." May sat down on her green sofa—the one built by Daniel and his brother. "That doesn't sound like it helped with your guilt in the slightest."

"Not in the slightest. I think I should go back."

"And say what?"

"I don't know, but I overheard men from the APL talk about shipping him off somewhere. Fort Oglethorpe, I think."

May cringed and sucked air through her teeth. "I suppose that's better than a lynching."

"I suppose." I held my head in my hands and dug my elbows into the tops of my thighs. "I can't believe we're even using the words 'That's better than a lynching.' What's wrong with the world right now?"

"What *isn't* wrong with it?" She sat back on the sofa and crossed her bare right leg over her left one. "Where did you spend the rest of the night, then? You didn't go back home, did you?"

"No! Absolutely not." I lifted my head. "I drove an ambulance for two Red Cross nurses who didn't know how to drive it themselves."

"What?" May laughed. " 'Tickling the Ivories with Ivy' also knows how to helm large automotives?"

"I do. I used to drive tractors and trucks on the family farm.

My father insisted everyone help with everything out there—even us women."

"Well, good for you."

"That part helped with the guilt a tad, but seeing how much people are suffering from this flu . . ." I closed my eyes and rubbed the balls of my fingers against the lids, finding the movement oddly soothing. "It was hard, witnessing all of that. I don't know if I have the courage and strength to do it again."

May reached over and patted my leg. "Go up and sleep in your new bed for a while. It'll make you feel better about everything, and it'll be far more comfortable than dozing in Eddie's grandfather's stodgy old chair like this."

Another sharp pain walloped me in the middle of my stomach, but I nodded and pushed myself out of the seat.

"Thank you for all of your help," I said before leaving that spot in the room. "I'm sorry if people ever . . ." I trailed off, not quite knowing how to articulate what I meant without uttering stupid phrases such as *I'm sorry people call you "Eddie's souvenir" and discuss the size of your bosom.*

"If people ever what?" she asked with a tilt of her head.

I took a deep breath. "I'm sorry if Buchanan hasn't always treated you kindly."

She nodded. "Well, thank you. But you don't need to take responsibility for the town's sins, too."

"I just . . ."

"Go up to bed, Ivy." She smiled and gestured with her head toward the stairs. "As my mother always told me, there's no use trying to face your troubles when you're tired. The troubles always win."

A LONG DAYTIME SLUMBER up in the attic's squishy bed, coupled with a late-evening bath, erased some of the strangeness and heartbreak of that long, lucid dream of a night. I donned a fresh pair of undergarments, a clean white middy blouse, and a honey-brown skirt I had sewn from extra fabric we didn't need after Billy left for the army. Mama had bought the fabric for a new pair of Sunday trousers she intended to make for him before his number was called, and there was no sense in allowing good wool to go to waste.

I followed the scent of freshly brewed coffee to May's kitchen and found her sitting by herself at a round table near the icebox. She played some sort of game with a board and a flat wooden pointer shaped halfway between a spade and a heart. Darkness had already descended over the world outside the window, and the board reflected the glare of the electric light shining down from a stained-glass lamp above the table.

"Hello." May peeked up at me from beneath her long lashes and pushed the wooden pointer to the word GOOD-BYE on the game board.

"Hello." I cleared my throat and leaned my hands against the back of one of her chairs. "What is that?"

"You've never seen a Ouija board?"

I jerked away from the table with a gasp.

May snickered. "Don't look so spooked, Ivy. The devil isn't

going to come crawling out of the board and snatch you away. It's perfectly safe."

"Are you sure about that?"

"Quite sure." She tucked the wooden pointer inside a small bag made of gray cloth. "And I'll have you know, I'm not the only Widow Street woman who employs Ouija boards and spirit mediums."

"You employ a medium?" I asked. "A séance sort of medium?"

"Yes, a highly reputable one, another former Chicago girl, in fact. Why?" She lifted the board's cardboard box off the floor. "Don't you believe in ghosts?"

"Oh, boy. What a question." I pulled out the chair with a loud screech of the wood and dropped down onto the seat.

"I'll take that response to mean that you do indeed believe," said May, a coy grin on her lips. "Might you have ghost stories of your own to share?"

"Well . . ." I folded my hands on the table to stop them from quaking. "To be most honest—and I'm only telling you this information because of your own Spiritualist beliefs . . ."

She nodded. "Go on."

"Well . . ." I inhaled a long breath with a lift of my shoulders. "The Rowan women are known to see the dead."

May raised her right eyebrow and settled the Ouija board inside its box. "The specifics, please."

"I've never once mentioned this peculiarity to another person outside the family," I said in a whisper, as if the spirits themselves—as if Eddie Dover—might actually hear me. "Not even my closest childhood friends. But my mother and I . . . well . . ." I licked my lips. "Rowan women tend to see the ghosts of loved ones right before someone dies."

May rubbed her lips together and seemed to digest my confession. "Harbinger spirits," she said with a pleased-looking nod. "Interesting."

I straightened my neck. "Is that something you know about?"

"Not entirely. But I've learned various theories about spirits through the medium."

"And what are her theories?"

"Well, she says"—May lowered the Ouija board's lid over the box with a soft squeak of the cardboard—"some spirits get stuck in the places where they died. The haunted-house sorts of ghosts, if you will. Some struggle to complete a task they didn't finish when they were alive. Others"—she brushed a sheet of dust off the curved letters of the word OUIJA on the lid—"they roam the earth, unsettled, restless, unsure what to do or where they belong. And then there are the lucky ones." She sank back in her chair and drew a deep sigh with a lift of her chest. "If only all spirits could follow their lead."

I leaned forward on my elbows. "What happens to the lucky ones?"

"They accept their fate"—she sighed again—"and just enjoy themselves."

"In heaven, you mean?"

"I was raised a strict Catholic, so I'm not sure if I can truly refer to a Spiritualist realm as heaven. But, yes, they're making the most of the afterlife. Have you ever heard that poem, 'Gather your roses while ye may'?"

"Yes, of course. It's 'To the . . .'" I cleared my throat, for the contents of the poem suddenly seemed quite personal, even if May misquoted the words a smidgen. "'To the Virgins, to Make Much of Time,' by Robert Herrick."

"Well, they're still gathering, still enjoying the party, the lucky bastards. I wish my poor Eddie could be one of them."

I stared at the way my fingers lay in a pale and quivery pile on the table, like an unsettling heap of squirming larvae. I spread out my hands and willed them to stay still. "Does Eddie visit you?"

May cast her eyes to the lamp shining above us, the warm light glistening against her moist eyes. "Yes."

"What does your medium say about his tendency to do so? What type of spirit is he?"

"A wanderer." She inhaled through her nose. "Those are the ones who tend to experience pangs of concern for their living loved ones. It's part of their restless nature."

"Do you think I'm witnessing wanderers, then?" I found myself leaning even farther forward, my elbows easing across the slick grain of the wood. "Are these spirits of lost loved ones worried about how I'll handle the news of death?"

"Perhaps." May returned her eyes to mine. "They might be attempting to comfort you."

"Unfortunately"—I glanced at the window beside us, mistaking the shadow of a tree limb for the silhouette of a man's arm—"they don't bring me one single shred of comfort. I'm actually scared to death one of them will show up at any moment, letting me know I'm about to lose someone else. This flu. That German." I shook my head. "I don't know. It just seems likely I'll see my brother whom I lost to the war, and then someone else I love will"—I swallowed and shuddered—"disappear."

May peeked at the window as well but seemed untroubled by the shadows. "So many people are dying out there right now, Ivy. I doubt there's time for spirits to bring warnings of every single fatality at the moment."

I shuddered again, and then I pushed myself to my feet. "I should get going."

"Where?"

"To see the German."

"But—"

"I know it sounds ridiculous after he threw me out, but there's a prickling deep in my bones that insists I have to go to him."

"Don't fall in love with him."

"I beg your pardon?"

"You heard what I said." Her eyes glinted with mischief, but her words carried more caution than cruelty. "Don't fall in love with the German. Unless"—she set the Ouija board box down into her lap—"you're absolutely sure"—she smiled and looked me straight in the eye—"you won't get caught."

Chapter 7

I rapped my knuckles against one of the rough-edged planks boarding up the Liberty Brothers door.

No one answered.

I peeked over my shoulder for signs of watchful eyes in the dark and then knocked again.

"Mr. Schendel?" I called inside. "It's Ivy. I would really like to speak to you."

I lowered my hand and leaned toward the door. My shadow seeped across the planks like black ink spilling across the surface. All around me, the yellow paint branched down the bricks in a frozen reminder of the violence hurled upon the store.

Nothing.

"Mr. Schendel? I know you're likely assuming I'm only here to rid myself of guilt. And you'd be partially right." I positioned my lips an inch away from the boards. "But I am concerned about you. And your family. And your business. In fact, I moved out of my parents' house because of what happened here. I thought you should know that. As much as I love my mother and worry about her staying with my father . . ." I covered my eyes and breathed through a sharp spike of pain in my head. "Oh, God, you don't know how much I worry about her right now. This flu, and . . . this . . . this murder hanging over that house. I worry about her, but I refuse to go back there. I refuse to acknowledge those two men as my father and brother. I'm done with them."

The air, cold as a root cellar, hung around me without the slightest whisper of a breeze rustling through the silence. I didn't hear anyone breathing on the other side of the door.

All those words I just confessed to him . . . wasted.

I turned to leave, and the door opened a crack. A pair of blue eyes peeked out from a shadowed face.

"Daniel?" I edged back to the door. "Did you . . . did you hear what I just said?"

"Is that true?" he asked.

"Which part?"

"You left your family? Because of this?"

I nodded. "Yes."

He didn't open the door another inch, and his face remained the only part of him I could see.

"I don't think"—he scratched at a chip on the door—"there's anything you can do for me."

"Are you sure about that?"

"I'm positive." He nodded. "There is nothing."

"I'd be willing to talk to the police . . ."

"The police already nosed about our store and did nothing. Did you see the bullshit in today's newspaper article?"

I drew back. "No. What did the article say?"

"I've stored a copy in the drawer near my cash register. If you want to witness the cold and brutal truth"—he peeked over his shoulder—"I'll go fetch it for you."

"It claims vagrants committed the murder, doesn't it?"

"The murder is only a small sliver of concern in that article. The writer complained about our lack of support in the latest Liberty Loan drive, which is a lie. He claimed we didn't register for the draft—another lie. Albrecht registered as soon as the U.S. declared war on Germany, but the army turned him down. They thought he wanted a free trip back home to the Fatherland."

"I . . ." I grabbed hold of the door. "I could talk to the news-paper. And the APL."

"No one will listen to you. It will help nothing. There is noth-ing you can do."

"There must be something. Please, let me inside so we can talk"—I pushed the door open with more force than I'd in-tended, knocking him off balance—"and so we can figure out—"

I stopped, for lamplight fell across Daniel's bare throat above the collar of the undershirt he wore instead of his shirtsleeves and vest. A vicious red line encircled his neck—a raw and ugly rope burn.

"Oh, God!" I clutched my own throat, which stung and closed up, as if someone had just clamped a rope around it.

"You need to go." He snatched my arm and steered me back toward the street.

"No! Tell me what happened." I pushed him off me and shoved my way into the heart of the store. "Did you try to hang yourself?"

"It doesn't matter—"

"Yes, it most certainly does matter. My family did this to you. They drove you to it."

"Please go, Ivy." He pointed toward the door.

"Tell me what I can do to help."

"Go."

"I don't want you killing yourself. Please, tell me what I can do to take away your pain."

"There is nothing."

"Tell me—"

"The only thing you can possibly do is to come to my bed with me."

I stepped back, and he lowered his arm and blinked as if his request had startled him as much as it had me.

"You want honesty, Fräulein?" he asked in that strange harsh and musical accent. "That is the only thing that would make me feel better, and I'm not even sure that would work."

My hands trembled, and my legs wobbled and dipped as if made out of rubber. "But . . . I-I-I can't. I'm a respectable woman . . ."

"This is wartime, Ivy. Morality and righteousness mean *nothing*."

"The war is overseas. Not here."

"Are you sure about that?" He glowered at the damaged chairs and the faded pink stains on the floor.

My skin chilled, and my eyes stung with tears—not from sorrow or shame or fear, but tears from that pustulant wound of guilt that oozed in the middle of my gut with unrelenting agony. I rubbed at the gooseflesh on my arms and thought of Peter's bruised fingers, Father's blood-spattered overalls, and the burn mark on Daniel's neck—that wicked ghost of a noose, which seemed to grow darker and redder the more I hesitated. The lining of my stomach boiled.

I turned my eyes toward the faded stains on the floor. "Do you really think it might help?"

"I don't know. As I said, I'm not sure . . ."

Out of the corner of my eye, I viewed his broad shoulders and the slim spread of his stomach, and a small flutter of unexpected arousal stirred inside me. Perhaps some primal call to procreate awakened—a deep human instinct for survival, spurred on by the threat of annihilation from the influenza and the war.

> *Gather ye rosebuds while ye may,*
> *Old time is still a-flying;*
> *And this same flower that smiles today*
> *Tomorrow will be dying.*

Daniel cleared his throat. "You don't have to—"

"You would have to promise to be gentle," I found myself

saying, and my face and neck warmed. I cupped my hands over my cheeks, imagining terrible splotchy patches, which, according to my brothers, is how my blushes often appeared.

Daniel swallowed and ran a hand through his hair. I thought he might grab my arm and toss me out of his store again, but instead he said in little more than a murmur, "My apartment is upstairs."

We locked eyes, and he seemed to test me, while I tested him, each of us waiting to call the other's bluff.

I drew a sharp breath. "Let's go upstairs then."

"All right. Let's go."

He turned, and I followed him toward a back doorway that led inside a sawdust-scented workroom crowded with planks of wood, tools, paints, glosses, harsh-smelling varnishes, fabrics, and wide worktables that reminded me of the picnic furniture out at Minter Lake. We trekked through golden flecks of wood that made my nose itch, and we reached a flight of stairs that bent up to the right. Neither of us said a word on our journey up to the second floor. Only our footsteps spoke, his more hurried than mine, although mine moved with far more urgency than I would have ever expected of such a moment. I found myself staring at the back of his neck . . . and wondering what he would taste like if I ran my tongue across that smooth patch of skin below his brown hair. I didn't normally wonder such things about men, but there it was—a strange and brazen urge. I pondered if his skin, up close, would smell of beer, as people insinuated about Germans.

Upstairs, we entered a small living room, well furnished, of course, considering the occupant. A Victrola with a painted brass horn sat on a mahogany stand in front of the leftmost window, and a photograph of a middle-aged couple in dark clothing and hats—his parents perhaps—stood on the mantelpiece of a brick fireplace. I saw a cream-colored cookstove and a wooden icebox through a doorway to the left.

"Do you live alone?" I asked.

"Yes." Daniel pursed his lips. "I do now."

"Oh. I-I'm sorry. I should have known." I glanced at the photograph of the couple again. "Are your parents—?"

"I live alone, and that's all you need to know. I have no other family anymore. Not here."

I nodded in understanding.

He sighed through his nose and continued onward through the apartment, past a closed door that made the hairs on the back of my neck bristle. I wondered, if I ventured inside the room within, whether I would find Albrecht's clothing and shoes and shaving brush, as well as other items that had touched his living body just a few days before. The room might still smell of Daniel's brother's cologne, or whatever scent he had carried upon him. Strands of his hair likely lingered in the teeth of his comb.

"It's in here." Daniel nodded his head toward another doorway, an open one. "My room, that is. Where I sleep."

I gave a little cough into my hand and followed him inside a sparse space lacking in color, aside from a navy-blue quilt on a wooden bed and tan-striped curtains hanging over a window that faced the street. Bare walnut panels lined the walls, a silver lamp sat on a chest of drawers, and a pen, a set of keys, and a brown document resembling a passport topped a small desk. A blond-wood guitar rested in the corner across from me.

Daniel rubbed the back of his neck and wandered around to the opposite side of the bed.

I eyed the quilt and the pillow, seeing the indentation of his body from the last time he had slept there. "Well . . ." I put my hands on my hips and breathed a sigh that parched my lips. "What am I supposed to do?"

He shoved his hands in the pockets of his trousers. "You've never been married?"

"No."

"A beautiful woman? Never married?"

My face warmed again. "No."

"No lovers either?"

"This is Illinois. We don't have lovers."

He barked a loud laugh—the type that comes out as a startling "Ha!" But then he hid his smile by wiping his hand across his mouth.

"What do I do?" I asked again.

"Well"—he looked toward the blue quilt and spoke more to the bed than to me—"you take off your clothes . . . and lie down."

"All of my clothes?"

"If you want. If it's comfortable."

"What do you want?"

"I want you to be comfortable."

I took off my coat, draped it over the foot of the bed, and reached up to the top button of my blouse. Daniel kept his eyes focused on the quilt, but I could tell by the way his breath grew louder and his body went still that he could see me in his peripheral vision. He was handsome for a German, I had to admit, with those deep blue eyes and short locks of tousled brown hair that curled along the sides of his forehead. Yet that red mark on his neck, the way he lingered by the bed in which he wanted me to join him—*everything* about him at the moment—reeked of death and lust. I didn't know what to make of it. I didn't know why I sort of liked it. If I looked into the mirror (if his room actually possessed a mirror), I'm not sure I would have even recognized the woman staring back at me.

> *The glorious lamp of heaven, the sun,*
> *The higher he's a-getting,*
> *The sooner will his race be run,*
> *And nearer he's to setting.*

I unhooked three more buttons and gave a shiver from the cool air nipping my bare skin. I could see the pale swell of my breasts and the white eyelet trim of my brassiere, and I thought of the long-ago summer when Wyatt Pettyjohn asked to touch my naked chest down by the lake, and how I let him, just to try it, before I told him, "I don't think I love you that way, Wyatt. I'm sorry. I've got too much to worry about at home for something like this."

A sudden jolt of music—that jazz band again—shot through Daniel's window, so loud, so close, that I could differentiate each individual instrument: a cornet, a clarinet, a trombone, drums, and a piano.

I unhooked the last button and asked, "What song is that?"

Daniel turned his left ear toward the window. " 'Tiger Rag.' Also by the Original Dixieland Jass Band."

"Why does it sound so much louder tonight?"

"They must have the windows open in the lodge." He glanced back at me. "Do you want me to open my window so you can hear it even better?"

"No! I don't want anyone out there to hear . . ." I straightened my blouse so it wouldn't hang cockeyed over my exposed Sears and Roebuck brassiere, which was the wildest thing about me, truth be told. Corsets and I had never agreed with each other because of farmwork. "Can you play it?"

"What?"

"The song? Can you play it on your guitar?"

With his hands on his waist, he swiveled his upper body toward the blond instrument leaning against the wall. Across the street, a new song commenced—a bouncier jazz number.

"You want me to play music for you?" he asked.

I nodded. "Could you? I want to hear how jazz sounds on a guitar. I've never heard it before, but I bet it's the berries."

He hesitated a moment, his hands still on his hips, his eyebrows raised, but after another nod from me, he sauntered over to the guitar. With gentle hands, like a father lifting a child from a crib, he picked up the instrument and settled down on the edge of the bed with the curve of the wood nestled against his lap. I stood there, not removing a single article of clothing, and watched him fiddle with the knobs on the neck as he tuned the silver strings.

He sat up straight and shifted himself toward the window, and I witnessed the music from the band work its way into his body. The transformation started at the top of him—his head bobbed, his eyes closed halfway. Then his shoulders rocked. He tapped his foot. His fingers lit upon the strings, and he joined right in and played that song as if, in an instant, he had become a long-distance member of the band.

I pinched my blouse shut between my right thumb and index finger and wandered over to his side of the bed, where I watched him strum with his head gently swaying.

" 'Joe Turner Blues,' " he said in his German accent, not stopping a beat, "by Wilbur Sweatman."

I perched on the far corner of the bed, and his lowest notes rumbled down through the center of my chest to the bottom of my stomach, vibrating through that guilty hollow that burbled inside me. He caressed those strings until his grief seemed to bleed straight out of his soul, and I wished my father and brother could have heard him.

The last note finished with an abrupt absence of sound, but then the band trumpeted their way into a brand-new song. Daniel placed the guitar back in its resting spot in the corner.

I rose to my feet and let my blouse fall back open.

"*Nein.*" He stepped toward me and, with delicate fingers that sent a tease of a chill down my spine, he refastened the buttons of my blouse, one by one, starting from the bottom of the garment. Our breaths blended in with one another, and the music spoke through our silence. His hands stopped before reaching the topmost button, and he pressed his left palm against my collarbone, running his thumb across the base of my throat with a touch butterfly soft.

"This . . ." He sighed against my neck. "This used to be my favorite part of a woman's body."

I exhaled a breath that must have brushed against his own neck, across the rope burn, and I wondered if I cooled some of the sting. "It's not your favorite part anymore?" I asked.

His eyes met mine. He kept his thumb on that small breadth of my skin. "Do you think I can take away your own pain? Is that why you keep coming here?"

I shook my head. "I don't know why I keep coming. I just . . ." My chest rose and fell below the spread of his palm. "There is a pain in me. A knife blade"—I balled my hand against my stomach—"wedged in my gut. I want to be rid of it. I want to finally live."

"You don't think that you've lived?"

I shook my head and swallowed. "I know I haven't. I've barely left my parents' house these past several years. I've never been with a man quite like this, and I'm . . ." I turned my eyes away from his. "The world's about to end. I can feel it in the marrow of my bones. I'm worried I'm about to miss out on a few things in life that shouldn't be missed."

He removed his hand from my skin. "Don't do anything here for the sake of your father and brother. They're not worth it."

"It wouldn't be for them."

"Are you sure about that?"

I stepped away from his touch and lifted my brown skirt and black petticoat above my knees. "Are you familiar with English-speaking poets, such as Emily Dickinson and Walt Whitman? Or Robert Herrick?"

He pinched his eyebrows together. "Why?"

"They all warn of the coming of death and teach us to embrace this world before we leave it." I slid my long cotton drawers down my legs and pulled them over each of my stockinged feet. "Shutting myself away from life, steeling myself against pleasure and pain, it's gotten me nowhere."

Before Daniel could say a word in response (his mouth hung open in an astonished dog sort of way), I kicked off my shoes. I then crawled across his bed on my hands and knees and lay back against the warm blue quilt, stirring up the smells of wood dust and spiced shaving soap. I closed my eyes and breathed in all of his scents—let my head fill up with them—while the drums and the horns of the jazz band pulsed through my blood.

"Are you sure about this?" he asked. "You don't know me at all . . ."

"I'm not sure in the slightest." I opened my eyes. "But it might be fun, and I would sell my soul for anything that's the complete opposite of death right now."

"But . . ."

"I want to try it, now that I'm here. Show me what all the fuss is about."

Daniel pulled his suspenders off his shoulders and tugged his white undershirt over his head, which made that raw red line on his neck stand out all the more. He slid toward me on the bed with a rustle of the quilt.

"Kiss me, please," I said, and I held his chin in my right hand, feeling the soft prickle of fresh stubble.

He leaned down and kissed my stomach, right above the guilty part, and I unclenched my hands and steadied my breathing. He then moved on to the length of my ribs and my breasts, as well as the spot at the base of my throat that he called his former favorite. His mouth didn't reach my lips; he didn't unbutton my clothing. He simply kissed my curves through all the layers of cotton and batiste and lace, and his hand reached up beneath my skirt. I closed my eyes and let my legs fall open, arched my back against the mattress, felt the knife blade loosen. The music pounded in my ears and wiggled its way through my torso and my hips, and when he was on me—in me—it was all I could hear and feel and taste. The headboard tapping against the wall, the beat of his breath against my ear, the electricity on my tongue, my strange, throaty cries. We were music. We were jazz.

We were alive.

Chapter 8

I blew out of that apartment with the speed of a gale whipping through rows of rustling cornstalks. Daniel slept, and I simply fled in a panic, sobered up by the fear of conceiving a *Boche* baby I would now have to explain to the rest of the world.

The band played "Jelly Roll Blues" again, and I struggled to keep my footsteps a muffled patter beneath the roar of the music blaring across the "Friendliest City in America." I buttoned up my coat and peered over my shoulder, expecting the shine of headlights at any moment.

"Ivy," said a voice from the shadows.

I sucked in my breath and came to a halt on the sidewalk across the street from the Chamber of Commerce.

A pair of round lenses glinted off the light of a streetlamp. Lucas, wearing his same charcoal-gray coat and hat from the other day, stepped out from his camouflaged position against the dark bricks of the music store. He looked just like a child playing detective.

"Where have you been?" he asked.

I kept my fingers on the top button of my coat. "What does it matter?"

He shrugged. "I just want to know what you're doing out at this late hour? Billy wouldn't have liked to think you were sneaking around."

I managed a laugh. "Billy *loved* to sneak out after dark. What are you talking about? He used to run off to your house whenever he was mad at our father, if I remember correctly."

"He wouldn't want his sister prowling around by herself though." Lucas reached into the breast pocket of his coat. "Will you do something for me, Ivy?"

I stiffened. "What?"

He pulled out a folded-up American flag and shook it out until the bottommost stripes hung down to his knees. "Will you kiss this flag for me? Show me how much you love this country?"

"Lucas . . ." I shook my head, confused. "I used to bandage up your knobby little knees whenever you'd fall down in our yard."

"Are you one hundred percent American, Ivy Rowan?"

"Of course I am."

"Then why do you smell like a German?"

My mouth fell open. I gaped at Lucas's still-round cheeks and magnified baby-brown eyes.

He stretched the flag out farther across his chest. The Stars and Stripes reflected off his lenses, and, again, he started to ask, "Why do you smell—?"

I grabbed hold of the fabric with both hands and kissed it loud enough to make an obnoxious smacking sound. I then raised my head and, not even caring that I spat as I spoke, I said in his face, "Billy would hate you for this."

"He'd hate you, too," he said, and he added, with a sting in his voice, "*whore.*"

I should have slapped him across his cheek. I really should have smacked that boy good and yelled at him for insulting the sister of his dear fallen friend. Fear of the APL paralyzed my hand, however.

Instead, I let go of the flag and fled.

I THREW MY WEIGHT against May's front door from the inside and turned a key to click the dead bolt into place. May's sewing machine whirred behind me, but the noise soon stopped, and May asked, "What's wrong?"

I shifted in her direction and found her staring at me through little silver glasses that reminded me of Granny Letty's spectacles. I would have found the look delightfully entertaining if Lucas hadn't just ripped my pride out of my chest.

"Someone caught me visiting the German," I said.

May removed her right fingers from the Singer's round hand crank. "Who?"

"A twenty-two-year-old busybody who used to be friends with my brother. He's part of the APL now." I hurtled myself over to her sofa and plopped down on the cushions before my head could go too dizzy, and, I swear, I could smell Daniel's workroom in the upholstery and the rich maple frame.

"Ivy." May swiveled toward me with a creak of her wooden chair. "If anyone ever corners you or threatens you again, there's only one thing you need to say."

"What?"

"You tell them, 'I'm the daughter and sister of men who dispose of Huns.' "

A chill shivered down my spine. The guilty spot in my stomach palpitated with squeezing shots of pain that made my mouth taste of metal. "I can't say *that*."

"If the APL is dragging you away and labeling you a traitor, you have every right to state the truth. You'll be untouchable."

I leaned forward on my elbows and pinched the bridge of my nose. "Maybe I should take my piano lesson earnings and buy a big, fat Liberty Bond tomorrow. Prove I'm one hundred percent American."

"Don't waste your money to please idiots terrified of looking like cowards. And by the way"—she set her glasses on the sewing table—"is this particular German worth so much fuss? I know he's in mourning and a tragic figure, which I'm sure melts your poetry-loving heart. But is he at least handsome and charming?"

My cheeks burned with another one of my splotchy blushes. "Oh, May. The truth of the matter is that Lucas was right to be suspicious of me. He called me a whore, and that's . . ." I covered my eyes with the heels of my palms. "That's actually the truth. The Herrick poem and all this death surrounding me inspired me to do something rather impulsive and stupid."

May's chair creaked again. "Ivy?" she asked. "Are you saying what I think you're saying?"

I nodded, my eyes still covered. "I gathered my rosebuds."

"Holy Moses!" She clapped her hands together and laughed in an impressed sort of way. "When you burst out of your cocoon, you come out in a full blaze of color and fireworks."

"Do you happen to know if there's anything I can do that would help prevent . . . ?" I lowered my hands. "I know Margaret Sanger published that pamphlet about birth control . . ."

"I don't have any douches or quinine, which she claims will help. But I do own a bottle of Nujol."

I winced. "I was hoping to sneak back out in the dark and drive that ambulance soon. I don't want a laxative in my system."

"A hot bath, then? That might help. Add a little Lysol to the water."

"Oh, God, no. That sounds horrid." I pushed myself to my feet. "In any case, I'm late for helping the girls with the ambulance."

"Why are you going straight back out there if APL busybodies are creeping around in the dark?"

"I don't want to just sit here and fret about everything. Ever since my father and brother came home the other night, I've only felt better when I'm doing something."

"What about the hot bath?"

"I'll just head off to my driving and pretend that everything will be all right."

May exhaled a curt laugh. "You can't just pretend away a pregnancy."

"I can try." I hustled toward her kitchen. "Pretending that unmentionable things never occurred is a Rowan family tradition. It's what we excel at."

"Are you sneaking out the back door?"

"Yes," I called to her from the kitchen, rounding her bulky black range. "If you don't mind, I'll steal across your yard and cut across the rest of the neighborhood so I don't have to run across any more APL snitches."

She might have minded—she might have warned me to be careful or to reconsider taking the Nujol, but I tore out of the door and into the damp-smelling air before she could talk me out of leaving.

THE AMBULANCE WHEEZED and choked in the distance again, drowning out the faraway bass line and the melody of the jazz. I sprinted down the sidewalk, terrified Nela had stalled the thing on the tracks a second night in a row.

When I rounded a corner, however, I spotted the ambulance parked in front of the brick and stone headquarters of the Buchanan Red Cross. My feet slowed. My arms swung back and forth across my waist as I brought myself to a stop in front of the vehicle. Nela crouched down in front of the grille again, puffing and reddening and turning the crank with both hands.

"Here." I bent down next to her. "Let me teach you how to turn the starter so you won't hurt yourself."

"Bah!" She stood up straight and kicked the grille with the toe of her boot. "I hate this goddamned truck!"

Addie's masked face peeked out from the passenger side, her eyebrows raised.

"It's all right." I waved at Addie, and I guided Nela aside by her elbow. "I'll show you what to do. Is the emergency brake set?"

Nela gave a brusque nod. "Yes."

"Good." I shoved the crank into place below the grille. "First of all—and this is highly important so you don't break your hand or lose an arm—you only use your left hand to turn the crank, and keep your thumb tucked next to your index finger. And only pull upward."

Nela set her hands on her hips and blew a lock of blond hair out of her eyes. "Yeah, OK. Left hand."

"Thumb tucked next to your hand," I said again, demonstrating the position with my fist.

"Left hand. Thumb tucked. Pull up."

I gave the handle a swift crank, and the motor sparked to life, popping and humming with the contented symphony of a working Ford Model T.

"Let's go." I patted the hood and scampered toward the driver's seat. "The APL is on the hunt again, and I don't want anyone stopping us from heading down to Southside."

ADDIE AND NELA NEVER TIRED THAT NIGHT, never stopped wanting to fetch one more patient. We carried the sick out of their houses on the sturdy canvas stretcher and delivered them to the comfort of Nela's home, where the fireplace burned and patients seemed to heal. Liliana had regained her strength enough to help tend to those whom we parked in the rooms upstairs. Mrs. O'Conner from next door brewed steaming cups of tea and bubbling pots of soup in the kitchen. Benjie played records on a Victrola in the front room. I didn't recognize the music that he chose, and instinctively I wondered if Daniel knew the names of the songs and the musicians. I almost even said aloud, *I bet you anything Daniel Schendel knows that tune and could cite the title and artist in less than two seconds.*

Eventually, morning broke out in patches of pale pink light. We passed a row of tired-looking houses with roofs that sagged as much as my shoulders, and the entire world struck me as a sickly thing in need of a strong shot of whiskey. Everything ailed. Even the cornfields in the distance looked unseasonably withered and brown for the first weeks of October.

"My eyes are getting bleary," I told Nela and Addie when the road ahead of me rippled into a snaking black ribbon. "I desperately need to stop and go home."

"Just one more patient." Nela squeezed her warm hand over my right knuckles on the steering wheel. "Please, Ivy. We've got to save at least one more before our shift ends. Please."

I sighed. "One more. But that's all I have left in me before risking a crash."

I drove the ambulance to a flu-marked house, one-story tall and paneled in wide red planks. A pair of floppy-eared dogs whined at us from the front windows. Nela and Addie fetched the stretcher while I knocked on the door below the scarlet letters of the influenza sign.

Behind me in the street, the Halloran's Dry Goods delivery wagon rattled by. I smelled the eye-watering stench of death and decay and guessed, with a heavy weight in my stomach, that the vehicle now delivered the deceased instead of merchandise. I returned my eyes to the little red door in front of me, not wanting to see any bodies where bolts of cloth and cooking utensils ought to have been.

No one answered my knocks, but the dogs barked from within. Their nails scratched against the floor on the other side of the wood, and from somewhere deep in the middle of the house, a child cried.

"Open the door," said Nela from the far end of the stretcher on the front path of broken bricks.

I did as she asked.

A dark hallway, lit by a flickering kerosene wall lamp, greeted us. One of the hounds, a skinny pup with a swollen belly and protruding ribs, turned and pattered toward the back of the house on tiny paws. We followed her down to a small bedroom in which a young black woman in a nightgown lay in bed with her right arm draped over her forehead. A baby with a thick head of hair slept in a crib below the window, and the ripe stench of soiled diapers hit my nose. The other child, the one I had heard bawling from outside, continued to wail in another room.

The woman turned toward us with dark eyes that bulged from a gaunt face. "What are you doing here?"

"It's all right, Mrs. Landers," said Addie. With Nela's help, she lowered the stretcher down beside the bed. "I'm working with the Red Cross now. I took over my sister Florence's duties. We're here to transport you to a medical facility where you can receive proper help."

"No." The woman curled onto her side and drew her knees to her chest. "No. I'm not going anywhere."

"It's all right, it's all right," we told her in soft coos, struggling to uncurl her rigid body and slide her toward the edge of the bed.

"Leave me alone!" she screamed. "No! You wicked women. No!"

The three of us leaned in with all our strength and somehow managed to lower her down to the stretcher on the floor, while she fought and shoved and scratched at our hands and faces.

"Please, don't panic," said Nela, unhooking the woman's fingers from her hair.

"Don't take me!"

"We're here to help," I said, receiving a sharp smack across my cheek.

The woman clawed the back of Addie's hand and slammed her palm into Nela's stomach. "Don't take me away from my babies! They've got no one else. Don't take me away. I'll kill you if you do! I'll kill you!"

Oh, God, I thought with tears welling in my eyes. *What type of world are we living in? What is this hellish illness and paranoid country doing to all of us?*

In the end, we left the young mother behind. She sobbed into her pillow as we closed the front door behind us, but there was simply nothing more we could do for her or her children, aside from obeying her wishes to be left alone. We possessed no medicine, no vaccine, no miraculous cure. None of us even carried a bottle of whiskey. We were but ferrymen—or ferrywomen—in the night, transporting the masses.

If anyone in the future were to ever ask me, *How bad was that strain of the flu that destroyed so many people around the time your brother died—that "Spanish influenza" that raged out of control when Albrecht Schendel was found murdered in his store?* I would tell them what I witnessed, all the pain and the grief and the seas of blood. Yet I don't think mere words, mere fumbled attempts to articulate the suffering, would be enough to convey the horror.

Even I didn't completely absorb the full impact of that disease those first nights of taxiing flu patients around South Buchanan, and I half convinced myself it was all a terrible nightmare stemming from my own flu fevers. I would soon wake up, and Albrecht Schendel would live, and no pandemic would exist out there, devouring the earth.

I DON'T EVEN REMEMBER arriving back at May's house that morning. Beyond the closed door of her bedroom, she tittered and chatted with someone, and I assumed her telephone was located in that particular part of the house. I didn't dare let my mind wander to her talk of Eddie's spirit. My brain ached too much to think of ghosts and Uninvited Guests.

Upstairs, I changed into my white nightgown and crawled toward the pillow across the bed like a blind pup in search of its mama.

Hours later, I opened my eyes on that lumpy attic mattress, and darkness squeezed around me again. Daytime had waned. Nighttime awoke. Time to fetch more of the sick.

The reported number of influenza cases, as well as fatalities resulting from influenza complications, continues to rise in Buchanan and the outlying regions. The Red Cross has issued another call for emergency volunteers. Interested parties, especially anyone with nursing or home health training, should report to the Red Cross headquarters on Lincoln Street. Furthermore, the Emergency Hospital, located in Polish Hall in South Buchanan, is in dire need of cots and blankets. Donations should be taken directly to the Red Cross, not to the hall itself. The city urges healthy members of the public to refrain from visiting Buchanan Hospital, Polish Hall, and any other facility tending to the sick.

The Buchanan Board of Health is discussing the mandatory use of three-ply gauze masks for all residents. In the meantime, police officers continue to strictly monitor all sneezing, coughing, and spitting No house should be exited without a handkerchief tucked inside one's pocket.

Mayor Hoyt, along with other noted officials, continues to remain in tip-top shape. City Hall has not reported any deaths among its employees and states that Buchanan is running "as smoothly as a ship in peaceful waters."

—Buchanan Sentinel, *October 8, 1918*

Chapter 9

I desperately required a reprieve.

After three nights in a row of driving and fetching and washing blood out of my blouse, reliving the sounds of flu victims choking in my sleep—remembering the sight of my own flu-stricken face in the mirror—my soul thirsted for music.

The jazz band complied.

I stood in the shadows in front of Daniel's store, not even caring if Lucas spied on me from somewhere nearby. I nearly even called out, *Hey, Lucas! Stop hiding in the doorways and come listen to this music. I'm tired of worrying about everything and just want to have some fun. Don't you?*

Up on the second floor across the street, beyond the open windows of the Masonic Lodge, the musicians serenaded our poor broken world with a fox-trot. No lights shone in Daniel's business behind my back, but I longed for him to open the door and join me—to imbibe the music meant for living and loving and dancing.

Two more songs passed, and yet I stood out there alone, afraid of knocking and fearful of leaving.

One more song, I told myself, peeking at the entrance of the store out of the corner of my eye. *And then I'll leave.*

No cars drove by in the street. No Lucases seemed to lurk nearby. I remained alone, accompanied by the jazz and the sweet promise of escape beyond those upstairs windows.

A minute or so later, the shop door opened with a jingle of the bell that hung above it. Daniel appeared in the lighted entryway and leaned his back against the doorjamb. He wore his shirt-sleeves and tweed vest again, and the red mark from the noose hid beneath his collar.

My lips parted, but no words slipped through them. He regarded me for several silent seconds, and I regarded him, while the music nudged us to inch closer together.

"Well," he finally asked, and he picked at a splinter hanging down from the doorframe above him, "do you now feel you understand what all the fuss was about?"

I sputtered a laugh. "Yes, I think I do."

He snapped the splinter off in one piece and tossed it out to the street. "I wasn't sure you'd ever come back."

"I've been helping out with the Red Cross quite a bit. I drive an ambulance and fetch flu victims down in Southside."

"Really?" He arched his eyebrows. "*You* fetch flu victims?"

"Yes, I do. I'm quite useful down there." I straightened my

posture. "Why? Are you the type of man who believes women ought to stay away from automobiles?"

"No."

"Do you think I wouldn't help the Southside sick, then?"

"Jesus Christ." He raised his hands in the air. "I wasn't trying to pick a fight."

"Well, anyway"—I turned my face back up to the Masonic Lodge windows above us—"that's what I've been doing." I watched him watching me in my peripheral vision. "Do you want to head across the street with me? They're playing fox trots tonight, so I assume there's dancing."

Daniel grimaced and swallowed as if I'd just force-fed him turpentine.

"Don't you dance?" I asked.

He picked at another splinter above his head. "It's been a long while."

"There's probably booze."

He shook his head. "I'm not in the mood for parties. I'd go for the booze, maybe, but not for anything else."

"The music's so loud over there. Not one person would hear that you have an accent."

He peeked up at the windows across the way and breathed a sigh that chilled to white fog in the crisp nighttime air.

"Please come, Daniel. I don't like the idea of you lingering here on your own with just dark thoughts for company."

"I'm not going to kill myself, if that's what troubles you."

"I'd believe you more if you escaped this place. Come with

me." I gestured with my head toward the street. "Let's go have a drink and relax in a corner of the room. We don't have to dance or talk to anyone else." I stepped toward him with my hands stuffed in my warm coat pockets. "I'll even come back here with you"—another step—"for a little while. Afterward."

"*Ach.*" He reached out and tucked a stray strand of my hair behind my ear. "*Du begehrst mich.*"

"What does that mean?"

"It doesn't matter." He glanced up at the lodge again. "Go up there for me, Fräulein. See what it's like. I'll wait in my window across the way, and you peek out and wave if it's to your liking."

I furrowed my brow. "You're just going to watch from across the street?"

"I'll listen to the music. I'll imagine you drinking and dancing. But"—he fixed my stray lock a second time, for it had fallen back in my face and tickled my cheek—"I am not going over there. You can come back and tell me about it afterward if you'd like." He unhooked the top button of my jacket. "I'll even look after your coat for you, so you don't have to worry about losing it when you're dancing."

"I probably won't dance . . ."

"But you'll get warm." He unfastened the rest of the buttons, and the skin of my chest prickled at the pressure of his so-close fingers. I smelled his rich shaving soap and the scent of sawdust, and my head went a little bit tipsy. I braced my right foot behind me.

He eased the coat off both my shoulders "Go. See what it's like. I'll be here."

THE BAND PLAYED "Livery Stable Blues" again. Once I entered the lodge, the instruments sounded muffled, as if hidden behind thick closed doors. A tantalizing treasure kept safe from the outside world.

I meandered down an upstairs hallway lined in a faded green rug the color of moss. The dark-wood walls smelled of age and oak and smoke, and upon them hung oil portraits of Masonic Grand Masters past, who stared at me with glints of distrust in their no-nonsense eyes. Weak electric light shone down from old lamps that flowered out of the ceiling with curved copper and frosted glass.

Toward the end of the hall stood a closed set of four-paneled doors that stretched high above my head. The knobs themselves spoke of grandness and secrecy, with an eye surrounded by a triangle carved into the patina-covered brass of each of them. From within the sealed off room beyond, the clarinet crowed like a rooster; the cornet whinnied like a horse. Laughter and music beckoned, *Come closer. Come see. Come see . . .*

I held my breath, turned one of the knobs with a brass eye pressing against my skin, and entered what looked to be a party inhabited by a couple dozen locals. I saw jewels, booze, a brick wall with five arched windows, gold-papered walls in the rest of the room, Sunday-best dresses, suits and ties, and round tables set up along the perimeter of a dance floor made of gleaming wood with black and white stripes on the edges. Three doughboys in olive-green U.S. Army uniforms poured glasses full of liquor at one of the back tables. An interracial band—the *only* interracial sight I'd ever witnessed in Buchanan, Illinois, aside from the patients at Polish Hall—blared "Livery Stable Blues" from the leftmost side of the room. A dozen couples fox-trotted around the polished boards, their upper bodies stiff, their legs and feet moving in perfect synchronization, as if the tips of their toes connected to their partners' shoes with invisible strings. I saw former classmates, unfamiliar couples, and more army boys in uniform, perhaps on leave from the training camp ten miles down the highway. The piano player—a young fellow with slicked dark hair that looked practically painted across his head—attacked those ivories with the same fervor I would have adored to use on that keyboard myself. My fingers itched with the urge to make music again. It had been far too long since I closed my keyboard cover at the beginning of October and retired upstairs with the first symptoms of the flu.

A wiry chap in a brown plaid suit brushed past my elbow and strutted into the room beside me. "So, this is where the jazz is," he said in a thick eastern European accent that resembled Nela's. He smiled, tugged his tweed cap off his blond head, and stepped farther inside with a little waddle of awe, as if he'd just wandered into a dream.

I drank in the entire scene around me and debated whether I

should scoot myself backward out of the room. I felt an intruder. A thief, stealing pleasure not meant for me.

Before I could retreat, a woman in a gauzy midnight-black dress—Eddie Dover's first sweetheart, Ruth Sellman—wiggled my way with two whiskey glasses in her hands. She wore her copper hair cut stunningly short, bobbed just below her chin, in the style of dancer Irene Castle, and she looked nothing at all like a war widow. I read in the paper that she had lost her husband, Jesse, to the Battle of Belleau Wood over the summer, but the toothy smile on her face and inebriated gleam in her eye spoke nothing of pain.

"Well, hello, Ivy." She bumped her broad hip against mine and dribbled a little whiskey onto the tips of her black shoes. "I never expected to see you here. You've been such a homebody since school ended ages ago."

"Yes . . . well"—I fussed with the limp collar of my blouse—"I live in town now, so I thought I'd come see what all the excitement was about."

"As you should. Here . . ." She handed me one of the glasses and sloshed more liquid over the rim. "Oops, sorry. Watch your feet there."

"It's all right." I turned my nose away from the sour smell that reminded me of Father and Peter charging into the house, spattered in blood. "Is this a party someone organized? Am I intruding on something private?"

"Not in the slightest. This is all a rather casual affair." She half-turned toward the musicians and talked over their loudening chorus. "The piano player came up here one recent night, feeling blue about everything going on in the world, and he just started attacking those ivories like he was living his last day on earth." She slung her arm around my shoulder and spoke close to my ear. "People heard him, and the other musicians and folks around town migrated over here like a herd of antelope answering the migratory call of nature."

"I don't blame them," I said, sidling away from her whiskey smells. "I've wanted to come up here for the same reason."

"Make yourself at home, Lively Ivy." She bumped my hip again. "Drink up. Don't give a thought about this damned killjoy flu or that nasty threat of Prohibition." She waved all those troubles away with a flick of her hand and a shimmer of airy black sleeves. "Somehow, the music will always play . . . and the booze will perpetually flow."

"Thank you."

She sashayed away and grabbed hold of a stocky, red-cheeked fellow by his emerald-green necktie. With one last peek back at me, she led the man across the floor and braced her arms around his for a go at the grizzly bear—a silly-looking dance involving showing one's teeth and yelling, "It's a bear!" I had once danced the thing with Wyatt at the hall beside the lake, years before.

I stood there on the edge of the dance floor, hovering on the borderland between the fun and the exit. The cries of the music tempted. I hesitated and wavered and rocked in place.

Come here. Come closer. Dance. Live. Love . . .

The song dwindled to an end, and without stopping for a

single breath, the band eased into a piece with a softer tempo. The couples slowed their pace, inched closer to one another, and rocked in each other's arms with a gentle grace that reminded me of September breezes brushing across the fields behind our house. I thought of Helen, Sigrid, and me playing hide-and-seek among green stalks of corn growing tall and pregnant with the coming harvest, our hair tied back with bows as large as the birds soaring overhead.

I slipped away to an open window framed by pale red curtains and glanced out at the sleeping street beyond. Across the way sat Daniel, perched on the sill of his own open window, whittling a piece of wood the size of a flat shoe.

I set down my whiskey glass and leaned my head out the window. "It's nice in here."

Daniel peeked up at me. A train whistled through the air from the west, and a wind rattled across the leaves of the maple below him. The night tasted electric, as if lightning lingered nearby.

"You should come over," I added.

He shook his head and returned to his whittling.

I frowned.

"Ivy?" asked a hesitant male voice from behind me. "Is that you?"

I turned around and discovered my old friend Wyatt walking toward me with his own sloshing glass of whiskey. He looked to be the same old usual Wyatt, with dark brown hair sticking up on the back of his head like the ruffled feathers of a duck, large ears, and a shirt in need of extra tucking beneath his gray coat. He still worked on his father's farm near the lake, the last I heard, and he and Sigrid owned their own little house on the edge of the property.

"I thought that was you," he said, and he joined me in front of the window, resting his glass next to mine on the sill. "How are you?"

"I . . ." I peeked across the street and found Daniel gone. The pounding of the nearby drums resonated inside my chest, which now felt hollow and empty. "I'm fine for now. I fell ill with that flu last week."

"Oh, God." Wyatt winced and pressed a hand against his forehead. "Please don't even say that word."

"Has it hit your house, too? Is Sigrid all right?"

"She and the children have been in the hospital for several days."

"Oh no." I touched his arm. "Oh, Wyatt. I'm so sorry. Is it bad? Are they going to be all right?"

"I don't know." He grabbed up his glass and gulped down the liquor with a swig that must have stung his throat. "I had to get away." He wiped his damp lips with the back of his hand. "I know I shouldn't be seeking out pleasures without her, but I had to escape the coughing and the fevers and all that other mess that goes with it. It's too much. You know what I mean? It's just too goddamned much for a person to take."

"Is there anything I can do for her? She was always so kind whenever any of us got sick as kids, making us little cards and bringing us home-picked flowers . . ."

"I really don't think there's anything any of us can do for her right now." He scratched at the red tip of his nose. "No one seems to know how to help. The doctor keeps giving her aspirin, but she just throws it up."

I turned my eyes toward the swaying couples on the dance floor. "I just—" I swallowed. "I know I've been a terrible friend to her these past seven years. I always felt a little awkward, seeing the two of you together . . . after you married. And everyone at home always needed my help. I had my piano lessons . . ."

He set his glass next to mine again. "How about you dance with me for a little while, for old times' sake, when life was so much easier? Remember the boat rides, and the motion pictures? And the dances by the lake?"

I dropped my hand away from his arm. "I don't . . . No, I'm sorry. It wouldn't feel right dancing with you, not with her lying ill in the hospital."

"I just want a dance, Ivy. Nothing else." He stepped nearer and caressed the sides of my arms with calloused hands that used to swallow up mine with their size. "I just need to be held by someone for a little while. I can't stand what's happening. How can you bear it? Why aren't you falling apart?"

I took another look across the street, in search of Daniel, while Wyatt breathed shaky breaths against my cheek. The drums beat so hard in my chest that they felt like a person whacking my heart with a club. My lungs squeezed shut. I couldn't breathe.

"Ivy, please . . ."

"I can't." I pushed against Wyatt's shoulder and nudged him away. "I'm sorry you're suffering, but I've got to go."

"But, Ivy—"

"No. I'm sorry. Other people need us."

He called my name again, but I cut through the center of the dancing couples. Elbows knocked against my arms, thick heels tromped on my toes, the scent of whiskey dizzied my head. Yet I managed to push through the crowd.

Before I pulled open the solid door and escaped into the hallway, Ruth called to me over the horns and the piano, "Don't be a stranger, Ivy sweetheart." She gave me a flirty wink, her arms still wrapped around the stocky fellow with the bright green tie. "Next time, wear your dancing shoes and stay for a while."

Chapter 10

Silhouettes of furniture—half-damaged, half-resurrected—stood in the darkness of Daniel's empty store. The sawdust air tickled my nose. The jazz music played on across the street, but the sound faded into a surreal and cottony memory of another world.

"Who was that fellow you were with?" asked Daniel from somewhere unseen, giving me a start.

I clutched my neck and drew a short breath. The *brush-brush-brush* of sandpaper rubbing against wood started up in the back workroom, hinting at his whereabouts. I followed the noise and found him sanding down the legs of a barstool by the light of a brass ceiling lamp that hung over one of the worktables.

He peeked up at me with only his eyes. "Do you know him?"

I shrugged. "What does it matter? You urged me to go up to investigate the music on my own, so I went."

"You said people in Illinois don't have lovers."

"He's not my lover. He's just . . ." I swept that same unpinned lock of hair from before out of my eyes. "He asked to marry me a long while back, when we were fresh out of school."

"And what happened?"

"I didn't wish to marry him. I enjoyed his company as a friend, but I didn't love him."

"Hmm." Daniel kept sanding. "Poor devil."

"I wouldn't feel too sorry for him." I crept farther inside the workroom with dull smacks of my soles for footsteps. "He ended up marrying a good friend of mine, and I've always wished them both well."

Daniel lifted an eyebrow. "His wife was at the dance, too?"

"No, she and the children are suffering from the flu, which has me worried. They're in the hospital. Wyatt said he needed an escape from everything."

Daniel stopped sanding and puffed a sigh through rounded lips.

"What's wrong?" I asked. "Surely you don't care about harmless Wyatt Pettyjohn—"

"What do you want to do?"

I straightened my neck. "I beg your pardon?"

"Do you want to stay here with me, or go back across the street, or . . . or . . ." He pursed his lips and braced his hands against the worktable. "I don't know why you keep coming here, Ivy."

"If you want to me to leave, I'll leave." I stepped backward. "I do have more important things I should be doing . . ."

"I'm not heading out of this building for silly dances. I have no desire to leave."

"I didn't say you had to."

"If you want to be with me—"

"I never said that either. I'm risking my neck just coming here. An APL informant out there already called me a whore."

Daniel's eyes darted toward the entrance to the main section of the store. "You spoke to someone who's watching you?"

"He used to be friends with my brother Billy. There are others like him out there, and they're keeping a close watch on you, too. I overheard a group of APL men talking about shipping you off to a fort of some sort."

Daniel let go of the table.

"I'm sorry to say it," I continued, "but you have the reputation of being the last German business owner in town. Everyone knows who you are. The APL is making sure the bank doesn't approve you for a loan."

"They specifically said my name?"

"Yes. I overheard the APL talking about the store when I left the other night. They pulled up in a car and talked about you without realizing I stood around the corner in the dark."

Daniel shook his head. "Why did Albrecht first come over here for a better life? Why in hell did he have to go and tempt me to follow him?"

"I'm sorry. I truly am."

He eyed the staircase, just behind me, to my right.

I glanced over my shoulder at the dim wooden steps. "I-I don't know if I should stay here with you. Lucas—that APL spy—he—"

"You know what I say to people who call me terrible names?"

"No." I peeked back at him. "What?"

"I tell them they're small and unimportant. They're just bullying other people because they're aware of their own insignificance. They're specks—which in German refers to bacon fat, but I'm talking about the English meaning. Little dots that carry no weight."

I couldn't help but smile.

"Come upstairs with me again," he said, and he wandered around the worktable and over to where I stood in front of shelves of paints and varnishes. With a gentle touch, he slid his left hand through my hair behind my right ear. "Let's escape this hell together. Who needs it?"

"Will you kiss me on the lips this time?"

He shook his head. "No. I'm not going to let myself do that."

"Why not?"

He lowered his eyes to my mouth. "A punishment."

"A punishment? For me, you mean?"

"No, for me." He brushed his cheek against mine and let his lips hover over the side of my neck. His breath warmed and tingled across my skin.

"Doing this with me," I said near his ear, "doing what you

did the other night with me—without kissing me—doesn't help your . . ."

He raised his head. "It doesn't help my what?"

"Your reputation. As a German." I swallowed. "They say . . ."

His mouth hardened, and he nodded for me to continue. "Go on. What do people say about us Krauts?"

"I'm sorry." I shook my head. "It doesn't matter. What does anything matter anymore?"

"They say we're animals, don't they? Lust-filled, beer-drinking beasts."

"If you just kissed me on the lips, it wouldn't feel that way."

"Come upstairs." He took my hand in his and stepped backward, toward the staircase. "I'll kiss you everywhere else—every other square inch of your American body, if you'd like—and I swear you'll go home not caring whether or not you were with an animal."

I squeezed down on his hand. "I don't think you're an animal, Daniel."

"I don't care if you do. Just let me take you upstairs again."

I turned my face to the dark wedge of the front counter visible beyond the doorway to the store.

"They're specks, Ivy," he reminded me. "Don't let them stop you from doing what you want to do."

I nodded. "You're right. To hell with them."

I RECALLED MY DREAM from the first night living outside of my house—the hazy reverie in which I had danced upon a table with bright-blue butterfly wings hanging off my naked back, while the jazz band wooed me with brass-fueled wails and moans. That same delicious breath of freedom visited me in Daniel's bed that second night, all my clothing and inhibitions gone.

My new metamorphosed self.

Ivy of the Night.

Afterward, we lay side by side in a tangle of sheets and bare legs and arms, our chests exposed, our faces flushed, our breathing blending in with the percussion of the band. My hair draped across his pillow in honey-blond sheets, freed from the pins that typically clamped it to the back of my head in intricate knots. When she worked at the bakery, Helen always compared my hairstyle to Mr. Weiss's fancy twisted breads.

Oh, Helen, I thought to myself with a sigh. *Just look at me now. I've done exactly what I scolded you for doing—involving myself with a German.*

Beside me, Daniel closed his eyes and drew a long breath through his nose. " 'Bull Frog Blues,' " he said in a voice lush and sleepy, "by the Six Brown Brothers."

I smiled. "You're a veritable jazz library."

He shrugged. "I spent so much time in the music store down the way. The owner's father was from Munich."

"Really? Mr. Smith is part German?"

"No, Mr. *Schmidt* is part German."

"He Americanized his name?"

"His father did, at Ellis Island, long before the war."

I rolled onto my right side, facing Daniel, and propped myself on my elbow. "What about back in Germany?"

"What about it?"

"Did you learn how to play the guitar there? Is that where your love of music began?"

He kept his eyes closed, and I noticed that his lashes carried flecks of both brown and gold. "My father owned a music store," he said, "and I grew up sampling instruments. Albrecht always loved carpentry, like our uncle, and I was the one who was supposed to go off and indulge in a gypsy life of performing."

I bit down on my bottom lip. "What happened?"

He turned his head toward me and blinked. "What do you think happened? I was a youth in 1914 Germany."

"The war?"

"Of course the war. It took away everything."

"Were you—?"

"No, you don't want to ask that next question, Ivy."

"How do you know what I'm going to ask?"

"You're going to ask if I was in the war, in the Kaiser's army."

"Well . . ." I pulled the sheet up over my chest, drawing its warmth around my skin. "Were you?"

He turned his face toward the ceiling and inhaled another long breath. "As I said, I was a youth in 1914 Germany. Of course I was put into the army."

I sank my head back down on the pillow.

"Bull Frog Blues" transitioned into a new song—a slow and aching melody that triggered tears in my eyes and hurt my throat.

A singer joined in, his words too garbled by the closed windows for me to hear them enough to understand what he sang, but his voice resonated with heartbreak and regret and loss. I eased down on my back and imagined Daniel four years younger, forced into a uniform like Billy, shipped off in a train to destinations unknown.

Daniel swallowed loud enough for me to hear him. "I'm sorry I made you cry."

I cleared my throat. Before I could respond and say I forgave him, he added, " . . . by Henry Burr."

"Oh." I sniffed and laughed a little. "Is that the song's title?"

He nodded. " 'I'm Sorry I Made You Cry.' "

Another verse passed, and he reached across the sheet and touched the back of my hand with the tips of his fingers.

We listened to the rest of the song with our hands pressed together and our eyes closed—or at least mine stayed closed the entire time, and his were shut when I lifted my lashes again. I then withdrew my hand from his, slipped out of bed, and fetched my long white drawers and my brassiere from the floorboards near his guitar.

"Did you ever see my card for piano lessons when you were visiting Mr. Smith's store?" I asked while tugging the undergarments over my hips. " 'Tickling the Ivories with Ivy.' "

"Oh . . . yes." He smiled. "I didn't know what that tickling the ivories expression meant at first. I thought it was something lewd."

"Oh no! Did you really?"

He chuckled from deep within his stomach. "I was tempted to telephone that Ivy during a particularly lonely night or two."

"Oh no!" I blushed and coughed up a laugh. "You would have been frightfully disappointed when a prim and proper piano teacher showed up at your door with sheet music."

"You're wrong." He curled onto his side. "I wouldn't have been disappointed at all."

I fumbled to fasten the brassiere around my chest and suppressed a smile that longed to stretch to ridiculous widths.

Another song rumbled awake across the street: a Scott Joplin composition, "Maple Leaf Rag."

"Ooh, I love ragtime," I said, standing up tall. "It's what first inspired me to plunk myself down on my grandmother's piano bench as a child. I begged Granny to teach me how to play it, and when she insisted on the classics, I taught myself Scott Joplin."

"And what did Granny say to that?"

"She told me I would have to give up any concert hall dreams if I insisted on playing Negro music."

Daniel snickered.

I wandered over to the window and debated lifting open the sash to hear better. My right fingers instinctively played the melody on the side of my leg.

"This music from across the street," said Daniel from the bed, "it's like a siren call to you, isn't it?"

I smiled and nodded. "Mm hmm."

"One day, you'll find yourself going to it . . . and never coming back."

"Well, that's a little ominous sounding." I rested my hand on his desk and brushed my palm against the brown passport-style document I'd seen sitting there two nights before.

I shouldn't have let my eyes veer toward that private piece of paper. I should have just kept listening to the music—I knew better. But the words on that front cover jumped straight off the page at me.

UNITED STATES OF AMERICA
DEPARTMENT OF JUSTICE
ALIEN REGISTRATION CARD

An official Department of Justice seal involving an eagle and the American flag filled the center of the page. The space at the bottom contained lines specifically pertaining to Daniel:

Issued to Wilhelm Daniel Schendel
Address 447 Willow Street
Buchanan, Ill.

I moved my hand away from the document and attempted to steady my breathing.

"What's wrong?" he asked from behind me, still lying on the bed. "Your back just went stiff."

"I'm sorry . . . I just . . ." I peeked over my shoulder at him. "Your registration card is sitting here on your desk."

"Oh. *That.*" He pushed himself up to a seated position. "My 'enemy alien' card, you mean."

"Yes." I lowered my eyes. "I suppose that's what they call it."

"What bothers you more about it?" He cocked his head at me. "The fact that I have it? Or my name written upon it?"

"Your real first name is Wilhelm?"

"Yes." He nodded. "Just like Kaiser Willie."

"Why don't you go by William?"

"I don't want to be called William. Daniel is one of my names, and it doesn't need to be twisted and misshapen to sound American."

I left the document and the window behind and picked up my black petticoat and skirt from the floor.

Daniel sank back against the sheets. "Are you finally feeling guilty about fucking a German?"

"Don't . . ." I shook my head and tugged both skirts up to my waist. "Don't say that word. It's ugly."

"Which word? Fucking? Or German?"

"No . . . don't."

"It's what you're doing, you know."

"I know."

I finished getting dressed, and he watched while the ragtime piano filled the empty gaps. I felt as if I'd swallowed a wasp or some sort of other stinging creature that pinched my tongue, burned my throat, and aggravated the guilty spot in my stomach. The pain seared and throbbed worse than ever.

I fastened the last button of my blouse and headed over to Daniel's side of the bed. My lips shook, and my voice threatened to crack, but I forced myself to speak.

"Don't call yourself an animal anymore," I said. "And don't assume I think the worst of you. I know there's something sick and wrong with our country right now, but don't make what we've done a part of its vileness."

He chewed on the inside of his cheek. "I don't think what we've done is vile."

"Neither do I."

"Are you certain about that?"

I hesitated a moment, but then I nodded.

"Will you come back again tomorrow night?" he asked.

"It's risky."

"Why? Because of those APL jackasses?"

"Because of the chance of me becoming in the family way."

"I can't get you pregnant."

"You can't?"

He picked at a small wrinkle in the sheets. "No."

"Are you quite certain about that?"

"Something happened. And I can't."

I tucked my blouse into my skirt until the fabric lay smooth and flat against my stomach. "That's another reason why I'm hesitant to come back again: you have far too many secrets. They make me uncomfortable."

"You're much better off not knowing my secrets."

"Then perhaps you should be on your own, Herr Wilhelm Schendel."

"Don't do that." He reached out and grabbed my hand. "Don't be cruel. My secrets are all a part of my past. There's simply no need to discuss them."

"But—"

"They won't change anything, and they can't hurt you. What's done is done."

"Are you . . ." I peeked over my shoulder, as if Lucas might actually be standing there in the room with us, eavesdropping on our conversation—and our lust. I shifted back toward Daniel and said in a whisper, "Am I safe with you, Daniel?"

"Nothing can hurt you here. I swear." He kissed the back of my hand with a touch that warmed and soothed. "Out there"—he nodded toward the window—"is chaos. In here, it's paradise. We found paradise, *Liebling.* But you have to keep coming back to make it stay."

I nodded with my lips pressed together. Tears blurred my eyes. "I'm sure I will. You know I will."

"Good," he said, although it sounded like *goot,* and he slid his fingers out of mine. "I'll be here."

Chapter 11

*T*he world outside smelled of rain. Beneath the streetlamps the sidewalks glistened with the dampness of a recent drizzle, and the trees dripped and made the world feel a tad cleaner. The jazz band played another song meant for two-stepping, and I heard the unmistakable hiss of a barn owl atop the roof of the bank building I passed.

I crossed the street and stopped in front of Weiss's Bakery. Inside the closed and darkened storefront, barely visible in the lack of light, sat the empty glass display counters that used to house cookies, cakes, breads, and pastries with long German names: *Franzbrötchen, Spritzkuchen, Streuselkuchen.* Before the war, we never thought twice about going into the little cream-colored shop, and I never worried about Helen working for Mr. Weiss—until all the talk started. Until we decided, *Yes, these people aren't like us. Their accents sound dangerous, not charming. Their countrymen back home are heathens and killers, so the ones living here must be the same.*

"Can you come see a picture with me?" Helen had asked me one afternoon just that past July.

"You know I get headaches whenever I head into town," I told her, and I almost didn't go. I saw her bloodshot eyes and the way her red curls hung in a tangled mess beneath her brown cloche, as if she had just squeezed the hat over her head to hide the disarray. But still, I hesitated.

"It's important," she had said, grabbing hold of my arm. "People just searched my apartment. They threw me across my own room when I told them the truth about Mr. Weiss and me. They tore open everything I own. I'm leaving tomorrow."

And she did. According to her mother, who spoke to my mother, Helen left Buchanan on the first morning train. I hoped—although I never knew for sure—that she made it safely to some faraway destination and forgot all about the ostracized Mr. Weiss, who supposedly failed to buy Liberty Bonds and caused all of her troubles to begin with. No letters from Helen ever arrived, though. She might not have wanted her postmarks traced. She might have needed my help, but I just stayed inside my house, worrying that the walls would collapse and the roof would cave in if I wasn't there, watching over everyone.

I blinked at the empty skeleton of the bakery in front of me.

Daniel was right: paradise hid behind closed doors. Outside, the "Friendliest Town in America" felt cold and ugly and stripped of life. *I* felt cold and ugly.

Without warning, an automobile engine roared around the corner. Headlights blared across my face, and my stomach dropped. I turned in the opposite direction and walked at as brisk a pace as possible without looking like I was running. The vehicle rumbled nearer, and I broke into a jog and darted around a corner, nearly slipping on the damp sidewalk. I launched into a full-fledged sprint, and the vehicle careened around the corner behind me and growled at my heels.

"Ivy!" called a familiar female voice that sounded like Addie's. "Why on earth are you running away from us?"

I stopped and turned. Addie and Nela—the bottom of their faces still swathed in gauze masks—peeked out from the windshield of the ambulance trailing behind me. Nela shifted a lever, and the engine sputtered and choked like a hundred-year-old man and died a brisk death. The street fell silent.

I clutched my chest and bent forward at my waist, and I laughed with relief. "Oh, thank God! I thought you were someone else."

"If you didn't want to help us tonight"—Nela slid out of the driver's side—"you should have told us. We've been looking for you for hours."

"I'm so sorry." I walked toward them. "I thought I said something about needing a short break tonight."

Nela snorted. "Our transports would like a break, too, but do you see anyone giving them one?"

"I know." I glanced down to the street's junction with Willow. "There's just—someone I've been worried about."

"We know all about that someone." Addie shifted to her right and dangled her legs out of the side of the ambulance. "Your German lover."

"What? What did you just say?" I hurried closer and lowered my voice to a whisper right in front of her. "Who on earth said that I had a lover?"

"Some man with thick glasses," said Addie, also in a whisper.

"You spoke to Lucas?"

She shrugged. "I don't know his name. We were looking for you and saw the man standing outside of that lodge back there that's playing jazz. He asked who we were searching for, and we told him."

I bit down on my bottom lip, feeling the pinch of my own teeth.

"Don't look so frightened, Ivy." Nela leaned her elbows against the ambulance's olive hood. "We don't care that this sweetheart of yours is a German. We just want to fetch you so we can fetch more patients. We've got to go."

"Thank you for not caring about what he is." I released another sigh. "And look at the two of you, racing through the streets! I'm overjoyed to see that you tried to drive by yourselves. You should have just gone over the tracks and started without me."

Nela shook her head. "I'm not driving over those tracks. I need your help."

"I'm not even an official volunteer. I don't have a uniform."

"It doesn't matter."

"I have a job I need to return to soon. I teach piano lessons to children, and I really should contact my students and let them know I've healed and can—"

"There aren't going to be any more piano lessons, Ivy," said Addie, gripping the edge of the seat. "Don't you see? Nothing is ever going to be the same. Nothing matters but taking the suffering out of their homes and helping them."

I shrank back, haunted by the words of the seventeen-year-old girl sitting in front of me. *There aren't going to be any more piano lessons.*

A segment of my soul seemed to physically leave at the thought of music draining away from the world.

"Please." Nela softened her voice. "We should go."

I nodded, with some reluctance. "But you've got to pay attention to how I drive. I might not always be able to be here. Will you try turning the starter crank again?"

Nela stiffened. "It took me five tries when I used your method earlier tonight."

"Just keep practicing exactly as I instructed," I said. "You won't get hurt, I promise."

Nela huffed a bit, but she climbed out of the ambulance and crouched down into position in front of the grille.

I rounded the vehicle to the driver's side and pulled all hand levers into a starting position. Then I turned the coil box switch to the left and called out, "Everything's ready."

Nela turned the crank only twice before the ambulance

sparked to life. I cheered, and she cheered, and she leapt into the passenger seat beside Addie.

"Watch how my feet control the three pedals on the floor," I said, "and how my hands work the various levers. Especially note how I keep this clutch lever beside my left leg in an upright position to keep the ambulance in neutral. That'll be helpful when you're still getting used to the vehicle, and it will keep you from stalling. If there's time, I'll let each of you drive for a bit."

"There won't be time," said Addie, straightening her gray hat.

"We'll make time." I pushed the clutch lever into neutral and increased the RPM by pulling down on the spark advance lever on the left side of the steering column. The ambulance hummed with contentment and cruised down the road.

"One day," I added over the loud purr of the motor, "if we finally receive a reprieve from this illness, I'll take you both to a place that serves jazz and booze and doesn't care about the location of your home or the color of your skin—or whether or not you stall a stubborn old mule of an ambulance."

I steered the vehicle around a bend to the right and guided us to Lincoln Street and the railroad tracks.

DURING OUR SEARCH for influenza signs on the front doors of neighborhood houses, I made the mistake of passing Polish Hall. Men in plain work clothes and dark caps carried three covered bodies out the front door. My eyes couldn't stop looking at the stretchers and the white sheets shaped around human forms.

The men loaded the dead into the Halloran's Dry Goods delivery wagon, as if carting away unwanted furniture.

I kept driving.

We delivered a young Polish priest to Nela's house after finding him slumped in the doorway of the cathedral. Nela's home had grown quite warm and bright, despite the influx of patients recuperating within those walls. Mrs. O'Conner and Liliana helped with the transportation of the priest up the staircase, while Benjie played records on the Victrola again, entertaining a group of five children, both black and white. The little ones sat in front of the fireplace with blankets wrapped around their little bodies, and a sentimental song that might have been a Henry Burr piece rose into the air along with the flames crackling in the hearth.

"Do you like jazz?" I called to Benjie after shutting the front door.

He sauntered toward me with his hands in his pockets, his eyes bright. "I adore jazz, miss. It's life."

"Oh, I absolutely agree with that statement." I put my hands on my hips and sized up his appearance. "My, you look much improved. So healthy."

"I told you I was already on the mend. I just wouldn't have lasted in Bloody Hall, as I call that wretched place."

"Well, if you get a chance to go out for a bit—if you need a little more music to cheer you up"—I gestured with my thumb over my shoulder, toward the front door—"I highly recommend heading to the Masonic Lodge in town. A band plays there every night, and they don't give a fig about the flu. Or race."

"They don't?"

"No." I smiled. "They're celebrating life. Head over there when you're strong enough. They'll welcome you there."

"I will. Thank you, miss."

Addie and Nela's thick Red Cross boots clomped down the stairs at a speed meant for hurrying, and so we swept back into the darkness of night.

MY FELLOW VOLUNTEERS refused to sit for driving lessons, even as daylight glowed above the flat fields to the east, beyond the towering mills that still seemed asleep. Not a single puff of smoke streamed from the stacks reaching up to the awakening sky.

"The time we're wasting fooling around with pedals and levers," said Addie, "could be spent fetching one more patient."

Nela nodded and shifted in the seat beside me. "Let's fetch one more."

"But . . ."

"Just one more," said Nela. "Please, Ivy, we've got to help. Think of the people alone in their homes, without a single doctor to check on them."

And so we indeed fetched yet another suffering patient—a young Russian girl who had just lost her mother to a wicked bout of pneumonia brought on by the flu. I helped in a blur of rushing and lifting and calming, and I prayed that such nights of ferrying the ill would end soon. I prayed that I, along with everyone else left on the crumbling earth, could actually head into the world and live.

Truly live.

Chapter 12

I returned to May's house and heard her whimper behind the closed door of her bedroom, and I swear by all that's holy, her sounds matched the labored breathing of flu victims struggling not to drown in the thick black fluid swimming in their lungs. I inched toward her bedroom door and leaned my head against the wood to hear better.

"Oh, Lord," she cried with a guttural moan. She gasped for air and called for the Lord again, and all I could think about was the sight of children bleeding from their eyes in Polish Hall and all those bodies traveling out to delivery wagons underneath bedsheets.

Without a knock of warning, I opened her bedroom door.

May, naked and sitting upright on her bed, gave a start and whipped her head toward me. A hand reached up to her bare right elbow.

Eddie Dover sat up from beneath her and stared me straight in the eye.

Eddie Dover—*dead*—but there.

"Oh, God!" I slammed the door shut and backed into the table that held Eddie's photograph, knocking the frame to the floor. The glass cracked down the middle. "Oh, God."

May called my name from within her room, but nothing on earth could have persuaded me to stay inside that house a moment longer. I turned and bolted.

Outside, the sun bled red into the eastern sky. I followed the brightening light of dawn down Willow Street, past other quaint and seemingly normal houses with pretty mailboxes out front, and then I marched beneath the white awnings of the business district. Shopkeepers unlocked their front doors and raised their American flags. On the corner of Lincoln and Willow, a newspaper boy set up a stack of the morning edition, and I caught the top headline: ALLIES GAIN VICTORIES IN THE BATTLE OF ST. QUENTIN CANAL. Another Red Cross ambulance—also manned by female volunteers in gray hats and coats—puttered northward on Farnsworth Street, toward the main hospital.

Someone is about to die was all I could think. *Harbinger spirits. Someone is going to die.*

I threw open Daniel's boarded-up door, which set off the bell hanging above.

"Daniel?" I called over the jingling. "Daniel, are you all right?"

He stirred upstairs. Footsteps hurried down the back stair-case.

"What is it?" He bustled out from the workshop with his hair uncombed and buttoned up a striped nightshirt. "What is wrong?"

"I had a terrible premonition someone's about to die."

"No, go get some rest." He walked over and cupped a cold hand around my right cheek. "Christ, you worked all night, didn't you?"

"You're all right, then?" I grabbed the front of his shirt between my fingers. "You don't feel ill or—?"

"Rest, Ivy. You're wearing yourself thin. You'll collapse."

"It's going to be my mother, then." I slipped away from his touch. "I should have never left her."

"Ivy."

"I've got to go."

I swung his door open and left.

A MILE OUTSIDE OF TOWN, I reached the graveled country road that led to our unassuming white farmhouse where Mama's side of the family had resided ever since the 1870s. Our home looked so empty sitting there, alone on endless fields sprouting shoots of winter wheat. Our nearest neighbors lived a half mile to the south, well beyond the long row of spruces planted to protect the crops from winds.

The closer I got to our property, the more I thought of my dear Emily Dickinson again.

I years had been from home,
And now, before the door,
I dared not open, lest a face
I never saw before

Stare vacant into mine
And ask my business there.
"My business, —just a life I left
Was such still dwelling there?"

Our rowdy pack of spaniels and retrievers galloped out to the edge of the property, their barks echoing across the countryside. Birds scattered from the old maple in front of the house. I patted the dogs' heads and snouts and told them, "Settle down, settle down. Let's not draw attention to Father if he's already out by the barn."

They lowered their ears and their long whipping tails and backed away.

I walked up to the house and ventured up the groaning steps to the front porch that housed a broom, a watering can, and two sun-faded chairs made of a red-tinged wood. Cobwebs clung to the eaves, betraying a lapse in Mama's penchant for cleanliness. Our front door—bright pippin apple green in color—stood before me in all its odd beauty. Mama had painted it that color shortly after Granny Letty died, simply because my grandmother adored that particular shade of green. Granny called it "whimsical." Even after Father struck Billy in the head in the stables—

even after Billy left home—the color always pleased me and somehow made me feel I belonged inside that house.

I opened the door and called out, "Mama?"

No answer.

I lunged for the staircase, convinced I'd find my mother lying upstairs in her bed with the flu, her skin bluish-black, her lips darker than a bruise.

"Mama!"

"Ivy?" she asked from behind me after I'd already flown up the first three steps.

I turned and lowered my shoulders in relief at the sight of her normal peaches and cream complexion.

She wiped down her old cast-iron skillet with a checkered dishcloth and wrinkled her forehead in confusion at me. Her pinned-up hair looked grayer and duller than I remembered. Her eyes lacked a spark.

"What are you doing here, darling?" she asked in a voice that struck me as nervous.

I stepped down two of the stairs. "I had an awful feeling about you and the influenza."

"Oh, honey." She set her pan and the cloth on the top of the upright piano. "You don't need to worry about me. If I were meant to get that flu, I would have fallen ill when you suffered from it."

"But"—I stepped off the bottommost step—"you don't understand. I just saw one of them. A Guest. Eddie Dover. In the house where I'm staying."

She straightened her posture. "You've been to Eddie Dover's house?"

"I'm rooming with his widow, and I saw him—just now. I'm certain someone is about to die. Oh, God, Mama, I could have sworn I'd come back here and find you dead."

Mama's eyes went bloodshot. She braced her hand against the piano and looked awfully pale.

"Are you all right?" I asked. "If it's not the flu—"

"So many people have been dying this past week, Ivy." She lowered herself to the bench with a slow and unsteady movement. I heard her knees pop and watched the way her veined and freckled hands grappled to find support against the closed keyboard. "I'm not quite sure what we survivors are meant to do, besides keeping others from losing their lives. I've been helping out with the neighbors. The illness has hit everyone in this vicinity hard."

"Polish Hall is overflowing with the sick." I stepped toward her with my hands balled into fists, my feet triggering creaks in the scuffed old floorboards. "There aren't enough doctors and nurses, but the regular hospital isn't allowing Southside residents inside."

She raised her eyebrows. "How do you know that?"

"I've been transporting the ill down there to a private residence in an ambulance. We'll likely run out of room in the house soon, but the emergency hospital has so few doctors and Red Cross volunteers. Girl Scouts are risking their lives to be of use. I saw little Ruby mopping up blood in there."

Mama cocked her head at me. "You've been driving an ambulance?"

"Yes, but that's beside the point. Could you write to the city? Maybe if we both wrote, or if several of us visited the Board of Health as a group . . ."

"I could try a letter. Perhaps I'll go visit the hall myself and—"

"No! Don't continue going near the sick. Please, Mama, keep yourself healthy."

She folded her hands in her lap and didn't respond. Nothing in that house made a squeak or a grumble of sound, aside from our gold clock ticking away time above the mantel. The silence of the place suddenly struck me as unsettling.

I glanced backward toward the stairs. "Where's Peter?"

"He enlisted."

"What?"

"He ran off to the recruitment office the day after . . ." She rolled back her shoulders. Her voice deepened. "After the murder."

I grabbed hold of my head and pressed my palms against my temples, for a little hairline fracture of pain split open in the center of my skull. "I should have stayed and spoken to Peter that night. I shouldn't have left."

"Peter is almost eighteen," said Mama. "He's doing what he needs to do, and I'd much rather have him join the army than sit around here, stewing with guilt and anger."

"And what about Father?"

Mama raised her chin. "What about him?"

"What is *he* doing now that he's gotten away with murder?"

"Ivy, don't—"

"I've seen Daniel Schendel, the slain German's brother. I've grown quite close to him, to be most honest. I told him I'd go to the police and the newspaper and tell them the truth, but he swears it will do no good."

"He's right—it won't. Our country is operating under a different set of rules right now."

"But—"

"You read about the trial for the Prager murder. The jury acquitted all eleven defendants and said the lynching was justified by 'unwritten law.' A Buchanan jury would do the same for Father and Peter." She stood up from the bench and rested her hands on her hips. Her back curved into the shape of the bowl of a spoon, and the front of her black mourning dress sagged from her chest, which looked small and malnourished—just like the rest of her.

"Your father's been drinking again," she said. "Hard."

I gritted my teeth and set my own hands on my hips. "Leave this house, Mama. Please! I don't want to have to keep worrying about you and Father's temper."

"You need to stop worrying about everyone in this place. That obsessive fretting has never done you a lick of good, Ivy, and it's kept you from acting like a normal young woman."

"But—"

"I know why you refused to leave." She shifted her weight between her feet. "I know you tried at first to live a normal life after what your father did to your brother." She swallowed and shook her head. "But it's always broken my heart to see the way you gradually holed yourself up inside this house and punished yourself every time you stepped one foot off this property. Billy recovered, by the grace of God, but I always felt like you were the one who actually got hit by that shovel."

I pursed my lips and blinked my eyes, and my throat swelled up. No words could have pushed their way out of me, even if they wanted to.

"And now—" Mama covered her mouth and muffled a sob. "You're suffering for the sake of that German, aren't you?"

I nodded, but I still couldn't speak. I wrapped my arms around my ribs and squeezed down on a soreness running through the bones beneath my blouse.

"Your profound empathy"—she swallowed again—"is probably related to your sensitive nature—your ability to see the Guests. But there's no need for it. There really isn't. You don't need to take on everyone else's pain as your own."

Again, no words formed on my lips. I felt myself shrinking down into the role of a small and unstable child, and I longed for her to hold me in her arms, to hug away the terrible hurt bearing down on my body.

"Ivy?"

I raised my eyes to hers. "What?"

"Go out there and find peace and happiness. Let their pain go. Forget the past. Please"—she clasped her hands together, as if she were praying—"promise me you'll do your best to move forward."

I managed a small nod. "All right. I'll try."

"Please do. It's for the best." She peeked over her shoulder. "Now go. Father's coming back inside again soon. I don't want you to have to see him."

"I have no intention of seeing him." I hustled closer to her. "Please be careful, Mama."

"I will, darling."

I kissed her cheek and left the house as quickly as I arrived.

Chapter 13

*K*nowing that my mother remained healthy, I next feared that my friend Sigrid would be the one to die—the one whom Eddie Dover came to warn me about. With the smooth soles and square heels of my shoes clip-clopping across more country roads, kicking up stones and dirt, I trekked out to the house Sigrid shared with Wyatt and their three children.

The young family resided on the northern edge of the Pettyjohns' farm, near Minter Lake, in a white colonial-style house with coal-black shutters framing every window. A cluster of thick, gnarled oak trees with half-bare limbs hung over the roof and scratched at the brick chimney. A swing made from a tractor tire hung still as stone from one of the thickest branches, above piles of pumpkin-colored leaves. Silence gripped the front yard. I didn't even hear the welcoming barks of Sigrid's three-legged spaniel, Knut—the one she had saved from her parents' house when her father wanted to shoot it for being a cripple.

I held my breath and knocked on the front door, not even caring if Wyatt showed up with his desperate eyes and his need to be held, as long as I could learn that Sigrid and the children were recuperating. Surviving.

She and the children have been in the hospital for several days, I remembered Wyatt telling me at the dance the night before.

I knocked again, and no one answered. The black door stared me down and reminded me that I had made myself a stranger to these two former friends who had once meant the world to me.

"Wyatt?" I called through the wood, determined not to run away—to be as nurturing and kind as the way Sigrid always treated me. "Wyatt? It's Ivy. I'm sorry if I seemed cold and rude last night. Please, if you're in there, open up and let me know how Sigrid and the children are faring."

He still didn't answer, so I turned the brass knob—so cold beneath my hand—and entered the house.

The door spilled into a wide entry hall, papered in gold and cherry red. To my left, I saw their parlor, in which a porcelain clock ticked a steady beat from a bookcase near the fireplace.

Tick-tock. Tick-tock. No-one. Is-home. Too-late. Good-bye.

A rag doll lay on the parlor floor, its arms and legs akimbo. The poor thing looked utterly uncomfortable and abandoned, as if its small owner had been forced to toss it aside in a terrible hurry. I walked over, picked the doll up, and brushed out its red loops of yarn hair. A soft trace of the scent of sugar clung to the fibers of the tiny blue doll dress and white pinafore—perhaps cookie crumbs, spilled into one of the little pinafore pockets.

"How is your owner, you poor thing?" I asked, and I kissed its cloth forehead and set it safely on the mantel, next to the framed photographs of Sigrid, Wyatt, the children, the grandparents, aunts, uncles . . .

A smaller photograph caught my eye—one that must have been taken at least fifteen years earlier. Sigrid, Helen, and I stood with our arms hooked around the backs of each other's waists in front of Grant Street School, a two-story brick structure, institutional and enormous, attended by all of Buchanan's school-aged children until the high school opened in 1905. The three of us wore our hair in braids and bows, and we wore ruffled dresses that hung down to our knees, over black stockings. Sigrid's older sister, Annelie, had saved up for a Brownie camera and loved taking photographs of daily life in Buchanan. I remembered her posing the three of us on the school's front steps and telling us to simply relax and act like ourselves. Sigrid, with her Norwegian blond hair and pretty smile, immediately threw her arms around our backs. Helen tickled my elbow, which made me laugh. In the photo, my mouth hung wide open, mid-chuckle, and my eyes were closed and squinty-looking. Not an attractive pose, I suppose, but it showed I knew how to live back then. As Robert Herrick said in "To the Virgins, to Make Much of Time"—

That age is best which is the first,
When youth and blood are warmer;
But being spent, the worse, and worst
Times still succeed the former.

❖

"No." I whispered, readjusting the photograph on the mantel so it didn't sit so crooked. "These couldn't have been our only good years. There still might be long and better lives ahead of us. This might not be the end. There still might be time."

I swept out of the Pettyjohns' home and shut the door behind me. Down the porch steps, I stopped and took a moment to pull three of the last scarlet blooms from one of Sigrid's rosebushes. Red petals brushed their velvet touch across my hands and scattered behind me on the road back to town.

TWO DELIVERY WAGONS carried crude pine caskets through the streets of Buchanan, toward the Protestant cemetery in the northeast section of town. I spotted several townspeople wearing the gauze surgical masks typically reserved for doctors or Red Cross volunteers like Nela and Addie. Advertisements for anti-influenza elixirs—DR. BELL'S PINE TAR HONEY, STUART'S CHARCOAL LOZENGES, SCHENCK'S MANDRAKE PILLS, BEECHAM'S PILLS, GLENN'S SULPHUR SOAP, MILLER'S ANTISEPTIC SNAKE OIL—hung in the front display window of the Buchanan Pharmacy, next to the Moonbeam Theater. Buchanan's green electric streetcar clattered along the rails down Willow Street but transported very few passengers within. All of them wore the white masks.

I headed northward on Farnsworth and walked three more blocks until I reached Buchanan Hospital, a stone castle of a mansion with turrets, square windows, and three brick chimneys breathing smoke into the bright morning air. The place was once the private residence of the owner of Buchanan's printing press, but he donated the building to the city when he died ten years earlier. A lush garden of coralbells and ivy grew around the edges of the structure, and wrought-iron benches nestled inside vine-covered alcoves every six or so feet along the walls.

I walked up the front steps to an arched entryway that led to a solid front door with a black metal latch. The sound of running feet pattered up from behind, and a young woman in a mink stole and a feathered hat sprinted up the steps beside me. She yanked open the door with an unladylike grunt, her arm shaking, teeth bared, and I entered behind her into a cavernous dark-wood lobby that smelled dank and feverish. A weighty lantern with orange glass hung from the ceiling on a thick chain. Closed doors—one of which was guarded by an orderly in a plain black coat—sealed off the rest of the hospital, but I heard footsteps echoing beyond. And coughing. A cacophony of coughing.

The woman in the stole flew at a nurse who stood behind an admissions desk.

"I need to see my husband!"

"I'm sorry, ma'am," said the nurse in a no-nonsense tone as crisp as her white cap and apron. "We're only allowing the sick into this building. You'll need to leave immediately."

"You don't understand." The woman slammed the palm of

her hand against the desk with a startling *thwack*. "My husband is a highly important man at the *Buchanan Sentinel*. His secretary told me an ambulance rushed him here this morning, but I want him transported to our home right now."

"No visitors," said the nurse. "I'm sorry. It's far too dangerous to expose outsiders to the germs." She nodded to the orderly, as if to signal him to step closer.

"Can we at least find out if certain individuals are still alive?" I asked, inching forward with Sigrid's roses in hand.

"This isn't right!" cried the woman in the stole.

"No visitors," said the nurse again, and the orderly tromped toward us with his hands clenched into two meaty fists.

The woman backed away, nearly treading on my foot. "I should be allowed to see my husband."

"You heard the nurse." The orderly opened the door. "No healthy people allowed. Out you go."

The woman huffed, and we both scuttled back out into the daylight, which blinded my eyes after the stark dimness of that dungeon of a lobby. The orderly whisked the door shut behind us.

"This isn't right," said the woman again from the top of the front steps. "I should be able to see him. I should . . . oh, God . . ." She clasped her hand over her mouth and squeezed her eyes closed.

"I'm sure they're treating him well," I told her, and I almost felt as though I should give her Sigrid's flowers to help her feel better. "I know how hard this is, but the care in this hospital is top-notch."

The woman burst into tears. The feathers on her hat shook with the sorrow trembling through her, and her nose ran.

"I'm so sorry," I said—the only thing I could say.

She turned and staggered down the stone stairs to an awaiting black Cadillac with polished wooden spokes. I considered reentering the hospital without her to see if they'd allow a woman who had already survived the flu to inquire about a patient, but a distraction stopped me: the rustle of leaves, as well as Wyatt's voice, from somewhere nearby.

"Ivy?"

I pressed my hands against the iron handrail and discovered Sigrid's husband journeying through the garden from the north side of the hospital. He took off his brown cap, which made his dark hair stick up, as usual, like a duck's tail.

I walked down the steps and joined him on the front sidewalk.

"They won't let you in to see Sigrid and the children either?" I asked.

He shook his head and pressed his cap over his heart. "I'm just going crazy wandering around out here. I could really use another drink from that party last night."

"Here." I handed him the roses. "I picked these for Sigrid from your garden. I thought she might want to see the last blooms of the year."

"You were at our house?"

"I worried about her after talking to you last night. Be careful of the thorns."

He tugged a handkerchief out of his breast pocket and wrapped up the stem with a delicate movement of his large hands. His gentleness stirred up more sadness and regret inside me. I should have been kinder to him years ago. I should never have led him to believe he might experience love and affection and physical pleasure with me.

"Is she still . . ." I cleared my throat. "She's still alive, isn't she?"

He nodded. "As far as I know."

"Have you slept at all since last night?"

"No. Have you?"

"No. I helped drive an ambulance late at night. And there's been . . . a strange thing happened this morning that . . ." I covered my eyes with my fingers and experienced a wave of tiredness for the first time since I had witnessed Eddie in May's room. "I'm exhausted actually. We should both go to our homes and get some sleep."

"I'll walk you home."

"No, no need. I don't live at the farm anymore. I'm renting a room in town."

"Really?" he asked with more than a hint of shock in his voice.

Another Red Cross ambulance charged our way on Farnsworth and rattled off to the hospital's back entrance around the corner. I felt the wind from its wake tangle through the unpinned strands of hair around my face.

"It had nothing to do with any of you, Wyatt." I lowered my hands to my cheeks. "Me, hiding away so often. I loved you as a friend—I truly did. And I loved Sigrid with all of my heart. It had everything to do with my father and the way he treated Billy out there on the farm."

Wyatt tipped his head sideways and squinted at me through the sunlight. "But Billy moved out of the house five years ago. And you still stayed inside."

"I know. I don't know what happened to me. I thought I could protect Peter, too, but he was—" I brushed out the wrinkles in my skirt. "He was always too much like Father." I lifted my face and looked Wyatt in the eye. "I just want you and Sigrid to know I'm sorry I never visited you or seemed to take an interest in getting to know your children. It was terrible of me, and I wish I could go back and change everything."

Wyatt pressed his lips together and nodded. "I'll give Sigrid the roses if I can."

"Thank you. I'd appreciate that."

I patted his arm and left him behind on those lush hospital grounds.

*Police interrogated Swedish-born Buchanan res-
ident Hanna Lindstrom, aged 22, after a neighbor
overheard her singing a song by German composer
Johannes Brahms. The neighbor reported Mrs. Lindstrom to the American Protective League, stat-
ing that the young woman also speaks Swedish in
public and refuses to post the United States Food
Administration pledge card in her window. The
police questioned Mrs. Lindstrom for two hours,
but they did not press charges, after failing
to find solid evidence of Espionage Act viola-
tions. Mrs. Lindstrom's husband, Isak Lindstrom,
is currently serving overseas in the U.S. Army.
The young mother of three claims to have been
singing a lullaby to her two-year-old daughter,
who was sick with influenza.*

*Local American Protective League chief Charles
Williams stated that Mrs. Lindstrom's interro-
gation is an opportunity to remind local residents of Buchanan's strict stance against German
music. "German propaganda, including subtle propaganda through art and literature, will not be
tolerated," said Mr. Williams. "If you celebrate
Bach, Beethoven, and Brahms, you are celebrating
German culture. We will question anyone caught
singing or playing enemy music. Influenza or no
influenza, we are still fighting Prussian dev-
ilry twenty-four hours a day. Germans—not germs—
remain our greatest adversary."*

—Buchanan Sentinel, October 9, 1918

Chapter 14

A group of four men in three-piece business suits and fedoras stood in front of Daniel's store, facing the boarded-up windows and door. They held their hands on their hips and folded their arms over their chests and discussed matters I couldn't hear from down the block.

My skin went cold. I crossed the street before any of them could see me and tucked myself around the corner of the Masonic Lodge's east-facing wall. As best as I could without being spotted, I watched them, my right hand braced against cold brick, my breathing irregular. I had wanted to check on Daniel before daring to return to May's for a rest, but I didn't realize ominous-looking strangers—most likely the APL—would be clustered in front of his door in the light of day. I had believed rats to scavenge mainly after dark.

Three of the men turned away from the store and walked westward, puffing on cigarettes and cigars, chuckling as they went.

One man remained.

Lucas.

He must have caught sight of me from across the street, for he lifted his chin and peered straight at me through his colossal lenses.

Another green streetcar rattled by. Steel wheels whirred against the tracks; electric wires bobbed and swayed overhead. I slipped around the corner and stole inside the front door of the Masonic Lodge before the vehicle could finish passing.

No one else made a peep inside the building. Assuming myself alone, I retraced my steps to the upstairs ballroom and hid myself behind the grand double doors with the brass eyes peering from the knobs. The ballroom lay empty and silent. Daylight streamed through the five closed windows framed by thin red curtains. No crumbs of party food littered the floors. No forgotten gloves or hair ribbons revealed hints of the enchantment of the nights. The mute piano rested against the wall, the keyboard cover down.

I sauntered over to the leftmost window and peeked out from behind the gauzy curtain. The fabric brushed against my cheek and smelled of perfumes and whiskey. No one stood in front of Daniel's store down below. I held my breath and listened for any indications of the lodge's front door opening—or any whines in the floorboards beyond the closed ballroom doors.

I simply disappeared in a puff of smoke behind the streetcar,

Lucas, I mentally willed to my brother's wayward friend, wherever he might have been. *Don't search for me.*

I DON'T KNOW how long I stood in front of the window, barely breathing, my eyes locked upon the sidewalk in front of Liberty Brothers Furniture. An amateur spy spying on APL spies. An amateur spy watching over the storefront of a potential German spy. Watching, watching, watching . . .

Another Emily Dickinson poem wandered through my brain—a rather odd and dramatic one, even by Miss Dickinson's standards.

> *Before I got my eye put out,*
> *I liked as well to see*
> *As other creatures, that have eyes,*
> *And know no other way.*

The image of a poked-out eye made my stomach tighten, and both of my eyes stung. Such torture seemed a highly feasible punishment for a person who lurked in the shadows and defied the U.S. government by wanting to protect an enemy alien.

My back ached from standing still for so long. Lucas didn't seem to be on the verge of throwing open the ballroom doors and dragging me down to the APL headquarters. Even if he waited for me somewhere inside the lodge, where could I possibly run? If I jumped out the window, the awning down below might break my fall a tad, but the ensuing injuries might be worse than an APL inquisition.

If anyone ever corners you or threatens you, there's only one thing you need to say, I remembered May instructing me. *You tell them, "I'm the daughter and sister of men who dispose of Huns."*

I stepped over to the piano, which tempted with its promise of comfort. I lifted the keyboard cover and exposed the black and white treasure chest that held all the songs yet to be played. I then scooted onto the hard wooden stool, my skirt swishing with the slide, and inhaled the regal and dusty smells of the instrument, as if breathing the perfume of fresh sweet corn. Or Sigrid's roses.

I leaned forward and embarked upon Beethoven's Piano Concerto No. 1—but, a moment later, my fingers jerked away from the keys.

Forbidden music.

German music.

I peeked over my shoulder to make sure such a blunder wouldn't send Lucas storming inside the double doors, and then I cracked my knuckles (a terrible habit, I know) and sorted through the musical files of my brain for a song that spoke nothing of patriotism or treachery. An older favorite, Irving Berlin's "Alexander's Ragtime Band," came to mind. I closed my eyes and poured my entire being into the notes, and the louder I played, the more the cruel world fell away. Nobody lay dead and buried in the ground, and no one hated and murdered and mangled and spied. Music consumed every particle of the darkness inside my mind, and I felt just like Alice sailing down the rabbit hole, fleeing the real world that waited miles and miles above.

I played the piano for at least an hour—maybe more. Nobody pushed open the ballroom doors. No one seemed to care. I made music until my exhausted head drooped down to the keys. After one last discordant note, played by my right cheek, I fell asleep, right there at the piano.

"MISS?" ASKED AN UNFAMILIAR VOICE—a tenor—and a warm hand touched my shoulder.

I awoke with a start and slammed my hands into the keys, creating a horrendous crash of notes that echoed across the room.

The pianist from the jazz band stood over me in his black tailcoat, his slicked hair shining on his head like oil spilled across his scalp. "Have you come to join us?" he asked with a smile on his thin face. He seemed to wear a little powder and rouge, now that I saw him up close.

The rest of the band members lugged in their instruments around me and grinned down at me as I slumped over the keys on the stool.

"I'm so sorry," I said, my face burning, and I darted out of the room like an intrusive mouse, caught by the owner of a house.

NELA AND ADDIE WAITED FOR ME in front of the Red Cross headquarters. I cranked the ambulance to a start and crawled into the driver's seat beside them.

"I'm so horribly embarrassed about what happened to me just now," I said, and I rubbed the sides of my face, causing my lips and cheeks to stretch all over the place. "I fell asleep at the piano of the Masonic Lodge. The jazz band I was telling you about had to wake me up."

"You can still drive, though, yes?" asked Nela.

My chin drifted toward my chest. "This is precisely what I meant about needing to teach you both how to drive. You can't rely on me. I haven't been myself since last Friday."

"Come on." Nela jostled my arm enough to stir me into an upright position. "We've got to go. Even if we're tired. We've got to help."

I lowered my hands from my face and gripped the black steering wheel. "Just . . . give me a moment . . ." My cheek sank forward and landed against my knuckles. My eyes fell shut, and I hovered between alertness and sleep. A deep breath, halfway to a snore, whispered free from my mouth.

"Ivy." Nela shoved me in the shoulder, knocking me to the left with such force that I nearly fell out of the ambulance.

"All right, all right." I sat up straight and discovered that the truck sat cockeyed in the road in front of the Red Cross building. "Did one of you try driving again?"

"I did." Addie raised her hand in the darkness beside Nela. "That's why it's parked so crooked."

"I'm awfully proud of you."

"I said it's crooked."

"It doesn't matter. You both simply need practice. No matter what anyone tells you, you don't need to be a man to handle a truck." I shifted the levers and poked my head out of the side of the ambulance to view the dark road behind us. "In fact, trucks are a little like men. They often require firm persuasion to get them to go where they're needed."

I pushed my foot into the reverse pedal and rolled the ambulance backward.

Without warning, a uniformed man—a soldier—showed up in the street behind us. I saw his face, clear and bright in the lamplight.

"Oh, God!" I slammed on the brakes.

"What's wrong?" asked Nela.

"Oh, God!" I jumped out of the truck and ran to the empty spot in the road where I'd just witnessed the figure. "Billy!"

Addie hustled around the ambulance from the other side. "What are you doing? Who's Billy?"

"I just saw my brother back here." I scanned the darkness with my hands threaded through my hair on my scalp. My heart pounded. Gooseflesh tingled across my arms. "He was just standing here. I saw him. I know I saw him."

"I don't see anyone."

"He was killed at the Battle of Saint-Mihiel in September, but I saw him. I swear"—my voice turned hoarse and painful—"he stood right here."

Nela hurried into view behind Addie. "What is happening?"

"Ivy just saw a ghost."

"There was another one this morning." I dug the heels of my

palms into the sockets of my eyes. "Oh, God. I don't know who I'm going to lose next. I hate this. Why are they coming here?"

Nela took hold of my arm. "As you said, you're tired. It was a trick of the mind." She lured me back to the driver's seat. Our two pairs of feet made a steady pitter-patter against the road, but I heard a third set of footsteps—not Addie's. Heavy, boot-clad feet wandered down the road, away from us.

"How about you drive and just stay in the ambulance while we fetch?" asked Nela. "You can sleep while we're carrying our patients."

"I should check on Daniel."

"Our shift already started." She held my arm and my waist and lowered me down to the padded seat, the way my mother used to assist my grandmother into chairs after she suffered her first stroke when I was nine. "Please—just drive, and we'll fetch."

THE PATIENTS WE TRANSPORTED all started to look alike, all of them poor immigrants and blacks with defeat dimming their eyes. We seemed to be cycling on an unending loop that would never allow for an end to the plague. No relief. No escape.

I stayed in the car while Addie and Nela fetched the patients, but just sitting there—helpless, useless, slumped against the leatherette upholstery—brought no relief to the fatigue fogging my brain. I joined in and helped them with the lifting and carrying until somewhere in the five o'clock hour, when my eyes turned bleary. I accidentally swerved too far to the right and ran the ambulance off the road. Pitch-black hedges clawed at the metal of the grille and the hood. Branches snapped. The car halted with a jolt that hurt my neck.

"That's it." I threw up my hands. "I'm now officially a hazard to the community. I'm done."

"Just—"

"No." I backed the truck out of the foliage with more scrapes and snaps from the branches. "Not just one more. I'm going to kill us all if I keep driving like this. I'm done."

I drove back in the direction of the Red Cross headquarters on the north side of town, and none of us spoke a word. Our bodies jostled together with the rhythm of the rumbling motor; we swayed against each other during the wide turns around corners. Morning light hovered on the edge of the eastern horizon, and I felt the urge to escape its brightness. To sleep during the darkness again would feel divine.

I parked alongside the curb, stumbled out of the car, and tripped my way toward Willow Street, and Daniel's place—not May's. No more talk of ghosts and death for me that day.

Chapter 15

*T*he Liberty Brothers shop bell jangled with a nervous clatter above me.

Daniel slid two nails out of his mouth and lowered the disembodied arm of an oak chair to the ground. "What happened to you?"

I ran my hands through my hair and found a bird's nest of tangles and sweat and dislodged pins. The room rolled beneath my feet and tipped me off balance. I fell back against the door with a rattle of the splintered glass.

"Ivy?" Daniel rushed over and took hold of my waist and left elbow. "Come sit down. You don't look well."

"I've barely slept."

He guided me toward the long front counter at the back. "Why didn't you come here sooner?"

"APL men huddled outside your door when I came by again yesterday."

"What?"

"You're right—there's nothing but chaos out there. I'm not sure how much longer I can tolerate it."

He guided me behind the counter and lowered me down to a pale wooden chair with a rose carved into the back. I thought of Sigrid lying somewhere inside that cold and cavernous hospital. And her children. Little gold spots buzzed before my eyes. I sank my face into my lap and interlocked my fingers behind my skull to squeeze the wooziness out of my brain.

"Ivy?" Daniel cupped the back of my neck with a warm hand, and I heard him kneel down on one knee beside me. "Are you all right? Is it more than just exhaustion?"

"I'm terrified that you or someone else I know is going to die."

"Why? Why did you come in here in such a panic yesterday morning?"

"I see—certain things—before someone close to me loses his life." I breathed into the folds of my skirt, heating my cheeks with the air. "I saw two of them in the past twenty-four hours."

Daniel's second knee dropped to the floor. "What is it that you see?"

"I don't want to say."

"Why not?"

"It'll sound like something's wrong with my head."

"I doubt it."

I managed to lift my face. "Just . . . please be extremely careful of this flu. Stay inside. Keep far away from others."

"That's what I've been doing. You know that."

"The world smells and tastes of death and fear right now. I can't even play Beethoven on a piano for a moment of escape. Someone will march in and take me away to wherever it is they talked about taking you."

He leaned his face closer. "Don't worry about those APL *Schweine* so much. No one's going to take you away."

"I saw the one who called me a whore again. He stood outside the store with the others, and he looked straight at me. I used to lend Billy and him my marbles when we were younger. I dried his tears when he fell down and scraped his knee at our house. Now he won't stop following me around like I'm a lethal criminal."

"Here"—Daniel offered his hand, his fingers trembling—"let's go upstairs and forget everything else."

"I'm too tired to go upstairs with you."

"No, not for that." He wrapped his hand around my palm and wrist and guided me up to my feet until we faced each other. "I'll draw you a hot bath, and then you can warm up by the fireplace and sleep in my bed."

My eyes strayed to the drawers below the brass cash register, no more than two feet away from us. "It's in there, isn't it?"

"What?"

"The article about the murder."

Daniel shifted his position and blocked the drawers with his body. "You don't want to see that right now. Not if you're exhausted and unsettled."

"What better time to read it than when I'm already unsettled?"

"I told you"—he squeezed my hand—"this is supposed to be paradise in here. Just you and me. Don't remind me of what happened here. Don't even think about it. Just come upstairs and forget about all these troubles."

"I don't . . ." I eyed the front door. "I don't know if I should. The women I'm working with—the Red Cross volunteers—they also know about you and me."

He shrugged. "And do they seem to care what you're doing?"

"I don't—"

"Have they called you names or threatened you?"

"No."

"Then what does it matter who knows? Everyone out there besides the APL is too busy saving their own necks to give a damn who's visiting whose bed. Come." He laced his fingers through mine and led me toward the workroom. "Let's take care of you. The rest of the world can just go to hell for all I care."

His hand relaxed on our way up the stairs, as did the stiffness in his shoulders and his back. His composure eased my own breathing and posture, and by the time we reached the top floor, we had melted into more tranquil versions of ourselves.

The band didn't play their jazz in that early-morning hour, and the apartment upstairs sat silent and still. The first fingers of daylight nudged through the living room curtains and turned the place into an entirely different scene from the mystique of our jazz- and sin-infused nights of lamplight and shadows.

"It's so quiet up here," I murmured.

"I'll play you a song on the guitar if you'd like."

"No, there's no need. I'm sure you're tired, too. I do miss the German composers, though. I will say that."

"I can tell you with absolute certainty that the music of Beethoven and Bach sounds nothing like German warfare. It's a ban created by idiots."

He led me over to the living room sofa, a beautiful piece of furniture upholstered in ivory linen, with a black lacquer finish on the wooden frame and legs.

"Sit here." He let go of my hand. "Get comfortable. I'll go draw you a bath."

I lowered myself to the sofa, and as promised, he disappeared into the little bathroom next to the kitchen. The spigot within the room squeaked with a high-pitched cry, and then water rushed through the pipes and splattered into the tub beyond. I sank back against the sofa and stared up at the mantel photograph of the couple whom I guessed to be his parents. The man sported a thick mustache and wore a three-piece suit with soft stripes. He held a pocket watch and a violin. The woman wore a dark dress and a wide hat with a large rosette, and she held on to the man's left elbow. They posed in front of a brick fireplace—not unlike the one right there in Daniel's apartment—in a house or a photography studio that must have stood thousands of miles away. Little half-smiles lit up their faces. They appeared content. Peaceful. Musical. Loving.

Daniel wandered back out to check on me while the water roared into the tub in the bathroom behind him.

"Are those your parents in that photograph?" I asked.

Without a glance at the photo, Daniel lowered himself to the rug in front of me and untied the lace of my right shoe. "Yes."

"Are they still alive?"

He slid the shoe off my foot. "Yes."

"In Germany?"

He peeked up at me from the tops of his eyes.

I sank my spine against the firm backing of the sofa. "All right." I sighed. "I won't ask questions."

He untied my other shoe and guided it off my left foot. He then slid the hem of my skirt up over my knees and past my thighs and unclasped my right stocking from its garter. I shifted my weight, surprised at the prickles of arousal that managed to awaken inside my limp and weighed-down body. Daniel leaned his face forward and kissed the inside of my right leg. Warmth spread from the pressure point of his lips to the far reaches of my thighs and my shins.

I touched his shoulder. "I'm so tired, Daniel."

"I know." His lips brushed my skin with a second kiss before he stood back up and returned to the bathwater.

Later, while he lit a fire for me in the hearth, I undressed amid a cloud of steam in the little whitewashed bathroom. My feet balanced on blue and white diamond-shaped tiles, and I struggled to remain awake and upright. I climbed into the bath, sank down into the water with a deep plunking sound, and curled onto my side in the heavenly heat. My head rested against the porcelain rim. The warmth nestled inside my nostrils and swallowed me up until I imagined myself becoming part of the vapor. I envisioned drifting up to the ceiling and landing in a wet circle high above. Little ripples of water lapped against the tub's walls.

I thought again of Eddie in May's bed, and of Billy standing behind the ambulance. My mind tried to talk itself into believing I'd imagined them all—there was no such thing as ghosts. Mama and I never actually experienced the Uninvited. We merely believed ourselves to be witnessing spirits because our minds couldn't bear the cruel and smothering anguish of grief. No one close to me would perish from the earth in a matter of hours, or even minutes. May simply slept with a lover who resembled her deceased husband. Mama remained healthy and alive. Sigrid and her children would survive. Daniel would be safe as long as he stayed away from others and kept his door locked tight against the APL and my father.

Father—who drank hard when upset—who just watched another son leave for the war—who might learn from Mama that I now spent my time with a German—who didn't care that I was standing right there in the barn when he slammed that shovel against the side of my brother's head.

I sat up straight in the tub.

Daniel never locked the door. I always walked straight inside the store, even at nighttime.

"Lock the door!"

I sprang out of the tub. Water rained down on the tiles from my hair and my arms. "Lock the door! Daniel!" I wrapped a towel around my middle. "Lock the front door—now!"

He flew into the bathroom. "What's wrong?"

"Go downstairs." I pushed his arm with a palm that soaked his shirt. "Lock the front door. My brother—Peter, Father's favorite—just enlisted. I told my mother I've been with you. My father's going to think more Germans are taking away his children. He'll kill you."

"He won't kill me."

"Yes, he will. You know he's done it before. He once even hit my brother Billy in the head with a shovel."

"If your father comes in this store"—Daniel stepped forward with feral, darkened eyes—"he's the one who's dying, Ivy. I'll take a knife and carve him up until he squeals like the pig that he is."

I shrank back and clasped the towel around my chest. Daniel blinked as if he had just realized what he'd said. He cupped his hand over his forehead and breathed with ragged gasps.

"Please, just lock the door," I said, and a sob burst from my lips.

Daniel turned and left without another word.

I sank down to the bathroom floor in my towel and held my stomach. Vomit rose to my throat. I covered my mouth, worried the foul black tar of flu victims would spill out of me.

Daniel returned with gentle footfalls. His eyes softened when he saw me down on the tiles.

"It's locked," he said, holding on to the bathroom door.

"Would you really kill him?"

"I don't know."

I clutched the towel. "Your eyes . . . they turned so wild and hateful when you talked about carving him up."

"I didn't . . ." He put his hands on his hips and sighed. "That Yank bastard who raised you brought murder into my home and my business. He ruined my brother and me. What do you expect me to think of him?"

I swallowed and stared up at him, remembering what I'd thought of him when I first saw him—how his head had seemed the ideal shape for a helmet of the Kaiser's army.

"Do you want to kill me, too?" I asked.

He sighed again, this time with a growl of frustration, and he offered his hand to me. "Come." He wiggled his fingers to get me to take them. "You'll get cold down there on the floor. I have clean, warm pajamas waiting for you to wear. They're my pajamas, but we can roll up the legs and hope the bottoms fit those lovely, rounded hips of yours."

I grabbed hold of his hand and let him lift me to my feet.

"The pajamas are in my room," he said with a nod toward the rest of the apartment, outside the bathroom. "Please, get dressed, and come get warm by the fire. The door is locked. We're safe. It's just the two of us, and no one is killing anyone. I swear to God."

THE GLARING LIGHT OF MORNING blinded my eyes on my way back to the sofa, and the pain reminded me of how little I'd slept. I rolled up the too-long sleeves of his striped pajamas and plunked myself down on the same ivory cushion where I had relaxed before the attempt at a bath.

Daniel sat in an armchair next to the Victrola and whittled the flat piece of wood I'd seen him carving when I peeked across the street at him from the Masonic Lodge window.

"If you really want to sleep well," he said, crossing his right foot over his left knee, "I could pour you a glass of strong German brandy."

"No." I smiled and tucked my legs beneath me on the sofa. "Not this early in the morning, thank you. If I ever take a night off from driving the ambulance, however, I'll gladly take you up on that offer."

"*Gut.* I hope you do. I have a strong suspicion you've never tried honest-to-goodness booze before."

I smiled. "No, I probably haven't."

The fire crackled in the hearth between us, and beyond the windows, the rest of the city stirred to life. The electric streetcar sang against its tracks. Wagons jostled down Willow Street, accompanied by the steady clip-clop of hooves and the jingle of reins.

Without warning, a Model T ambulance dashed through the street down below—I recognized the particular pops and rumbles of the motor and the sound of the size of the vehicle. I lowered my feet back to the floor and sat up straight.

"I hear an ambulance," I said.

Daniel set his knife on his lap. "You're off duty, Ivy."

"I know." I glanced over the back of the sofa, toward a window covered by a thin brown burlap curtain.

Daniel left his whittling behind and joined me on the sofa. "Don't pay any attention to the world out there. It can function without you for the next twelve hours. Come"—he patted his lap—"lay your head down and close your eyes. Rest and get warm."

I hesitated. Laying my head down on his legs in such a way would suggest tenderness. Nurturing companionship. Even love.

"Are you sure you want me to—?"

"Lie down." He patted his lap again. "It's all right. No one is coming in here to arrest you for being with me. I swear. People have better things to do right now."

I lowered my head against his leg, and my cheek settled against his trousers. My legs stretched across the sofa's smooth linen, and I reached my toes as far as they could go before bumping the curved arm. The smoky scent of his fireplace settled inside my nose, and I remembered how I used to believe, with such terrible prejudice, that all German homes smelled of beer and sauerkraut.

"Am I keeping you from the shop?" I asked with my eyes half closed.

"I worked all night. I think someone might be coming by to measure for new windows this afternoon, but this morning"—he laid the palm of his left hand against my hair—"I plan to rest, too."

"Were you hoping to open the store back up soon? I heard the APL say—"

"No—don't say those three letters anymore. They're officially banned from paradise."

"All right. That's a reasonable request."

He stroked my hair and made my scalp tingle, and I felt as though we were playing at husband and wife. I wondered if Wyatt and Sigrid shared such moments together. Or my mother and father—before we children came along.

"Ivy," he said, breaking the delicate silence.

"Mm hmm," I murmured, on the edge of sleep.

"When you first came to the store, you said you'd been sick."

"Yes, I had been."

"With this flu?"

"Yes." I sighed through my nose. "At first, I thought I wasn't feeling well because of the news of the death of my brother. I fell ill the same day we received the telegram about Billy."

Daniel's hand came to a stop above my ear. "Did you suffer much? From the illness?"

"No." I shook my head. "At least, I don't remember too much about it. My temperature spiked to a troubling number, apparently, and I remember my family sitting with me, holding my hand. At one point, even Peter, my . . ." I cleared my throat. "The brother who caused trouble here . . . he brought me flowers. My mother kept watch over me"—I nestled my head further against Daniel's legs—"deep into the nights."

"But you weren't in pain?"

"I hallucinated and slept and shivered, all of that awful stuff that comes with the flu. But I was never afraid, because I didn't know this flu would be such a vicious killer. I don't even know how I managed to contract it." I stopped and opened my eyes, and my stomach clenched. "Oh, God." I shot up to a seated position. "It must have been one of the children I teach. They'd come to my house for lessons, and—" I slapped my hand over my mouth. "I wonder if whichever child it was . . . I wonder if he—or she—is still alive."

A second ambulance tore down the street outside the window. I jumped and covered my ears and heard the engine squalling through my brain.

Daniel left the sofa and clicked open a cupboard door on the Victrola's mahogany stand. I removed my hands from my ears and watched him sift through dozens of record sleeves that crinkled from his touch.

"What are you doing?" I asked.

"Aha!" he cried. *"Da ist es!"*

"What are you saying?"

He stood up straight and slid a record out of a thin tan sleeve. "I'm going to play my favorite song for you so we can both block out the world outside. It's my fault for bringing up the *verdammt* flu."

He lowered the record onto the phonograph's turntable and wound the silver crank on the right-hand side. With the gentlest of movements, as when he had picked up his guitar during my first night in his bedroom, he leaned forward and placed the needle onto the crackling grooves.

" 'Slippery Hank,' " he said, lifting his face toward me with an arch of his left eyebrow, "by Earl Fuller's Famous Jazz Band."

A second later, one of the fastest and most frenzied jazz songs I'd ever heard volleyed across the apartment walls. A cornet trumpeted, and music zigged and zagged all over inside of me.

I laughed. "That's marvelous. It sounds like watching a circus while on cocaine."

"You've tried cocaine?"

"No, I've just read newspaper articles about it. Or—I know—the sound of people chasing one another around in a Fatty Arbuckle comedy."

"You like the song?"

"I love it."

He plopped down next to me on the sofa again, and I lowered my head back to his lap. The clatter and chaos of the outside world fell away—no more ambulances, no wagons ambling down the street with the dead wrapped in sheets. The wood-paneled walls and little brick fireplace, and even the brown burlap curtains blocking out the sun, seemed to brighten and nestle us closer together.

Once again, it was simply Daniel and me and beautiful, boisterous jazz.

Chapter 16

*E*ventually, we retired to his bedroom and slept in his bed the entire rest of the day. Not once did I awaken until the band from the Masonic Lodge sent its nighttime music sailing through the thin glass panes of Daniel's window. The pull of Nela and Addie and our transports drew me out of the snug sheets, where I had slept with Daniel's right leg over my left one. I washed my face in his bathroom and borrowed a swig of mouthwash to make up for my lack of a toothbrush and the fuzzy taste in my mouth. My skirt and blouse from the day before replaced the comfort of his oversized striped cotton pajamas.

"Are you leaving already?" he asked from the bed, dressed in only a pair of white pajama bottoms. He stretched his arms over his head and looked so lovely with his bare chest and mussed-up hair, I felt half-tempted to jump straight back into bed with him and continue hibernating.

"Nela and Addie, those Red Cross volunteers, will be counting on me to drive the ambulance again tonight." I sank my backside down on the mattress next to him.

"Stay a little longer." He raised himself up to a seated position. "Why hurry to rush back into hell?"

"I promised them I'd help." I reached forward and sifted my fingers through the close-trimmed hair above his left ear. We had never before sat and just looked at each other like that, I realized, face-to-face, eye-to-eye. I stroked his soft curls as if I'd known him for years, and even though, for whatever reason, he had inflicted his personal punishment upon himself, banning himself from kisses, he rubbed his lips together in a way that conveyed a need for me to lean my face close to his. I bent forward and pressed my mouth against his mouth, and for the first time in our short yet intimate relationship, we kissed.

He froze, and his breath fluttered through his nose in a quiet patter, breezing against my cheek. When I lifted my head, he turned his eyes away and inhaled a sharp breath.

"How old are you?" I asked.

He looked at me again. "Why do you ask?"

"You suddenly seem so much younger than before."

He adjusted his weight with a creak of the bed. "I'm twenty-four."

"Really?" My mouth fell open. "You're a year younger than me?"

"You're twenty-five?"

"Yes. I thought you were older."

"No." He shook his head. "Just twenty-four. I feel decades

older, though, and I probably look it, too. I've already pulled out a few white hairs after leaving Germany."

"No, you look just fine." I stroked his hair again and tried to read the stoic expression in his blue eyes, which watched me as much as I watched them. "You must have been no more than twenty when they put you in the army."

"I left home for war on my twentieth birthday, but I certainly wasn't the youngest one in the army." He lured my hand away from his hair and rubbed his thumb over the backs of my fingers. "Don't ever think of me as an innocent babe, Ivy. As anyone back home would tell you, I was a hellion who craved girls, booze, and adventure from far too young an age. I was begging for trouble."

"If I asked you why you left Germany . . . and the war"—I gave the strained smile of a person who's certain she's bound to encounter rejection—"would you tell me?"

He turned his face away again, toward the bare wooden wall.

"Were you injured?" I asked.

"I left Germany"—he swallowed—"in 1915, but there's no need for me to say anything more about it. That's all over now."

"I'm not going to betray any of your secrets to the authorities, if that's what worries you." I cleared my throat and felt heat rise to my cheeks. "I'm not even the first person I've known to take a German lover."

He didn't respond, or move, so I continued. "My friend Helen—"

"Helmut Weiss's mistress."

I sat up straight. "You know about Helen and Mr. Weiss?"

"Helmut is my father's cousin. That's why Albrecht moved to this specific town after he left Germany—after his wife and baby died. He wanted to leave his troubles behind in Deutschland but still be close to family."

"Oh. I didn't realize that." I blinked a few more times and tried to digest the connection between Daniel and Helen's German. "Well, anyway," I continued, "last July I went to see a motion picture with Helen—I don't even remember which one, something with Douglas Fairbanks in it—and one of those Four Minute Men got up in front of the audience while the projectionist changed the reels."

"*Ach,* I really hate those Four Minute idiots."

I smiled. "I've never been fond of them either. This one gave his little speech about Liberty Loans or saving peach pits for gas masks, something along those lines. And Helen leaned over to me and said, 'I'm worried someone will hang Mr. Weiss like they did Robert Prager.'" I sighed and shook my head. "At the moment, I didn't care a fig about Mr. Weiss. I just thought of him as a lecherous, forty-year-old German adulterer who should have never involved himself with one of my friends. Now I have to wonder, though"—I sighed again—"what was his life like over here? Was he a good man, deep down, despite his flaws, if someone as smart and vibrant as Helen fell in love with him?"

A little pucker of discontent formed between Daniel's eyebrows.

I nudged the back of his hand. "What's wrong?"

"Do you know who reported Helmut to the American Protective League and lied about him failing to buy Liberty Bonds?"

"I thought we weren't bringing up the APL anymore."

"You brought up Cousin Helmut. It's impossible not to talk about him without mentioning those *Schweine*."

"Who, then?" I asked. "One of his customers?"

"No, his American-born wife. She found him with his hussy back in the bakery kitchen and immediately went to the authorities. Those terrible APL idiots showed up at his store and instructed him to leave town or else suffer dire consequences." Daniel glanced at me out of the corners of his eyes. "There's a prison camp for German-American civilians at Fort Oglethorpe in Georgia. Another one exists at Fort Douglas in Utah. At one time or another, we all received the threat of detainment, but that didn't worry any of us half as much as the real possibility of a lynching."

I swallowed the taste of bile and muttered, "Helen Fay wasn't a hussy."

"And Helmut Weiss wasn't a traitor. He was just a *Dummkopf* who cheated on his wife."

I lowered my head and kneaded my lips together.

Across the street the band played a song I recognized, "Nightingale Rag," and I wondered what it would take to get Daniel to join me over in the lodge, just to escape all that talk of traitors and prison camps and lynching. He covered my right hand with his hot palm and managed to slow my breathing. Until that moment, I hadn't even realized my lungs were contracting and expanding at a brisk and unhealthy pace.

"Never mind all that." He swallowed. "Come back early in the morning, after you've finished carting those poor bastards around town. Sleep here again."

"I should probably pay my landlady first, so she doesn't think I've run off. I was supposed to be the first-ever boarder of the Dover Home for Women of Independent Means."

"Haven't you run off?"

"I don't know." I managed a halfhearted grin. "I honestly don't know where I belong anymore. No place feels quite right."

"Bring your things to my place. Stay here."

I shook my head. "I can't live here, Daniel."

"Why not? We'll be no worse off than Helen and Helmut." He snorted. "Oh, *Scheisse*. Even their names make them sound like a comical, doomed pair, no?"

"Precisely. They *were* doomed, and we'll be no different. The authorities ripped apart her apartment and threw her across the room. I don't even know if she's alive anymore."

He squeezed his hands around mine. "Stop worrying about everyone and everything. Come live here and drink away all your woes with me."

I pulled my hands out of his and shifted sideways on the bed. "I don't understand you."

"What?" He leaned toward me. "What don't you understand?"

"You won't kiss my lips or tell me a thing about you—why you're not in the German army anymore, who your parents are. Yet you want me to abandon my last precarious remnants of respectability so we can live together in sin."

"It's not sin."

"Yes, it is." My voice turned louder than expected, echoing off the walls. "To the rest of the world I'll be a hussy, like you just said of Helen. People like Lucas will keep calling me the whore of a German spy."

"I am not a spy."

"How do I know that? What proof have you ever given me to show that the German government didn't send you over here to—?"

"I'm a deserter."

I stiffened. "What?"

His jaw hardened. "I'm a deserter. I'd be executed if I ever returned to Germany. My parents don't even know where I am."

"You deserted the German armed forces?"

He nodded.

I gasped. "How? How did you not get killed?"

"I very nearly did—several times. But I made it. That's why I'm here."

He didn't elaborate, so I sat back on my hands and let the ragtime music settle inside my blood, longing to find a way to lure more of his story out of him. I imagined myself as a magician in a silk top hat and Daniel's history as colorful scarves I could draw out of his sleeves and view in all their clarity. *Truth is a torch,* as the poet Goethe had warned, but I didn't care if Daniel's stories scorched and blinded me.

I wanted the truth in one giant dose.

Daniel pushed the sheets off his legs with a sudden movement that made me stiffen. He climbed out of bed, put on his undershirt, and with a leonine grace that betrayed nothing of his status as a deserter and a refugee, he sauntered over to his guitar. I watched him ease down on the other side of the mattress with the instrument poised on his lap. He fussed with the strings and the knobs for no more than a minute, and then he strummed a subdued version of the jazz band's song that drifted through the window.

"It was during a furlough back home," he said as he played, his back toward me, his shoulders rocking with the smallest fraction of a sway. "Instead of returning to my post, I burned my uniform and somehow managed to escape to Holland without getting shot. Then I snuck aboard a steamer bound for New York. I hid down in the dark filth of a coal bunker and traveled at sea like a rat in a hole for nearly two weeks—nearly died of starvation. I honestly don't know how I made it here alive. I arrived in America as a sack of skin and bones." He withdrew his left fingers from the strings and swiveled in my direction. The music across the street played on without him.

"That's why I could never enlist in the U.S. Army," he said. "The newspaper article got that one detail correct: I never registered for the draft. I'm a wanted enemy of the Fatherland, and I can't return to Europe."

My lips parted to respond, but then he added, "I killed a great number of people in the war, Ivy. I'm not worthy of a kiss from your lips, so don't ever feel you're being deprived of something sacred if we never share the type of love you might be hoping to share. I'm a killer and a deserter, and no one wants me in their country. Not Germany, not America or Canada or any other place involved in the war. I'm considered an enemy of everyone."

I trembled from head to toe, all alone on my side of the bed; the battlefields of Europe had never edged so uncomfortably close to Buchanan, Illinois.

Daniel lowered his guitar to the floor with a soft tap of the wood against the boards. He sat up straight again and said, "I can't allow myself to love you. But I'll continue to take away your pain, if that's what you need of me. God knows, you're saving me from my pain."

"I'm glad," I said with my shoulders hunched, my voice cracking. "I'm glad I've helped."

He walked over to me on silent footfalls and stroked the hair above my right ear, as I'd just done to him. "Do you want me to give you a quick tumble before you leave?" He leaned down and kissed the top of my head, spilling a chill down to my toes. "So we can forget this ugliness? Would that help?"

I nodded, and even though it made no sense to pull down my drawers after hearing his grueling accounts of hardships and near death, I couldn't get my underclothes off my legs fast enough. Daniel tugged down his pants and laid me back on the edge of his bed. While the jazz band wailed a song as frantic and fervent as "Slippery Hank," I wrapped my legs around his waist and imagined the two of us as sticks of kindling, striking together, desperate for the taste of fire.

Chapter 17

I found the Red Cross ambulance parked alongside the curb outside Daniel's store, rumbling, shaking, ready to drive.

Addie's mask-covered face turned my way from the passenger side, and she sat up straight in the seat. "There she is."

Nela's eyes popped into view above her own swath of gauze beside Addie. "You can always bring him with you, you know," she called to me. "It wouldn't hurt to have a man around for the heavier lifting."

I buttoned up my coat and wished my face didn't heat up like a chimney every time anyone alluded to sex or Daniel.

"If you're driving four blocks away from the Red Cross headquarters"—I hopped into the empty driver's seat beside Nela—"then you can certainly drive down to Southside on your own. Why are you waiting here for me?"

Neither passenger answered. Nela fussed with the black Red

Cross–issued necktie hanging down her chest. Addie picked at a spot of dirt or dust or something equally miniscule on the dashboard.

"You've helmed a massive automotive," I said, "*and* parked it nicely alongside a curb, I might add. Not an easy task in the slightest. Why did you wait around for me when I know you must be longing to drive off as soon as possible?"

"I don't want to cross the railroad tracks," said Nela. She tugged on her necktie with so much nervous strength, she unraveled the knot. "I don't want to stall in front of a locomotive ever again."

"You won't. You've gotten so much more adept at driving. You can get yourself over the tracks just as easily as you drove down this street. Here . . ." I jumped out of the vehicle and waved for Nela to do the same. "Let's trade places. You drive, and I'll be sitting right next to you if anything happens."

"Oh, Lord, have mercy on our souls," said Addie into the thick gray collar of her coat.

Nela slid across the seat, her mouth tight, her body rigid. She stepped out of the ambulance so that I could scoot in between them.

I'd never heard such a troubled sigh as when Nela dropped down into the driver's position.

"You'll be absolutely fine." I nudged my arm against hers. "I promise."

Nela lowered her face. "I'm just a stupid woman, Ivy. And a foreigner at that."

"Poppycock!—as my granny Letty would have said." I raised my chin. "I've been driving my family's trucks and tractors since I was fifteen years old, and not once did my womb or my breasts get in the way of steering and braking."

Both Nela and Addie laughed throaty chuckles.

"American birth certificates aren't required to power the vehicles either," I added. "You can do this, Nela. You merely require confidence and practice."

"All right." Nela released the emergency brake—as well as another sigh that seemed to derive from the bottom of her lungs. "Let us go." She pulled on the throttle and spark advance levers with beautiful synchronicity, rolled the ambulance forward, and drove us four blocks west to Lincoln Street, just past the Hotel America. Her left turn around the corner felt brilliant, as smooth as a July boat ride on Minter Lake. The engine sighed with satisfied little *pop-pop-pop*s.

"You're doing brilliantly, you see?" I asked. "Just keep doing what you're doing."

The steel tracks and railway-crossing sign glowed up ahead in the light of the moon. Nela's breathing heightened. Her fingers whitened on the steering wheel. The ambulance slowed and whined.

"Keep driving," I said in the voice I typically reserved for piano pupils whose fingers tripped over keys. "There's no need to stop until just before we reach the tracks. We'll look and listen for signs of any locomotives, and then you'll guide the ambulance straight over those tracks, the same way you set off down

Willow Street without a hitch. Keep the clutch lever straight up, in neutral."

I heard the sounds of whispering beside me and realized Addie was reciting the Lord's Prayer under her breath. The car jerked and sputtered with Nela's dimming confidence.

"Keep the clutch pedal pushed all the way forward in first gear," I said, "and you won't stall. You'll simply stop for a moment so we can listen for trains. Keep going a little farther."

Nela propelled the ambulance forward with too much throttle. We came so close to those tracks, I could have practically reached out to touch them.

"Stop!" I cried.

She slammed her foot against the brake, and our heads whipped forward on our necks.

"*Cholera!*" Nela smacked the steering wheel with the palms of her hands.

"What?" I leaned forward and squinted into the darkness. "Do you see signs . . . ? Are people now sick from cholera, too?"

"No, it's a Polish way to swear. I don't like sitting this close to the tracks. *Cholera jasna!*"

"Oh, Jesus." Addie braced her hands against the dashboard. "Don't scare us to death with your swear words, too, Nela."

"It's all right." I gasped and rubbed a stitch in my left side. "The engine didn't stall, so you'll just need to adjust the levers and roll us forward. Addie, you keep your eyes and ears positioned to the right, and I'll watch the left. There aren't any patients in the back of the ambulance, correct?"

"Nope, it's empty," said Addie, scooting toward the open doorway.

"Where are you going?" I grabbed her by the arm.

"She doesn't trust me." Nela squirmed. "No one should trust me. I'm going to put us straight in the path of a train again."

"I'm not leaving—I'm right here," said Addie, but she twisted her body to the right and clamped her hand around the side bar, as if ready to eject herself from the ambulance at a moment's notice.

I scanned the dark expanse of tracks to the left and strained to hear whether a whistle pierced the night air in the distance. A bat screeched its eerie cry from somewhere in the black sky overhead, but the tracks lay silent.

Just to be certain, in case Addie was getting too ready to jump to pay close enough attention, I checked the right side, too.

"I don't see or hear any signs of a train," I said. "We're clear."

Addie whimpered and started right back up with the Lord's Prayer. Nela gasped for air like a fish thrown on land.

"Just relax. It's all right." I cupped my fingers around the back of Nela's hand. "Sing a song to calm yourself if you need to."

"I only know Polish songs. That damned America Protective League will drag me away if I start singing in Polish this close to North Buchanan." She clutched the steering wheel with all her might and continued to breathe in a panic. She even burped from sucking in so much air. I worried she might vomit.

" 'Father and I went down to camp,' " sang Addie in a small voice beside me. " 'Along with Captain Gooding . . .' "

I turned my face toward her and saw her wide-open eyes peering at mine through the darkness.

Addie continued: " 'And there we saw the men and boys . . .' "

I nodded and joined in. " 'As thick as hasty pudding.' "

Nela's left hand grabbed hold of the emergency brake.

" 'Yankee Doodle keep it up,' " I sang with Addie, and we craned our necks to see down the tracks. " 'Yankee Doodle dandy / Mind the music and the step . . .' "

With a squeal of rubber, Nela threw the ambulance into gear and launched us over the tracks as if shooting us to the moon. Wind tore through our hair and split across our faces, and the shimmering metal rails fell into the distance behind us.

Nela kept on driving with reckless abandon to the south side of town, and at the top of her lungs she sang out, " 'Mind the music and the step / And with the girls be handy.' *Cholera!* That was fun!"

WE DIDN'T FIND ANY red and white influenza notices hanging on front doors that night. Nela drove the ambulance up and down the lamplit streets of houses clustered throughout Southside, but all indicators of the flu seemed to have lifted from the earth. Few lights shone behind windows. Less clothing hung from the web of lines crisscrossing the alleyways and side yards. An unnerving emptiness and silence inhabited the entire region.

I scooted to the edge of the seat in case I had simply missed the signs because of my new center position in the vehicle.

"Where are the notices?" I asked. "I can't honestly believe people stopped getting sick that quickly. Can you?"

Addie shook her head. "I told you before, those influenza signs are as embarrassing as all heck. They tried to make us post one on our door right before we lost my sister Florence. Mama said it made her feel dirty as a dog." Addie rocked against me to the beat of the ambulance puttering through the sleeping neighborhoods. "I bet people are pulling the signs down to keep their pride."

Nela steered us onto a new road, where the wheels crunched across crisp autumn leaves scattered across dirt and gravel.

"I suppose we have to hope people will hear us driving by," I said, "and come outside to wave us down."

"That's not good enough," muttered Nela under her breath.

"How else are we supposed to find people, then?"

Neither of them answered my question. I couldn't answer it myself. An air of defeat settled over all of us in that chilly, open driving compartment.

We crept through the streets for close to a half hour, and during that entire time we came across only one sign, posted on the door of a tiny wooden structure almost small enough to be a milk shed. The home sat on the southwesternmost edge of Southside, just before the land opened up to fields of autumn crops. Dark outlines of pumpkins lay just beyond a rusted collection of harrows and plows.

No one answered the front door. The knob wouldn't budge when Nela jiggled it. We got back into the ambulance with wilted postures and frustrated breaths, and we pressed onward.

"Maybe we should just get out of the ambulance"—Nela steered us back onto the first street we had scanned—"and go door to door, knocking."

"No!" said Addie. "Are you crazy? It's the middle of the night. We'll wake up both the sick *and* the healthy. No one needs that right now."

"There is a daytime set of volunteers that drives down here, isn't there?" I asked.

"Yes." Nela gave a brusque nod. "But that doesn't mean we're not needed right now. The flu doesn't care about night and day."

"We had a fine doctor in our neighborhood." Addie sank back into the seat and crossed her arms over her gray coat. "Before he answered the call for medical help overseas. Stupid, selfish war."

"Benjie's father?" I asked.

Addie nodded. "He would have been one of the first to help here in Southside. People of all colors trusted him."

"This is madness." Nela slammed her foot onto the brake, and the ambulance skidded to a stop—miraculously, without stalling. "People must be lying in their homes, desperate for help."

"Should we transport more of the sick out of Polish Hall?" I asked. "Like we did with Benjie?"

Both women spun their heads my way as if I'd just proposed carting the sick to Germany.

"We volunteered to fetch people from their homes," said Nela. "We've got to keep doing what they sent us out to do."

"I sort of feel . . ." I buttoned up my coat against the cold. "I just . . . I don't think driving around all night in the dark is going to help anyone. I feel we should either relieve the emergency hospital of their work and take people to your house, where the recovery rate seems high. Or else stop for the night."

"We can't stop." Nela released the emergency brake and set us driving again. "And we can't show up at a hospital and steal their patients."

"It's not even a real hospital," I said. "It's more of a desperation ward. A 'We Don't Know How to Properly Take Care of Our Residents Here in Buchanan' Ward."

"We're not even supposed to be driving this truck," said Addie.

I swiveled toward her with a shift of my knees. "What?"

"Addie!" hissed Nela, and she stopped the truck again. "You were never supposed to tell her that. I warned you—"

"She might as well know the truth after coming this far with us." Addie sank back into the seat, her arms still locked across her chest. "I'm not even a registered Red Cross nurse. This is my sister's uniform."

"But . . . what?" I turned back to Nela. "Have you been stealing this ambulance every night?"

"No, it's not quite like that . . ." Nela unbuttoned a pocket on the breast of her coat. "I'm a card-carrying Red Cross volunteer with hygiene courses and hospital volunteer hours completed. Liliana had trained to drive ambulances in the hopes of volunteering overseas." She pulled out a Red Cross card and shoved it at me. I saw an official Red Cross stamp and certification that referred to her as "Mrs. Fred Stone."

"Who's Mrs. Stone?" I asked.

"Me." Nela grabbed the card out of my hand and wedged it back into her pocket. "I told you the first night I met you, my husband is American. I'm not lying about who I am, and I didn't steal this ambulance."

"Then why did Addie just say—?"

"Liliana and I answered the call for help at the end of September, after watching people suffer without anyone coming to save them. She fell sick one night when we were on duty, and I needed to drive her. No one else was there with me except for Addie—this crazy girl who was mad as the devil from losing her sister and desperate to help. So we jumped into the ambulance and went."

"No one knows you're driving this truck every night?" I asked.

"It doesn't matter!" Nela slammed her hands against the steering wheel and caused Addie and me to jump. "People need help. I don't even care that this seventeen-year-old girl hasn't had one single hour of hospital training. I don't care that her skin is as black as coal. She's strong enough to carry a stretcher. She's willing to walk through Southside muck to save people's lives. That's all that matters right now, Ivy. Nothing else matters."

I sat stock-still and opened my mouth to mutter drivel about the American Protective League watching out for all types of subversive activity, but before I could utter a word, Nela jumped out of the ambulance with the motor still running, and marched toward a two-story house beside us that looked like nothing more than a home-shaped shadow.

"Don't wake them up." Addie leapt out of the truck and ran after Nela. "Stop it, Nela! If we make them mad, they'll report us. We won't be allowed to help."

"Let's go to Polish Hall and ask if they want our help." I scooted over to the driver's side. "I'll drive again so if anyone catches us . . ."

"I don't give a damn if they catch me," said Nela, shaking herself free of Addie. "They need to know we don't have enough care down here. We need at least two more emergency hospitals and care for children with sick parents. We need doctors and translators and medicine. We need a way to convince people hiding in their homes to seek help when they need it. We need Americans like you to push the high and mighty to open their blind eyes and see us struggling down here."

"I'll do what I can, Nela. I swear I will. But, please, for now, let's start by checking on Polish Hall. Let's ask the volunteers who are knee-deep in assisting the ill what they need. There's nothing else we can do out here in the dark."

"Come on." Addie took Nela by the hand and led her toward the ambulance. The hems of their gray Red Cross skirts swayed below their knees.

Nela came to a stop beside me at the driver's-side door. The smell of gasoline from the Ford began to bother me, as did the whole difficult venture.

"We volunteered to fetch people from their homes," said Nela again. "We've got to keep doing what they sent us out to do."

I squeezed my eyes shut and tried to remain calm. I wanted to tell her again how useless we seemed, puttering around in the dark, not knowing where to find patients, but the entire conversation seemed circular and endless.

"Fine." I opened my eyes. "I'll drive for another half hour. And then I'll drop you back off at your house, where patients are already lying, in need of your help. Will you promise to only be out here for a half hour?"

She screwed up her face and shook from head to toe, and I worried for a moment that something might not be right with her head. Maybe she experienced skull-splitting moments of terror similar to the ones I used to endure whenever I attempted to leave home.

"All right." She relaxed her shoulders. "We drive for another half hour. And then I help Liliana with the people in my house."

"Good." I grabbed hold of the steering wheel. "Jump inside. Let's get going."

WE MANAGED TO FIND one additional influenza sign during that half hour. We knocked on a thin wooden door, and no one answered, so Nela—more determined than ever to discover someone to transport—handed me her end of the stretcher and pushed her way inside.

Another darkened house. More smells of sickness and dirty diapers. Addie and I carried the stretcher upstairs, behind Nela, and we poked our heads into the rooms of the sleeping.

How frightening it would be to wake up, I thought, *delirious with a fever, to find two masked females and an exhausted American woman peeking into one's bedroom.*

We roamed the hallways and scanned each bed of sleepers, but only one person stood out: a girl around the age of eleven, with auburn braids. She huddled in a dim corner of a hallway in a nightgown, her bare toes sticking out from beneath the frayed white hem.

"Hello." Nela hurried over to her and embarked upon a few questions, all spoken in Polish.

The girl stared up at her with enormous dark eyes that made me shiver. Something about the child's lost expression and motionless body gave me gooseflesh and set my heart galloping in my chest. I remembered May sitting over her Ouija board, saying to me in her calm and steady voice, *Some spirits get stuck in the places where they died.*

"Is she alive?" I asked before I could even think how odd my question sounded.

Nela peeked back at me. "Of course. She's just ill and frightened." Nela spoke in Polish again, and the girl shook her head and pushed her away.

Addie lowered the front end of the stretcher a few feet from the child. "Tell her we have music at your house, Nela. Tell her there are other sick children there, and they'll want to play with her when she feels better."

Nela translated Addie's words with encouraging little nods of her head, and the girl eased her stiff posture against the wall. Finally she spoke, also in Polish.

Nela turned on her heels toward Addie and me. "She'll come, but the stretcher scares her. She'd rather walk."

"Is she able?" I asked.

"She says she is."

Addie and I picked up the stretcher and carried it away, while Nela slid her arm behind the girl's shoulders and helped her to a standing position.

"Are there any others here who are sick?" Addie called over her shoulder.

I heard more exchanges in Polish before Nela answered, "She says the others are recuperating."

We lugged the empty stretcher down the unlit staircase, careful not to bang the walls or walk with too loud a tread.

I backed out the front door and asked, "How is that poor girl going to ride in the back with the stretcher if it frightens her?"

"I can ride back there," said Addie. "I don't mind. She can ride in front."

"Absolutely not!" I stopped in my tracks. "If you haven't contracted the flu yet, you shouldn't be anywhere near a compartment where we carry the sick."

"I'm near the sick all the time, and I'm doing just fine."

I glanced over my shoulder to see where I was going and heard someone call the name "Wendy Darling."

Across the street a figure in an army tunic and breeches stood beneath a lamp and smoked a cigarette.

Billy.

"No!" I dropped my side of the stretcher, and the handles crashed against the sidewalk.

"What's happening?" asked Addie.

"No, no, no!" I crouched on the ground and covered my ears, closed my eyes, shook from head to toe.

"What is it?" Nela's Red Cross boots clomped over to me, and I heard the shuffle of the girl's bare feet beside her. "What is wrong?"

"Will you look across the street"—I stayed on the ground with my hands pressed against the sides of my head—"and tell me if you see a United States soldier smoking a cigarette beneath that lamp."

"There's a training camp—"

"I know there's a training camp not more than ten miles away, but this soldier looked familiar to me."

"Your brother?" asked Addie.

"Please, tell me if you see him."

No one answered for a moment, which made me tremble all the harder.

"Well?"

"I scc no one," said Nela.

"Are you certain?"

"Look for yourself. No one is standing under that lamp."

With utmost caution, I stretched myself back up to a standing position and shifted toward the street.

He was gone.

"Go home." Nela nudged my arm. "Your eyes are looking—how did you say it? 'Bleary'? I remember that hedge you killed the last time you were like this."

"But . . . you're all still working so hard. All those people at your house . . ."

"You going home to rest will give us room to put the girl in the front seat," suggested Addie.

"Let me at least . . ." I grabbed up my end of the stretcher. "Let me help you put this back in the ambulance. I don't . . ." I glanced back at the empty streetlamp where I thought I'd seen Billy. "I'm sorry. I wish I didn't see them. I really do."

Addie and I returned to the back of the ambulance and slid the stretcher inside the dark compartment that smelled of sickness and damp canvas.

"Go"—Addie tapped my shoulder—"before Nela changes her mind and gives you any guilt. We know where to find you if we desperately need you again."

"But—"

"Go! This isn't where you need to be right now."

I turned and left, and the knife blade of guilt tried to dig its way back into my gut, but I pushed it away as best as I could.

Chapter 18

I walked through the midnight streets on my own with my arms clasped around my torso. The echoes of my footsteps ricocheted off the Southside houses and sounded as though a second pair of feet traveled through Buchanan with me, and I worried I'd hear Billy's voice again, calling to me, *Wendy Darling.*

From the eaves of one of the homes, another barn owl hissed—a disturbing noise akin to leaking gas. Across the street, a couple argued on their front porch in Russian, and their tension sliced straight through me. I pressed onward, glancing over my shoulder every half minute. Thankfully, no one stepped out into the road behind me, but that didn't stop me from checking with obsessive regularity.

On the northern side of the railroad tracks, the music of the jazz band enlivened the slumbering businesses lined in their neat and organized grid of brick and stone. The sound sizzled like static across my skin. The piano beckoned. Seduced. It tempted me to turn toward the direction of Daniel and the Masonic Lodge.

Don't be a stranger, Ivy sweetheart, I remembered Ruth Sellman calling to me across the dance floor. *Next time, wear your dancing shoes and stay for a while.*

I turned west on Willow, however, ignoring the pull of music and rapture, and continued onward until I reached May's house.

My cheeks warmed with shame. I stared up at the dormer window that belonged to my new room in the attic and thought back to the man lying below May on her bed. My brain now could not convince my eyes that they had genuinely viewed Eddie Dover. A fair-haired man had lain with May, it's true, but, honestly, Eddie wasn't the only blond male who ever graced that part of the world.

I still carried my key in my coat pocket, but I found the front door unlocked, just as Daniel's front door often sat free of any protection—which deepened my concern over Buchanan residents' naïve trust in their neighbors.

No lights lit the front room, but my eyes adjusted to darkness after my trek through the nighttime streets. With my upper body stiff and my lungs tight, I managed to steal across the house, past the closed doorway of May's silent bedroom, and up the staircase.

I navigated my way through all of May and Eddie's belongings on the attic floor, lifting my knees high in the air as though wading through mud, and reached for the cold base of the gold lamp standing next to the bed. I pulled a chain and clicked on the light.

A surprise awaited me.

Across the white ruffles of the bedspread lay a pair of human-sized butterfly wings made of shimmering periwinkle fabric. Someone—May, I assumed—had sewn little jeweled bracelets to the tops of the wings so that the costume could be slipped over one's arms to be worn. A note rested on top of the creation:

Where did you fly off to, little butterfly?

I picked up the small piece of white paper and pressed my hand against my forehead to dim another wave of humiliation.

"Well?" asked a voice from behind me.

I spun around, finding May at the top of the attic stairs, dressed in the red silk robe I remembered from before. She wore her hair down, and her thick motion-picture star curls fell to her waist.

"Where *did* you go?" she asked with a lift of her dark eyebrows.

"I'm sorry I took off like that." I grabbed my leather handbag from the floor below the chest of drawers and clicked open the gold clasp. "I just . . . um . . ." I pulled several dollars out of the purse. "Let me go ahead and pay you. I'm really sorry I've been a terrible boarder, but I—"

"Ivy."

I snapped my face upright and fully met her eyes for the

first time since I had caught her with the man who looked like Eddie.

May stepped farther inside the room with her hands on the black sash of her robe. "Are you leaving me?"

"Yes." I handed her the bills. "Here's some rent money."

She wrinkled her nose. "That's more than enough. You weren't even here a full week."

"Take it, for your troubles." I held out the money with the tips of my fingers until she grabbed hold of the bills.

She folded her arms across her chest. "Where are you going to live?"

"Um . . . a friend . . ." I scratched at my ear. "A friend invited me to stay."

"A friend?" The right side of her mouth edged into a grin.

"Yes. A close friend."

"You said your only good friend in Buchanan moved away over the summer."

"Yes, well . . ." I turned back to the dresser and slid open the top drawer. "There's another friend."

"The German?"

I didn't answer.

"Ivy?"

"What?" I peeked back at her.

"Are you sure you're ready for this?"

"No, I'm not, but—" I stopped and raised both my hands in the air, for a terrible realization occurred to me. "Oh, Christ!

I'm covered in germs. I can't touch my clothing and then wear it around him. Why have I been going near him afterward?" I spun toward May, my hands still raised. "I shouldn't be near you either. I'm going to kill everyone. This is why I saw Billy."

"Who's Billy?"

"My brother, the one killed in the war. Why do I keep going near all of you after being around all those sick people we're transporting? *I'm* the reason someone is going to die."

"Come downstairs." May waved me over to the top of the staircase. "You can take a bath before you go to your German Romeo. Wash your hair, disinfect your shoes with my bottle of Lysol, and throw those clothes you're wearing out to my leaf piles I'll eventually burn. But don't panic so much, Sarah Bernhardt."

My feet refused to budge. "May."

She turned back toward me. "What?"

"Who did I see you with in your bedroom?"

She sank down to the topmost step, and her dark eyes grew large and childlike. "Does it matter?"

"Is he here right now?"

She shook her head, her dark curls wobbling. "No. Not until three o'clock. He always arrives at three in the morning. The witching hour." She disappeared down two more steps; all I could see were the tops of her eyes and her head of black hair, and she made my blood run cold peering at me that way. "You have two and a half hours to bathe before he arrives," she said.

"Flap your wings and get flying off to that bath if you don't want to see him."

MAY MONITORED MY BATHWATER in her plumbed downstairs bathroom, while I shivered outside on her back porch for fear of infiltrating her house with influenza. I longed to dunk my entire body into scalding water and burn away every last trace of the germs.

With a deep moan of the wood, I lowered myself down to a seated position on the top step, and I leaned my head against a post. Out in the backyard rose silhouettes of trees with thick autumn leaves waiting to plummet to the earth. I feared a shadowed figure in an army uniform would step out from behind one of the trunks, and I'd see the glow of Billy's cigarette. Or Lucas's eyes behind his glasses.

May opened the bathroom window behind me and called out, "It's ready. Take off your clothes and toss them onto one of the leaf piles."

I stood up and craned my neck to survey the proximity of the backyard to the nearest windows of the neighboring houses. "Will any of your neighbors be able to see?"

"It's dark. They're asleep. They're other widows anyway, with children."

"Are you sure you're alone in there?"

"Yes. I'm alone right now. Don't be so modest, Ivy. Take off your clothes."

I flung my beloved green overcoat into the yard and heard it splat across the brittle leaves. Not wanting to risk wearing one stitch of flu-infested clothing, I stripped all the way down to the buff, hurled my garments into the night, and ran inside.

May stood in the kitchen and held open the door to the adjoining bathroom for me. I covered my chest and my privates and hurried past her on bare feet that squeaked against the tiled floor.

"Don't be such a prude," she said with a laugh. "You've got a body like the Venus de Milo's. Flaunt it."

I climbed into her claw-foot bathtub, and before she could say another word about my nakedness, I sank down on my back and submerged my head in the warm and silent waters, watching my long hair drift to the surface above me like undulating blades of river grass.

A CLOCK IN MAY'S FRONT ROOM CHIMED one thirty in the morning. Dressed in fresh clothing and Lysol-disinfected shoes, I meandered downstairs with my packed-up bags in hand and the butterfly wings tucked beneath my left arm. I managed to pin up my wet hair, but it still dripped plump drops onto the back of my clean white blouse.

May stood up from her armchair, a mug of steaming tea in hand.

"Well." I set down my bags by my sides. "I guess this is goodbye."

"I guess so." She lowered her mug to a table. "That was an awfully short stay. We were supposed to have heaps of fun."

"I'm sorry. It's just . . ." I tried my best not to glance back at her bedroom door. "Thank you for housing me, even if it was so temporary."

"You're welcome."

I grabbed up the handles of my bags again and hoisted the luggage to the front door.

"I know it doesn't make any sense," she said from behind me before I could reach for the knob.

I shifted around to face her.

She pulled her robe a little farther over her chest and folded her hands together. "I can't explain how he arrives, but his presence doesn't ever frighten me. We're happy as clams during those heavenly moments in the early-morning hours." She smiled. "Truly we are."

I stood there and gawked with my mouth tipped open too far.

"You don't need to feel frightened for me," she said. "Or worried. I'm fine. Just"—she raised her shoulders to her ears in a sort of shrug—"a little lonely during the remaining hours of the day."

"I'll come visit again," I offered. "Once it's not so dangerous to be outside. I feel I should hole myself up with Daniel in his apartment for a while until the rapid spread of infection passes. I want to keep him safe."

"I understand." She nodded, and her smile looked strained. Her eyes moistened.

"Will you be all right?"

"Oh sure. I've got company coming soon." She wiped her eyes

and glanced at the clock. "I'll be fine, Ivy. Go. Take those wings and fly."

"Are you sure?"

"Yes. You deserve a little zig-zig."

"A little what?"

She winked and nodded toward the door. "Go. I'm sure he's waiting."

"Our Own Robert Prager"
A Message from a Murdered Man's Brother

Six months have passed since three to four hundred men and boys wrapped Robert P. Prager in an American flag and hung him from a tree branch one mile west of Collinsville, Ill. Prager, a German-born coalminer, was accused of making disloyal and Socialist remarks to other miners and died at the hands of ordinary United States citizens—citizens later acquitted of the crime of his murder.

In August 1917, vigilantes lynched IWW organizer Frank Little near Butte, Montana. Less than a month before Prager's death, four men—a Polish Catholic priest included—were tarred and feathered in Christopher, Ill., to Collinsville's south. Two other men were previously tarred and feathered in the same region. Only God knows how many other attacks upon immigrants and Socialists have gone unreported within this state and elsewhere.

Almost six months to the exact date of the Prager lynching, my own brother lost his life at the hands of vigilantes right here in Buchanan, Ill. The Buchanan Sentinel claims that "vagrants" wandered into our place of business and brutally beat and killed him in a random moment of patriotic passion. However, because of the particular condition of our store in the aftermath of the crime and the specific tools and yellow paint carried to the scene, I believe his death resulted from local "superpatriots" hellbent on driving Germans and other foreigners out of the region.

Since my immigration, I have learned that Americans have belittled, beaten, and killed their black and native citizens for centuries. The recent number of abused and murdered Germans and other foreign-born residents seems relatively small in comparison to the crimes against the nonwhites of this country. Yet this added surge of hatred only proves that America has no right sailing to foreign lands in the name of protecting freedom—not when we're steeped in the mire of violent inequality here at home.

I do not believe my brother will ever receive justice for his death. I could hire detectives and hunt down his killers, yet I know their criminal behavior will not only be pardoned, but also celebrated. I read the accounts of the trial of Robert Prager's acquitted killers. I know a band played "The Star-Spangled Banner" in the courthouse rotunda, and after the "not-guilty" verdict was handed out, a juryman shouted, "Well, I guess nobody can say we aren't loyal now." And yet I sincerely hope that Buchanan residents will read my words and join together to protect other persecuted individuals from similar deaths by everyday citizens taking the law into their own hands. I am tempted to wallow in drink and pity myself because of what happened; to cower in terror and expect to one day soon find an over-zealous mob coming my way, carrying a noose and a flag. I know that's what my brother's attackers expect of me, but I refuse to cower.

I pray that my brother rests in peace, but I will not rest until I finish speaking my mind about his brutal and unnecessary death.

—THE BUCHANAN WORKMAN, October 10, 1918

Chapter 19

With my bags still in hand, I used my left elbow to knock on the front door of Liberty Brothers Furniture. Across the street, long and jubilant slides of the trombone suggested that the night was meant for celebrating, not for fretting about ghosts and one's uselessness.

Daniel answered the door in his shirtsleeves and trousers.

I lifted up my bags, and the jeweled bracelets of the wings clanked down my left arm. "How about that glass of German brandy you promised, Mr. Schendel?"

He threw the door open farther and smiled wider than I'd ever seen him do before—wider than I'd seen *anyone* smile before. I stepped across the threshold and lowered my bags, and as soon as he closed the door and latched the lock, he wrapped his arms around my waist and peppered my neck with kisses. "*Willkommen,*" he said near my ear. "Why is your hair all wet?"

"I washed up to ensure I wouldn't bring any germs into your home. I want to hunker down with you during the rest of this epidemic and make sure you stay safe."

"You smell delicious." He planted one more tickle of a kiss on my throat. "Let's go put your bags away and have that drink."

We deposited my belongings up in his bedroom, and he grabbed my hand and steered me across the apartment to the kitchen. "Here, before we get comfortable and relaxed"—he led me to an oak table built for two, across from a cream-colored cookstove that smelled of burnt wood—"I have some things to show you."

He stopped us in front of three photographs, laid out in a tidy little line across the table's smooth surface. The collection included an image of Daniel himself, attached to the inside of his Alien Registration card, above his inky thumbprint.

"Oh." I squeezed his hand. "You don't have to share these if you don't want to. I know how much you desire your privacy."

"So"—he lifted the framed image of his parents from the mantel—"this is indeed my mother and father—*Mutter* and *Vater,* as we say over there. They still live in Germany, as you asked, in the same home where I grew up. And this is Albrecht and his late wife, Gertrud, on their wedding day in 1911."

He laid his left hand next to the unframed photograph of a young man who resembled Daniel, but with straighter hair and larger teeth. The bride wore a high-collared white gown and a rounded headdress that looked like the sun rising behind her fair hair.

"So, that's . . . that's how he looked," I murmured, and I held the rounded edge of the table to steady myself. Putting a face to Father and Peter's victim, picturing Albrecht Schendel as a real human being and not just a tragic name, caused the entire scene of the murder to flare to life inside my mind. I imagined that face in the photo a little fuller with age, and I envisioned it all—Father pinning Albrecht down on the ground of the store; Peter pummeling Albrecht's nose and teeth with a fist that swelled and bruised from the force of the impact; Albrecht crawling on the floor to get away, blood pouring from his mouth and nostrils; Father kicking Albrecht in the ribs with his thick farm boots until the bones cracked.

I pinched my nose to stave off a headache. "Did they really beat him to death?"

"I didn't . . ." Daniel turned over the photo of his brother and his long-ago bride. "I didn't show this picture to you to make you feel guilty. I assumed you've been wondering what he looks like."

I nodded. "I have been wondering, and before long I would have asked. But"—I flipped the photo back to its upright position—"I want to know, did they truly beat him to death with their own bare hands?"

Daniel traced an index finger down the leftmost edge of the photo. "They beat him badly, to the point where he could no longer move or cry out for help. And then"—he cleared his throat—"they used something else, to finish the task."

I winced. "Oh . . . Daniel . . ." I covered my mouth and dug my fingers into my cheeks. "I didn't know there was also a weapon. What did they use?"

He turned the picture over to its back side again, and all I could see were Albrecht and Gertrud's names, along with a note I assumed to be the date—*18. März 1911*—written in the center of the paper in a lovely display of slanted handwriting.

"I don't want to talk about what they used." Daniel moved on to his brown registration card and released a breath from his chest. "And this is me, of course. I wanted to use an entirely different name when I escaped over here, but Albrecht had already obtained papers for me in my own name. So, at the beginning of this year, when they forced all of us Germans to register as alien enemies within five days, I had to indeed use 'Wilhelm Schendel.'"

I picked up his card and smiled a little at his defiant glare in the photograph. His squished-together line of a mouth looked as though he were trying not to spit at the camera's lens.

"One would assume," I said, "that the U.S. would have been far kinder to a man who abandoned the army of the enemy."

"One would assume that." He gathered up all the photographs in his hands, one by one. "But this is not the fantastical land of liberty that people portray in stories. The melting pot does nothing but scald and blister right now."

He carried the pictures out to the other room, and I eyed the wine and brandy parked on a shelf below the kitchen worktable, next to the icebox. I longed to dive straight into one of those beautiful brown or green bottles and drown myself in an ocean of brain-stupefying liquor.

Daniel returned with a loud clap of his hands. "Now, the brandy."

"I have to warn you"—I stood up straight—"I'm not usually much of a drinker . . ."

"As I said"—he reached down below the worktable and sifted through the bottles with gentle clinks of the glass—"I'm sure you have never experienced a glass of real, honest-to-goodness booze. The type that will make you howl at the moon and run through the streets naked."

I laughed.

"Here . . ." He carried over a green bottle with a red and brown label, written in German. "This is from Albrecht's collection he imported before the war. Sit down." He scooted out a chair for me. "Make yourself at home."

He fetched two brandy snifters and a corkscrew from a cupboard. Then he stood over the table across from me and hummed along with the band across the street while twisting the cork off the top of the bottle. An explosive pop shot across the kitchen. The scent of brandy rushed through my nostrils, practically turning me pie-eyed from the fumes alone.

Daniel planted himself in a chair and poured us each a glass of an amber-red liquid that swirled inside the bulbous bottoms of the snifters. "Well . . ." He set down the bottle and kneaded the stem of his glass between his fingers. "What should we drink to, Fräulein?"

"Hmm. How about . . . ?" I lifted my glass into the air and tapped the tip of my left index finger against my lips. "How about to life?"

"All right, then." He lifted his glass as well. "To life. *Prost!*"

I took a deep breath and braced myself for the sting, and we both leaned back our heads and drank a hearty swig. Fire scoured my throat, and I coughed and cringed and wiped my lips with a knuckle, while Daniel snickered from across the table.

"*Das ist gut,* no?" he asked with a glimmer in his eyes. "Can you handle it, *Amerikanerin?*"

"*Ja,* Mr. Schendel." I sat up straight with my elbows digging into the table and asked, "What should we drink to next?"

His smile faded to a somber expression that caused the skin between his eyebrows to crinkle. "To fate."

We lifted our glasses to our lips, and after another deep breath, I downed a second swig along with him. I then braced my hands against the table and pushed the burning air from my lungs like a fire-breathing dragon—or a woman panting through the throes of labor pains.

He laughed again. "It gets better soon, after you get used to the bite. Keep trying."

Once the heat settled, I raised my snifter again and said, "To your brother, Albrecht."

"And to your brother—"

"Billy." I took a third swig, a deep one that burned with a little less ferociousness, and then I lifted my glass even higher, above my head, and said, "To Wilhelm Daniel Schendel."

Ah, that particular sip tasted divine. My tongue tingled, and I delighted in the sensation of running the tip of it across my slippery teeth. Daniel tapped the neck of the bottle against our snifters and topped off our drinks.

"And to Ivy . . ." he said. "Ummm . . . to Ivy . . ." Daniel held up his glass and blinked at me. "Oh, *Scheisse.*" He snickered. "I don't even know your last name."

"You don't? But what about—" I quickly shut my mouth before any references to that damned newspaper article flew out of it. As I remembered Daniel saying, the paper didn't mention one word about Frank and Peter Rowan. "It's Rowan," I said. "Ivy Anne Rowan."

"To Ivy Anne Rowan, then." He smiled and brought his glass to his lips. "And all her lovely loveliness."

I closed my eyes and enjoyed another swallow just as the band across the way switched to a familiar song. "Oh!" I straightened up tall in my chair. "To 'Livery Stavle—'"

" 'Stable,' " Daniel corrected me.

" 'Stavle—' "

"To 'Liberty *Stable* Blues.' "

Our glasses soon sat empty.

Daniel poured again.

I planted my elbows on the table and wiggled my shoulders and hips to the rhythm of the music. "Do you know how to dance, Wilhelm Daniel?"

"I haven't danced since before the war."

"You haven't? Do you know how to fox-trot? Or do you just polka?"

"Oh, *Gott.*" He rolled his eyes. "Miss Ivy Anne Rowan, we don't just dance the polka in Deutschland. Shame on you."

I laughed louder than necessary and flopped back in my chair. "I don't know these things. I'm a naïve American, remember?"

"Well, I can one-step as well as any Yank."

"I think maybe we should dance."

"I think maybe I'll need to drink a little more before we do that."

We imbibed several more sips, and before long we were standing in his living room with my left hand atop his shoulder, his right hand snuggled up to my waist, and our other fingers locked firmly together. He counted to three, and we rocked our torsos side to side while our feet stepped to the beat of a song from across the way.

" 'Gun-Cotton Rag,' " he said over the horns, "by Merle von Hagen."

The music increased in tempo, so we sped up our steps and the rate of our turns, and we ended up spinning straight into a table lamp. The poor thing crashed to the floor with a shatter of cobalt-blue glass. Shards scattered across the rug. All we could do was cover our mouths and laugh at the damage.

"We killed it," said Daniel, and he slung his arm around my waist again. We kept right on dancing.

We stopped between songs for another drink, and the next

thing I knew I was dancing in my undergarments, with May's gauzy butterfly wings strapped to my arms and back and Daniel in just his trousers and his suspenders. One of my black stockings dangled down his naked chest like a necktie, and his hair was all mussed from my hands. His shirt and vest and the rest of my clothing buried the wreckage of the lamp, and we avoided the mess and giggled like children, and then another lamp broke, and before long I was straddling him down on the floor, gripping his shoulders, watching him close his eyes and moan while we both struggled to find some sort of relief. None was to be had, so we yanked our undergarments back up our legs and drank again, and a pistol somehow made its way into my hands. A pair of safety goggles protected my eyes, and Daniel stood behind me, his warm torso snug against my back. He helped me point the silver barrel toward one of the glasses on the table, but my target wobbled and blurred into two brandy snifters.

"You just squeeze," he said near my ear, his breath hot on my skin, and a thrill of danger surged through me, followed by another loud fit of laughter.

"Squeeze," he said again, and I pulled the trigger and fired a bullet into a wall, hoping to God no one lived next door.

He helped me fire a second time, and the snifter burst to thousands of pieces before my eyes. Brandy bled across the table and trickled down to the floor in a thick stream of red. I started to think of the flu and nosebleeds, so I took the barrel of the gun and smashed the second glass to pieces, just to hear it shatter.

The music played faster and faster, and we ran our tongues all over each other and climbed on top of each other, and somehow we damaged more of that apartment. Glass kept breaking. Booze stained the floor. End tables collapsed on their sides. I bit Daniel's neck and clawed his back and howled with a primitive roar.

The last thing I remember of that bacchanalian night was lying on my stomach in his bed, with him on top of me, and I was crying into his pillow. I sobbed for the dead, and for him and me, and he crawled off of me and ran his hands through my hair, begging me not to cry, pleading with me to stay with him.

Chapter 20

A man's voice called out, "What the hell happened in here?"

I jolted awake and found the midday sun plowing through the striped curtains of Daniel's room, heating my bare feet, which dangled over the strings of his guitar at the end of the bed. I moved my leg and accidentally strummed an off-key chord with one of my big toes.

Daniel slept on his back beside me, not moving.

I attributed the voice to a dream. Or maybe a passerby on the sidewalk outside.

Nothing to worry about, I told myself. *Go back to sleep.*

I tucked myself under the covers and nuzzled down inside a pocket of heat and safety.

Just as I got myself good and cozy, the floorboards outside the bedroom door whined with the weight of footsteps. Glass clattered and tinkled, as if someone were cleaning up our wreckage from the night before.

"*Was ist das?*" asked that unknown voice I'd heard before. "What the hell happened?"

I shrank down under the covers and whispered, "Daniel! Oh, God. Daniel, wake up! Hurry!"

Daniel didn't stir, and my chest nearly burst, for a man suddenly edged his way inside the room. His face and brown hair matched that of Albrecht Schendel in the wedding photograph, and I knew it was happening again.

No, no, no, no, no!

I struggled to breathe and stay stock-still at the same time. My heart burned as though it bled throughout my chest.

The man meandered across the bedroom floor, his neck tense, eyes narrowed, but, to my relief, he didn't seem to notice his brother and me lying in the bed. He slid the guitar off the end of the mattress, spilling an aching-cold chill across my feet, and positioned the instrument in the corner where it usually rested. I heard the plunk of the neck bumping the juncture in the walls.

He turned and walked over to Daniel's desk. With the softest whisper of his fingers, he rubbed his hand across the wood, his back toward me. No matter how much I told my eyes to stop seeing him, Albrecht Schendel would not go away. He refused to become a figment of my imagination.

I drew another short breath, rolled over to Daniel's side, and struggled to burrow my body into the small slip of space between him and the mattress. Daniel's skin felt as frigid as a block of ice next to mine. He didn't move. I shuddered with the fear that he lay dead beside me—the flu or the alcohol had killed him. His murdered brother's spirit stood in the room with us, while Daniel's stiff and lifeless body sheltered my left side.

Albrecht retreated, and I stayed in my paralyzed state, my cheeks sopping wet and my lips salty with tears. Footsteps retreated down the staircase. The front door shut down below.

I sat up in bed and squeezed my nails into Daniel's left arm.

His eyes shot open. *"Autsch! Scheisse!"* He grabbed his damaged skin. "What are you doing?"

"I saw your brother."

His face went still and pale. "What?"

"He came into the room with us, just now." I peered over my shoulder to the parts of the room where I'd just seen Albrecht, half-expecting him to manifest again. "He rested your guitar back in the corner where it belongs."

"No, he didn't," said Daniel without a trace of doubt in his voice. He didn't even sit up to look at the guitar. "You imagined it."

"I tend to see spirits—harbinger spirits—before people close to me die, and—"

"You imagined it." He pulled me back down to the mattress beside him, and my right cheek fell against the cold sheet. "Get some more sleep. We're both just exhausted."

"But—"

"Go to sleep, *Liebling*. We need to rest so we don't feel sick as dogs when we come to again. You're probably already in the grip of a hangover. There's no such thing as ghosts. You imagined him."

I closed my eyes and listened to the stark silence of the streets outside, which should have been bustling with the sounds of bicycles and Model Ts and the chatter of workers and shoppers. Instead, the world resembled a music box that had wound itself all the way down and breathed its last chiming note.

WHEN I AWOKE AGAIN, the darkness of night had settled back over the room, and the band lulled the town with a piano-heavy piece that reminded me of childhood nights, when Mama soothed me on her lap after nightmares spoiled my sleep.

Daniel's eyes blinked open beside me.

"Are you all right?" I asked him.

He nodded. "Are you?"

I rubbed my eyes with the heels of my palms. "I don't feel as sick as I thought I would. Maybe, after that monster flu and the migraines I used to suffer, a hangover feels like nothing more than a dull headache."

"Or maybe"—he smiled and stretched an arm above the pillow—"your body is simply built to enjoy German imports."

I barked a laugh and propped myself up on my right elbow. An object lying in the bed next to his head immediately caught my eye and dampened my mood.

I shrank back. "Why is that gun in the bed with us?"

He tilted his head to peek back at the weapon, which lay halfway under the pillow behind his head, the barrel and wide-open mouth exposed. "I don't know," he said. "I don't remember which one of us brought it in here. God knows what we were doing with it." With a rustle of the sheet, he flipped himself onto his stomach and clicked a lever on the gun.

"Daniel!" I scooted away on the mattress. "What are you doing?"

"It's all right." He plunked the pistol in the upper corner of the bed and rolled onto his back again. "God, I haven't had that much fun while drunk since before the war."

"Why do you have a pistol?"

He shrugged. "Albrecht kept it, to protect us and the store. He stored it in one of the drawers by the cash register."

"Was he not able to reach it, then?"

Daniel blinked. "What?"

"Was he up in his room when they came the night of the murder?"

"He was at his girl Nora's house, but—"

"Then how . . ." I wrinkled my brow. "Did he walk in on them vandalizing the place? Is that what happened? How did it happen?"

"Oh, Christ, Ivy." Daniel wrapped a hand around mine, and his eyes turned damp and bloodshot. His nostrils fluttered. "Stop asking me questions like that. I don't want to say anything more about the murder. You've already heard enough."

"I can't stop asking." I lowered my head against his chest. "I'm sorry, but I can't let it go. They didn't hurt you, too, did they? Were you here? Did you see it happen?"

"No, they didn't hurt me. Stop talking about them."

"I hope you're able to forgive me."

"Forgive you for what? You weren't the one who did anything."

"Their names . . ." A sharp ache rippled down my throat. "Their names are Frank and Peter Rowan." I squeezed my eyes shut and felt Daniel go rigid beneath me. "I don't know if you ever learned that information about them, but they were drunk and angry about Billy's death in the war. They had no right to come in here and kill anyone. I still can't bear the thought of what they did, and I keep seeing them beat your brother over and over inside my head. Please, I need to know, do you forgive me for sharing the same blood as them?"

"I forgive you, but there's honestly no reason to, Ivy. Stop bearing their guilt for them."

"Don't kill yourself because of them." I lifted my head and winced yet again at the sight of the gun at the head of the bed. "Please, I'm still so worried you'll do something to yourself."

"I'm not going to kill myself."

"Do you promise? Swear to God. Swear upon your brother's grave."

"Ivy." He pulled me down close to him. "Come here. I want to tell you something."

My heart lurched. I readjusted my hands against both his chest and the mattress to steady myself. "What? You're scaring me."

"Don't be nervous. I just want to tell you that this poor world would actually be better off without me. I'm not saying that because I'm planning to commit suicide, but you should know, I've killed . . ."

"I know. You told me that. The war . . ."

"I've killed women and children."

My lips parted, and a shaky stream of air pattered out of my mouth and rustled through his hair.

"On my twentieth birthday, in the summer of 1914"—his hand trembled on my shoulder—"the German army put me on a train with all the other new recruits without telling us where we were heading. We traveled for well over a day and eventually found ourselves at the Belgian-German frontier. A few days later, we marched into Belgium with orders to make war against the Belgian armed forces." He stopped for breaths of air, his chest expanding and contracting below my palm. "Even though they instructed us to shoot only soldiers, they encouraged us to defend our lives and the Fatherland against any citizens who rebelled against our invasion. We killed farmers and young men wanting to protect their towns and their country, and the regular part of my brain shut down. We had to turn into unthinking killers. One of my friends couldn't do it—he panicked and tried to run—so they made us shoot him, to teach us all a lesson. I stood in a firing squad and shot him to death, my own friend, and I forced myself to feel nothing."

I dug my teeth into my bottom lip and made no response, aside from a soft whimper I hadn't intended to produce. I myself attempted to feel nothing, but a terrible weight pushed down on my lungs and my heart.

Daniel turned his face away from me and blinked with a long and dreamlike movement, as if succumbing to sleep. "And then we invaded homes. Attacked civilians. Men. Women. Children. We had to show them we were in charge, and it felt good for a while, turning off that human side, reaping the spoils of a victor. But then, sometime later, I'm not even sure which date it was or how long I'd been in Belgium, we came upon a farmhouse, and my commanding officer wanted me to bayonet a girl, no more than eighteen, while he watched." Daniel closed his eyes and swallowed with a sharp bob of his Adam's apple. "We were in her family's barn, and I think he was testing me— making sure I wasn't one of the weak ones about to turn on the army."

His breathing weakened to a choppy sound. He grimaced and, with his free hand, he rubbed the pink line encircling his throat, as though the mark still burned and strangled. "I had to stab her," he said, "several times, to get her to die. Blood spilled out of her mouth as she lay there beneath me, her life draining away, and I thought to myself, 'Oh, *Gott*. How can I keep fighting for the Fatherland—how can I ever kiss the lips of a woman again—after seeing what I've done to this poor girl?' "

I rose up to a seated position and rested my elbows against the sheet on my knees, not looking at him, not touching him. The band played on, teasing of normalcy and mirth, but each note of the piano became an unseen hand that wrung my heart—squeezing it, pulverizing it—until I couldn't stand to breathe.

Daniel reached out and rubbed my lower back, which stiffened at his touch. "As I told you before," he said, "I risked my neck and escaped. I wanted to start my life over with my brother in America, knowing he started over when life soured for him in Europe. But it's never quite worked. I've never felt needed or whole or redeemed"—he swallowed loud enough for me to hear, and his hand went still on my back—"until you showed up and asked me to ease your pain."

I didn't answer. I couldn't stop imagining him stabbing a Belgian girl with a bayonet, even though I knew, deep down, that our dear Billy must have killed people, and that beautiful Eddie Dover showered men with bullets from his flying war machine. I saw her, though—a dying girl with a mouth and chin covered in dark-red blood, like all those poor, suffering victims in agony from the Spanish influenza—while he stood above her with the stained tip of his bayonet.

He withdrew his hand from my spine. "This is why I didn't want to share my secrets." His voice hardened. "You won't even look at me now, will you?"

"I don't know what to say. I know it's war and you were following orders, but—" I tossed the sheet off my legs. "I don't know what to say."

I fetched clean clothing out of my luggage and made a beeline toward the bathroom next to the kitchen, past the broken lamps and all the other damage we had hurled upon the place in our hedonistic idiocy. I washed my face and dressed myself while my legs shook with the urge to run.

I passed back through the apartment to fetch my shoes.

Daniel, fully dressed and cleaning up one of the lamps in the living room, stood up straight with a shard of blue glass in his hand. "Where are you going?"

"I've got to see if Addie and Nela need me to drive the ambulance."

He followed me into his bedroom. "And if they don't?"

"I don't know." I shoved my right foot into a shoe and tied the laces. "I need to walk for a while. I need air. I've got to go somewhere. I can't breathe."

"You don't understand, do you?" He parked himself in front of me with the shard still gripped in his fingers. "You can walk and walk to the ends of the earth, but that pain inside you, you know the one you're always telling me about?"

I forced the other shoe over my left foot with a grunt.

"It will never go away, Ivy. Not until you make peace with everything that's happened here. It'll always follow you, and you'll never get away from it."

"I've got to go." I knotted the laces. "You've blocked yourself from loving me because of Belgium. Now I'm going to block myself from loving you so I don't have to worry about you ever again. I'm tired of this."

"I'm not going to die."

"Yes, you are. I saw your brother and know you're marked for death—I can practically smell it on you." I jumped to my feet and pushed him aside. "I've got to go."

"You spend so much time worrying about people dying on

you and forgiving you"—he chased after me—"but nothing will ever change for you until you forgive everyone else—your father, your brother, me, yourself for not being strong."

"I am strong." I hurried down the stairs with my feet thumping and skidding, and he followed.

"You seem awfully weak right now, Ivy," he said, "running away like this. You're always running away, aren't you? You didn't hide out in your parents' house for years because you were worried about your family. You worried about yourself in the big, bad world because emotions terrify you."

"You're the one who can't love." I tore through the darkened store. "Don't talk to me about emotions."

"A sadistic military operation carved my heart out of me. What's your excuse, Fräulein?"

"Don't bother waiting for me anymore. I'm not coming back. I'm done." I grabbed for the door, but he yanked me backward by my elbow.

"Don't leave," he said, his face close to mine.

"Why should I stay? You lied. This isn't paradise."

"It could be if you stop asking me questions about everything. Just forget the rest of the world—"

I pulled away, yet he tugged me right back.

"Let me go!"

"Ivy—"

"Let me go"—I pushed his hand off me—"you disgusting Kraut bastard. You fucking German animal."

He shrank back and blanched, and I could almost see the red

sting of my words slapped across his face in the shape of a hand-print. My mouth tasted rotten and filthy, and I knew if I stayed in the shop another moment, I'd vomit up all the rest of the poison brewing inside me. I backed away and slipped out the door to the black streets of Buchanan.

Chapter 21

I only made it as far as the sidewalk in front of Weiss's Bakery before my legs gave out. The air smelled of rain, and moisture on the cement dampened my skirt and my outstretched palms and fingers. I couldn't move. I could only crouch on my hands and knees and imagine Daniel stabbing a girl to death and Father and Peter beating Albrecht's face until their hands swelled to twice their normal sizes. A bayonet. Four fists. A bayonet. Flu victims spitting up black liquid. Daniel hanging from a rope. Father hitting Billy with a shovel. So much death. So much violence. I pressed my palms against the sidewalk and shook with convulsions that turned the sidewalk blurry. My eyes watered, and tears stung my skin, and I groaned in pain, as if I were the one being stabbed and beaten and strangled.

"Do you know what I wonder?" asked a voice nearby.

I lifted my head with a start and saw Lucas peering at me

from the shadows between the protruding display windows of the tobacco shop next door. The lenses of his spectacles reflected a trace of moonlight, and I could just barely see the thin line of his lips that didn't smile or glower or show any other discernible emotion.

"I wonder," he said, "if the Kaiser's army dispersed handsome young men across the United States and instructed them to fill women's heads with pity and their wombs with *Boche* babies."

I scowled at him from down on the ground, my chest heaving.

"That hedonistic life you just shared with that Kraut?" he said with a nod down toward Daniel's store. "All that naughty pleasure? I'm willing to bet that was just another German tactic to dominate the world. As you just said"—Lucas swallowed, and I could see the ripple in his throat—"he's a disgusting Kraut bastard. An animal. A fucking animal."

I pushed myself to my feet and grabbed Lucas's spectacles off his nose. He cried out in shock, but I shoved him away and threw the glasses out to the street with a satisfying crack of the lenses breaking against asphalt.

"Ivy!" Lucas covered his naked eyes. "What did you do?"

"Stop spying on me!" I shoved him again.

"You broke my glasses!"

"What I do with Daniel Schendel is none of your business." I grabbed his left arm and squeezed it tight enough to make him cry out in pain. "It's not anyone's business but mine and his. Do you hear me?"

"Yes."

I shook him. "Are you sure about that?"

"Yes, I hear you!"

"Stop working for the APL and do something better with your life. Nobody here is an enemy of this country except for all of you Peeping Toms who rob us of our freedom. We're all just trying to survive—that's all."

From down the street, the instruments of the band hollered through the streets of Buchanan with voices even louder than mine. Still bearing down on Lucas's skinny biceps, I swung us both around and faced the direction of the Masonic Lodge. My arms and legs vibrated with the urge to sprint down the sidewalk and scale the brick walls to reach the music as fast as I was able.

It's like a siren call to you, isn't it? Daniel had asked me during one of our first nights together. *One day, you'll find yourself going to it . . . and never coming back.*

Lucas sputtered up a sob. "I want my glasses. I can't see a damn thing but blurry dark shapes. I'm blind."

I clenched my eyes shut. "I've just made a terrible mistake."

"I'll say you did."

"No, I don't mean your glasses. Oh, God." I rubbed my throat with my free hand. "Why did I say those things to him?"

"Do you see them in the street? Are they salvageable?"

I let go of Lucas's arm.

"Wait! Stop!" He grabbed hold of my left shoulder with a force that toppled me off balance. "Don't go anywhere. I can't see."

"Don't panic. You'll push me over."

"Go get them—please!"

"Here, I'll make a deal with you." I yanked his fingers off me. "I'll help you with your spectacles, but only after you do a tremendous favor for me."

"What favor?"

I tipped my head to the right and listened with my left ear, in search of any sounds of other APL spies creeping around us. The jazz music rollicked across the town like a tipsy party guest, slamming into walls, rattling windows, snuffing out all other noises.

"Lucas," I said in a whisper, "I'm about to do something highly unpatriotic."

"But"—he snorted—"you've already been doing something highly—"

"Please, just listen." I inched another step closer, getting right in front of his panicky brown eyes that looked so tiny and mouse-like without the spectacles. "There's something I've got to do to make amends with Daniel Schendel, but it violates the Sedition Act by inciting disloyalty. Or, at least, the APL's definition of disloyalty. Tomorrow"—I glanced backward for a fleeting moment, worried I'd just seen a shadow scuttle beneath a streetlamp—"if you feel the need to turn me in, you may do so. But only as long as you swear to make the APL leave Mr. Schendel alone for the rest of his living days."

Lucas's lips quivered, and his blind eyes widened. "But . . . what are you . . . ?" He gulped. "What are you going to do?"

"My father and Peter killed Mr. Schendel's brother last week. They forced themselves into their store and beat him to death."

"I didn't . . ." Lucas shook his head. "I didn't know that."

"Really?" I lifted my brows. "Other members of your group have talked all about it. I've heard them."

"Those other fellas in the APL don't always take me seriously, on account of me being the youngest member. They don't tell me everything."

I put my hand on his shoulder. "Swear upon everything dear to you that Daniel Schendel will be all right. If you want to turn me in to your fellow volunteers to prove your worth, go ahead and do so. I don't care. Just keep him safe."

"I just want my glasses, Ivy. I'm tired and want to get back home."

"I'll take you home and arrange to have your glasses mended and paid for immediately, but only if you promise to help him. Otherwise"—I bent close to his ear and dropped my voice to a whisper that I hoped gave his neck chills—"I'm leaving you here, alone in the street."

His lips trembled again. "That's not like you, Ivy."

"That's how I felt about you when you first flashed your APL badge at me and asked about Peter joining the war. We've all turned into brutes, when what we should be doing is helping one another."

He scraped his teeth across his bottom lip and seemed to weigh my words with care.

"Help me." I squeezed his left shoulder. "And I'll help you. All right?"

He nodded and sniffed. "All right. I swear. You and Mr. Schendel will both stay safe. Just . . . get me my glasses now, OK?"

I stepped away from him, keeping my eyes upon him for any twitches of his mouth or alterations in his expression that might indicate he was lying about our safety. My feet sidled toward the spectacles lying in the middle of the road. I leaned over and picked them up, feeling the dense weight of the bottle cap lenses, and when I took my eyes off Lucas to survey the damage, my jaw dropped.

The glasses remained intact.

I hadn't broken them at all.

"How bad are they?" asked Lucas from the curb, holding his arms around himself, rocking. He looked more like the little boy I remembered from the past—the one with skinned-up knees who would come running into our yard, his brown cap flying off his head, shoes untied, to see if Billy could play.

"Well . . . umm . . ." I lifted the lenses up to the lamplight and inspected for signs of hairline fractures.

"Did both lenses break?" His voice cracked. "Do you think . . . c-c-could I at least see out of one of the lenses?"

"The glasses are fine, Lucas." I plodded back to him to the beat of the drums down the way. "Somehow, they didn't get damaged in the slightest. I could have sworn I heard them splinter, but . . ."

He reached out his hand, and I placed the spectacles on his palm.

His jaw stiffened. He situated the handles of the frames over his ears with a brusque movement that made my stomach dip. His magnified brown eyes glared at me without blinking.

"You'll still help though, won't you?" I asked, rubbing my hands over the gooseflesh below my sleeves. "You're a kind person. You've always been kind, ever since you first started coming to play at our house."

He pushed his glasses farther up his nose and backed away, slipping into shadow, the same way I'd found him. "I don't help whores and traitors, Miss Rowan."

"Lucas—"

"If you're planning to violate the Sedition Act"—his nose and his lenses disappeared into darkness, but he flashed his silver American Protective League badge, which managed to catch a glint of moonlight from beneath his coat—"then you'll need to do so at your own risk."

The blackness of night swallowed him up completely.

He was gone.

Chapter 22

The ballroom had escalated in elegance.

Instead of one dozen dancing couples, two to three dozen young pairs, dressed in bright evening gowns and dark suits with silk neckties, fox-trotted around the hardwood floor. At least three dozen more guests sipped champagne at tables draped in ivory cloths. At a long buffet-style table on the far right of the room, a chestnut-haired fellow in a white coat—a professional bartender, it seemed—poured bottles of the sweet-scented booze into sparkling flutes and slid them across the surface for those who waited. No one wore flu masks. No one peeked over her shoulder as if worried the APL might tap her on the back and demand that she kiss the American flag. The wild number blasting from the band's gleaming instruments sang a song of utter denial.

Pain lifted from my body and evaporated into the air. My

brain went a little dizzy from all the jewels and bright crystal chandeliers and the couples spinning together like silken cogs inside a grand machine. I veered away from the rightmost side of the establishment, where uniformed doughboys gathered around the freshly poured drinks. They laughed and ogled the ladies with the lowest necklines, and I envisioned them separating in two different directions, like a parting olive curtain, to reveal Billy standing at dead center, smoking his cigarette, asking with his eyes, *Have you figured out yet who's going to die, sis?*

I cupped my hand over my brow and locked my knees against the sensation of the floor buckling beneath my feet.

"Hey there, Miss Rowan," said a male voice that struck me as familiar.

I lowered my hand to find Benjie from Nela's house strolling toward me in a smart black coat and striped gray pants. He smiled and looked nothing at all like the flu patient who had grabbed hold of my leg in a panic on the bloodstained floor of Polish Hall.

"Hello, Benjie." I smiled in return and relaxed my knees and my shoulders. "You found the place."

"How could I miss it? I heard the jazz clear across town."

"The band's swell, aren't they?"

"They're sweller than swell." He beamed with a broad grin and tucked his hands in his coat pockets. "I'm just glad they let me in the place. It's not as lily white as I expected for this part of town."

"That's true. I'm awfully glad it isn't."

"Just look at everyone out there." Benjie turned toward the dance floor and inhaled with satisfaction.

I scanned the room and saw that every single soul in the place veritably pulsated with music. The band—that beating heart of jazz and pleasure—seemed to ensure that every man and woman, whatever color or background they might have been, danced and lived and breathed inside those gleaming golden walls. If anyone were to ever say to me that music wasted one's time, I would urge them to climb the stairs to that Buchanan Masonic Lodge ballroom and experience their own toes tapping to the rhythm of hot jazz, their own blood throbbing with vitality.

The doughboys around the buffet table ensnared my attention again, so I turned my back on their uniforms and faced Benjie more fully. "I'm actually about to make a rather strange request of the band. If a little fellow in thick spectacles charges into the room, please point him in my direction and let him know I'm the one to blame."

Benjie laughed and shook his head in confusion. "What the devil are you talking about?"

I glanced back at the five windows that peeked across at Daniel's store from the brick outer wall, and I could have sworn those windows stood a little taller and wider than I remembered. Brand-new curtains framed the panes—thick velvet ones in a royal shade of red, quite pleasing to the eye.

"Miss Rowan?" asked Benjie. "Are you all right?"

"Umm . . ." I cradled my forehead in my hand. "I just . . . I'm not quite myself right now. I've had a terrible falling-out with someone and need to do something to help."

"Your sweetheart?"

I pressed my fingers against my skull and managed a pained smile. "Yes. Although *sweet* doesn't seem the right term to describe us."

"I'd ask you to dance so you could forget about him"—he peered back at the other couples, none of whom merged black with white—"but, I don't know."

"No, thank you. I've got to give my strange request to the band and make amends. I'm much too old to dance with you anyway."

"Oh, I don't know about that, miss." Benjie flashed another broad grin and leaned back on his heels. "You look mighty young and fine to a poor boy who's just left the clutches of death."

"Find a girl your own age, Benjie." I backed away. "One who doesn't have so much trouble hanging on her shoulders."

I turned around and bumped straight into Ruth Sellman, who carried a flute of champagne and wore a bright-blue dress that seemed alive with swaying fringe and glimmering beads. "Well, hello. Our homebody's back." She grabbed my hand and yanked me toward the dance floor. "Wyatt Pettyjohn's here, and he's been looking for a dance partner."

"No!" I dug my heels into the floor and brought us to a halt. "I can't dance right now."

"Why not?"

"I have a special song request I need to make."

With a snort, Ruth looked toward the band. "Please don't tell me it's a war song, meant to rally the boys. If I hear 'Over There' one more time, I swear I'll smack—"

"No, it's not that at all." I unknotted my fingers from hers. "Tell Wyatt"—I caught sight of Wyatt's forlorn eyes and his shirt that needed extra tucking into his gray pants, coming toward us around the perimeter of the dancers—"tell him I'm actually here for a purpose other than dancing and visiting at the moment."

"I highly recommend that you get a drink and make yourself at home instead," she said. "You're going to spoil everyone's fun by turning down dances and acting peculiar. This is a party. It's supposed to be scrumptious."

"But . . ."

"It's a party!" she said with a small bite to her voice, and she wandered away while half-turned toward me. Her heels clicked across the smooth floorboards, and her hips wiggled beneath that blue fringed dress. She set her champagne flute on a table, went straight over to the lost-looking Wyatt, and grabbed his arm and his hand for a dance.

I ignored her pressure to drink and entertain married men and instead pushed through the crowd of partygoers, which seemed to have swollen into a louder and larger mass of undulating bodies, fueled by jazz and juice and desire. People bumped against me and pummeled my toes with their sharp heels, but I somehow forged my way to the band.

The drummer, the clarinetist, and the trombonist perched on the ends of their wooden chairs, their bodies rocking and swaying, their posteriors barely planted on the seats, as if the music possessed the power to launch them off the earth at any moment. The cornet player stood with his legs apart, his knees bent, his back arched, and he wailed on his horn until his puffed-up cheeks turned redder than turnips. The piano player with the slicked oil-paint hair sat nearest to me, and he stormed those keys with the fury of a madman, his eyes squeezed shut, his head rattling back and forth, his lips wobbling.

I walked over to the group and leaned my right elbow against the smooth top of the upright piano. The vibrations of the notes thrummed through the wood and traveled up my arm and down to the farthest reaches of my toes with a pleasurable sensation that made my eyelids flutter. I breathed a small sigh and struggled to keep my wits about me.

The piano player lifted his hands from the keys. After only one short beat, he seemed about to thrust his hands straight back down to the ivories for another number.

I knocked on the top of the piano and quickly said, "Excuse me."

His hands stopped in midair, and he looked my way. "Yes?"

"Am I able to make a song request?"

The drummer behind him—a blue-eyed gentleman with skin that blended the boundaries between black and white—tapped the opening beat of a song, but the pianist held up his right hand and said, "Wait a minute. The lady wants to make a request."

"I'm really sorry to interrupt your performance like this," I said, shifting my weight between my legs, "but first of all, I was wondering if you'd ever be interested in having a guitarist join your ensemble."

The five members of the band eyed each other with their faces molded into the little frowns people make when considering an idea they've never contemplated before.

"I know a guitarist, you see," I continued. "He's extraordinarily talented and learns music by ear. He knows jazz as well as he knows himself."

"It's hard to hear a guitar over the rest of our ruckus," said the trombone player, a black fellow with a rich voice that rumbled in my knees. "He'd have to play loud and fierce."

"He does. He's remarkable. I've never heard anything quite like him."

"Well"—the piano player swiveled toward me on his stool—"bring him over here then. Let us hear this fella."

"Well, there's one problem. He's nervous about coming here, because he's . . ." I picked at the corner of the piano below my elbow. "He's German."

The piano player and the drummer both broke into snickers.

"What's so funny?" I asked.

"Ernest Ford"—using his thumb, the piano player gestured toward the drummer over his shoulder—"this handsome blue-eyed fella sitting behind me, his daddy's one hundred percent Negro and his mama's one hundred percent German, but somehow he adds up to be one hundred percent all-American jazz. As long as this guitarist joe doesn't wander in here with a German bayonet pointed at all of us . . ."

I stiffened. "No, no, no."

"We'd be happy to meet him," said Ernest at the drums.

"Hey!" called one of the uniformed boys out on the dance floor. "Where's the music?"

"Hold your horses." The piano player swiveled back to the keys. "Did you say you had a music request, too, miss?"

"Yes." I rubbed my lips together. "I was wondering if you might play a little Beethoven."

The heads of all five band members whipped toward me.

"My guitarist friend will need proof to feel welcome over here," I explained. "He lives across the street, and I know if he heard the music of a German composer blaring out of these windows . . ." I stopped, for they all wrinkled their foreheads as if I'd just asked them to don German helmets and speak in the tongue of the Kaiser. "I know that Beethoven has been banned, but—"

"That's not the problem, darlin'," said the trombonist, leaning forward with his elbow on his right leg. "Beethoven isn't jazz."

I tapped my fingers against the top of the piano. "The fourth movement of Symphony No. 9 could be."

They furrowed their brows again, and the balding clarinetist chuckled and scratched his thumb against his cheek. I slid myself around the piano, bent over the keys next to the pianist, and tapped out a bass line with my left hand. Two bars later, my right hand launched into the melody of Beethoven's "Ode to

Joy"—played in the hot, modern style of the Original Dixieland Jass Band.

The rest of the room fell still with a silence that startled me at first, but my fingers continued to pound those ivories as if the safety of the world depended on an improvised jazz rendition of a nearly one-hundred-year-old symphony movement. Behind me the trombone burst awake with a fanciful slide. The clarinetist joined in with embellishments and echoes. The blue-eyed, half-German drummer tapped out the timing. The cornet player accompanied me on the melody, and the rouged and pomaded piano player lunged into the lower keys beside me with complicated flourishes and harmony that made old Beethoven sing. Germany, America, classical music, and jazz collided and mated and set the entire room dancing in a jubilant one-step that could have ended the war right then and there.

I lifted my fingers from the keys and let the piano player take full rein of the ivories. No doubt existed in my mind that "Ode to Joy" rang throughout the nighttime streets and permeated Daniel's closed-up store and apartment. I strode over to the same open window where I'd stood before and watched the lights burst to life behind Daniel's drapes. He slid open the curtains, raised the sash, and stuck his head into the glorious Beethoven air with his mouth hanging open. A breeze stirred through both his hair and mine, and every element on earth seemed to move and sing and cry out for us to celebrate. Daniel's eyes met mine from across the street dividing us, but we didn't say one word to each other.

We simply listened.

I bit down on my lip, determined not to miss a single note by allowing myself to cry, and I mentally willed Daniel to stay at his window and experience the song for however long the band decided to make it last. The music rose to astounding heights. Daniel's lips moved as if he mouthed the words in German. The lights in his bedroom seemed to brighten around him, illuminating his hair and his clothing.

The song lasted for another full minute, and then it ended amid a thundering round of applause from the dancers behind me. I already missed the thrill of the symphony inside me.

"That was for you," I called across to Daniel, poking my head out as far as it would go without losing my balance and falling out the window. "The band members want you to know you'd be more than welcome over here. They could use a guitarist."

Daniel rested his elbows against his sill. "It's not the band members' opinions that I care about."

"*I* want you to know you're welcome over here, and I don't give a rap who hears the music of a German composer blasting through the streets. Playing Beethoven was my idea. I'm sorry about what I said, and I hate myself for saying it."

The trombone player blew a startling slide, and a conventional jazz number exploded across the lodge, drowning any chance of my properly hearing a response from Daniel.

I pointed down to his front door and shouted over the horns, "Please—meet me downstairs. I want to talk to you."

He stood up straight and closed his window, an action I took to mean that he was either complying with my request or shutting me out of his life. Hoping for the former, I left my own window and clasped my hands together in a gesture of thanks in the direction of the band.

My feet galloped down the Masonic Lodge stairs, and I almost slipped twice in my haste.

Once again, I set off to right a Rowan wrong against Mr. Wilhelm Daniel Schendel.

Chapter 23

*H*is front door remained shut. I slowed to a stop in front of the boarded-up glass and rapped my knuckles against one of the rough planks with a sound that came out dull and hollow.

"Daniel?" I tried the brass knob but found it locked. "Please open up. I want to apologize for what I said." I turned my ear toward the door and held my breath, but my pulse beat in my head like a clattering locomotive and muffled even the sounds of the band.

"Please, Daniel. Talk to me. You know I said those terrible words in a moment of panic. Let's not end things like this." I inched closer to the door. My voice shook. "The very idea of you walking away from all that horror over there—risking your life to do so—makes you a far braver and better person than I could ever be. I'm sorry I reacted so poorly. I know the war forces people to do atrocious things they wouldn't normally do."

The door clicked open, and Daniel stood in front of me with one hand on the doorknob and the other massaging his throat below his shirt collar.

"That word 'Kraut,'" he said with a wince and a sharp swallow, as if the German slur burned at his mouth and stung his throat, "it never sounded so ugly as it did coming out of your mouth."

"I know." I pressed a hand against my stomach. "I'm sorry. I didn't mean it. Those were horrific things to say."

"I don't even know what we should do, the two of us." He leaned his left shoulder against the doorjamb and breathed a weighty sigh. "The more truth you pull out of me, the worse things will get between us, and this whole beautiful world we created will keep shattering to pieces."

"What do you mean by 'the more truth'?" I stepped closer. "Are there other secrets you're hiding from me?"

He averted his eyes to the Masonic Lodge windows up above.

"Daniel? What else are you keeping from me?"

"Those people up there in the lodge . . ." He nodded up to the music. "What do they say about you and me?"

"I told you, they don't care that you're German. Their drummer is half black, half German, and they're kind as can be to him."

"That's not what I mean. What do people say about the world?" He tipped his head to the right and narrowed his eyes at me. "Those friends of yours in the ambulance, that man

Wyatt you spoke with the other night. What do they think is happening?"

I shook my head, perplexed. "I don't understand what you mean. Everyone feels the world is crumbling to pieces, but mainly people are looking to either help each other or escape. Or both." I rested my left hand against the door and felt the pressure of his hand holding the nearby knob. "You know I'm terrified you'll get this flu, but it would be awfully nice to go somewhere with you tonight and leave behind everything that's haunting us inside this store. It doesn't even have to be up in the dance hall. We could go somewhere private."

He rubbed at his throat again, and he refused to meet my eyes. "I'm not going anywhere, Ivy."

"No one will hurt you out here, Daniel. I swear. Please"—I took his right hand and sandwiched it between my shaking palms—"come with me. Let's take a walk or—"

"I'm not going with you."

"I know you're still upset with me, but—"

"It's not that."

"Then come with me."

He pulled his hand out of mine with a force that made me lose my balance. "I can't go with you."

"Why not?"

"I just can't."

"But—".

"I can't leave the store, damn it! Don't you hear me?" Without warning, he kicked the door inward with a startling bang that made me jump. "I can't *ever* leave this goddamned building."

I stepped backward, toward the street, and a cold rush of blood shot through my veins. The hairs on the backs of my arms and neck stood on end.

"But . . . no . . ." I shook my head. Every part of me trembled and ached with a terrible chill that hurt more than the knife blade scraping at my stomach. "I d-d-don't understand."

He gritted his teeth and turned his face away from me again, and I heard Goethe whisper in my ear, *Truth is a torch . . . we all try to reach it with closed eyes, lest we should be scorched.*

I pushed past Daniel and forced my way into the unlit shop, taking care not to trip over the silhouettes of chairs and tables propped on the floor at unsettling angles.

"Where are you going?" he asked from behind me.

I rounded the mahogany counter at the back of the store.

"Ivy?"

I reached for the top drawer below the register.

"No!" Daniel locked both his arms around my chest and hoisted me away before I could grab the knob and pull.

"Let me see the article."

"No!" He carried me away, toward the front door.

"Daniel!" I kicked my legs and wriggled to break free. "Let me see it!"

"You'll spoil everything."

"It's already spoiled. Show it to me. Let me see the name of the man they murdered. I want to see it."

He threw me out to the sidewalk, where I fell to the ground and banged my knees against hard cement. The door slammed shut behind me. The lock clicked into place.

I stared at the boards vibrating against the glass and quaked as violently as they quaked.

Some spirits get stuck in the places where they died, May had said as she sat at her table with all those letters spread before her on the Ouija board. *Some spirits get stuck in the places where they died.*

I pushed myself to my feet, meeting with the pain of a twisted ankle, and I limped eastward on Willow-not-Werner Street, toward my family's home.

You don't understand, do you? Daniel had asked me the first night I met him. *You are—how do you say it over here—naïve? Is that a word in English?*

My secrets won't change anything, he had also said, two nights later, after I'd somehow been with him—*twice* by then. *They can't hurt you. What's done is done.*

My Uninvited Guests always signaled loss. Their presence suggested that the wall dividing the living and the dead had opened a crack. I kept seeing and seeing and seeing him, and people all around me in Buchanan died at an astounding rate that turned grocery wagons into hearses, social halls into morgues. He had stood over the blood on the night of the murder, his hands stuffed in the pockets of his tan trousers, his face directed toward the dark stain marring the floorboards, and if I really stretched myself back into time and truly thought about that night, my mind would show me his face again, and I'd see the truth blazing in his eyes. His brother had slept at his sweetheart Nora's house that night, while Daniel remained at home—alone—until two strong men with revenge in their eyes burst into his store to kill.

Chapter 24

"Mama!" I called up the staircase, not caring who I woke. "Come downstairs. Please! Hurry!"

I paced the floorboards and clasped my temples to keep my skull from breaking in half. When my mother didn't hustle down fast enough, I grabbed an old studio photograph of my brothers and me as children—one that teased of happier times from above the piano—and hurled it at the opposite wall with a wild shattering of glass. "Mother!"

"Ivy?" Mama tiptoed into view at the bottom of the stairs and pulled her white cambric robe around her nightgown. "Why are you here so late—and so upset?"

I squared my shoulders at her and lifted my chin. "What is the name of the man they murdered?"

Her face drained to the color of that robe.

"You must have seen the article," I said. "What was his name? Which Schendel brother did they kill?"

"What's going on down there?" asked Father from their bedroom upstairs.

"It's nothing, Frank. Go back to sleep." She turned back to me and gripped the square newel post at the bottom of the stairs. "Oh, Ivy . . ."

"Tell me!" I said. "Why won't anyone tell me anything? Stop treating me like I'm a delicate piece of china that mustn't be broken."

"Wait here." She held out her hand, as if instructing one of the dogs to stay put, and pattered off to the kitchen on the bare soles of her feet.

I heard the pop of a tin lid coming off of a can, a sound that always betrayed Mama's secret sips from a flask of booze she kept hidden in a biscuit container—her emergency dose of comfort, consumed whenever Father pushed her to the edge of sanity and composure. A newspaper rustled out there in the kitchen, and then Mama crept back around the corner and walked toward me with her hands tucked behind her back.

"Do you truly want to see it, darling?" she asked. "Are you absolutely certain this is what you want?"

I thrust my right hand at her. "Show me."

She pushed a newspaper my way, and I saw the face of the victim—*his* face—along with his name: WILHELM DANIEL SCHEN-DEL. Key details about his condition at the time of death shot at me like stinging bullets:

> Multiple bruises and lacerations . . . broken nose . . .
> fractured ribs . . . ruptured spleen . . . a rope wrapped
> around his neck . . . strangled . . .

And that opening sentence—*oh, God.*

> Friday night a band of vagrants broke into Liberty
> Brothers Furniture Store and attacked and killed
> Wilhelm Daniel Schendel, aged 24, a German enemy
> of the U.S. who resided in downtown Buchanan.

I dropped to the floorboards with a jolt of my neck that hurt down to my knees.

"Oh . . . darling . . ." Mama stepped toward me with an offer of a trembling hand.

I recoiled. "I don't understand! It doesn't make sense. Why is it him? It doesn't make sense."

"Ivy . . ." She kneeled down in front of me. "My poor girl . . ."

"I was with him." I shook the newspaper in her face until she blinked and flinched. "*With* him. Multiple times. How could I have been with a man my family killed over Billy's death?"

Mama's chin shook, and she could no longer look me in the eye.

"What?" I slammed the paper to the floor and heard a rip in the newsprint. "Talk to me. Why won't anyone talk to me? What's happening?"

"It wasn't Billy's death that set them off."

"I don't . . ." I wrinkled my brow. "Then what? What set them off?"

"This flu . . . it's taken so many lives." She bent her face toward her knees and grabbed hold of her stomach, as if she shared my same knife blade of pain. Her mouth twisted into a grimace, and she squeezed her eyes shut tight, deepening the lines of her crow's-feet. "Your father got it into his head that the Germans dumped the germs into an American theater," she continued. "He wanted to spill German blood for revenge. I know he was sometimes cold and harsh, that it often seemed he didn't care, but he loved you so much, Ivy."

"No, he didn't."

"Yes"—she nodded—"he truly did. He said that hearing you play the piano was the best part of his day after toiling in the fields until his back and fingers ached. He loved you so much that he . . ." She covered her eyes with one hand, and her lips quavered and sputtered. Her nose ran. "He loved you so much, Ivy . . ." She braced her left hand on her lower back. "He loved you so much that he killed a man."

I braced my hands against the floor. Daniel's face stared up at me from the newspaper down below, his mouth set in that defiant pose, his eyes both frightened and furious as he stood for a camera that captured the images of Germans.

I shut my eyes against the sight of him in that hellish article that didn't make one damn bit of sense. "I don't . . ." I shook my head. "I don't understand anything that you're saying. What's happening here? What's happening?"

Mama broke into tears. I kept my eyes closed, but I heard her weep, the same way she had cried the night Father and Peter slammed their way inside the house with blood on their clothes and their fingers—while I, fresh out of bed from the flu, had followed after everyone in my nightgown.

I followed after them, and no one but Mama had paid me any heed.

I stood there and watched them . . . and no one had noticed.

I opened my eyes. The fingers of my right hand reached down to the *Sentinel* and dared to curl back the front page with the soft crinkle of newsprint. On page 3, a list awaited—a collection of names of the Buchanan residents who had perished from the flu from October 1 through October 5, 1918. My pulse pounded in my ears; the air in the house felt too thick to breathe.

Eight of the names of the dead jumped off the page and pierced my heart:

May Belmont Dover, widow of Edward C. Dover, aged 25

Howard Greene, owner, Hotel America, aged 42

Lucas Hart, American Protective League volunteer,
     aged 22

Benjamin Kelley, Negro, aged 19

Margaret O'Conner, grandmother and mother, aged 47

Wyatt Pettyjohn, farmer, aged 25

Ivy Rowan, daughter of Frank Rowan, aged 25

Ruth Sellman, widow of Jesse Sellman, aged 26

I rose to my feet, my legs burning to escape, to keep going, to keep wandering—to run.

Others, May had said, *they roam the earth, unsettled, restless, unsure what to do or where they belong.*

"This . . . no . . ." I kicked the newspaper away and backed toward the door. "I speak with all sorts of people out there. Not just Daniel and May and Wyatt. I've been driving an ambulance around town, helping people in need—people stuck in their homes because they can't get any care . . ."

Some spirits get stuck in the places where they died.

I squeezed my head between my hands. Pain simmered across my skull the way a fever burns in a brain until your very soul feels on fire. "Don't sit there and tell me the flu took my life," I said through blinding waves of pressure. Stinging black spots danced before my eyes. My ears rang with a screeching holler that couldn't be silenced no matter how hard I swallowed. "We're all alive. Everyone I see out there is alive."

"Ivy . . ." Mama—just a blurry movement of arms and legs on the ground—fetched a handkerchief from the pocket of her robe. "The influenza has taken the lives of ninety-three Buchanan residents just in these first two weeks of October. If you add Wilhelm Schendel's death to the count, plus those of three young Red Cross volunteers killed in a horrible train accident shortly before we lost you . . ."

"No." My back banged against the door, and the cold knob dug into my spine.

She wiped her eyes. "That makes ninety-seven brand-new October souls from this one small town alone. Lord knows how many Buchanan servicemen have perished overseas or in training camps during that same amount of time."

"Stop!" I slapped my hands over my ears. "Stop saying these things. This is a terrible trick you're playing. Why are you saying these things?"

"I'm sorry, Ivy, but it's God's honest truth. I see you so clearly that it breaks my heart. I know it means that the wall between the living and the dead has cracked wide open, and more and more people will be lost in the coming days. I wish I could hold you and comfort you. I wish that you could comfort me . . ."

I cowered against the door and grabbed my chest and remembered the agony of my lungs suffocating with fluid. I shut my eyes and fought to push away the memory of my own sufferings from the influenza—memories that crouched in my brain, hiding behind all my other recent recollections, like a naughty child avoiding punishment.

"Please . . . don't be frightened." My mother got to her feet and stood up tall. "I'm helping those in need like you asked. I went to Polish Hall and saw the lack of care, and I complained to the city's Committee of Public Safety. We're going to be recruiting more volunteers and opening more emergency hospitals. I'll do my best to save lives in your name. You don't need to worry about a thing anymore, sweetheart. And Granny Letty is always here, watching over me . . ."

I turned away from the rocking chair, for I saw her—Granny

Letty, with her silver hair pinned in a topknot and her gray eyes crinkling with a smile.

"Go back to that young German man," said Mama, her voice as soft as when she used to read me stories of castles and magic and airy promises of happily ever after. "Go take comfort with him and everyone else you find out there. Enjoy yourself. Be free." She squeezed her arms around her middle. "I'll think of you every time I hear a strain of music, and I'll tell myself, 'My Ivy is in those notes. I know she is. I can hear her.'"

I turned and blew out of the house with a slam of the door that rattled across the windows and set the dogs barking. Tears swam in my eyes and turned the road ahead of me into a long and wavering black snake, but I gritted my teeth and pounded my soles against gravel all the way back to downtown Buchanan. For that's all I seemed fated to do—to wander, to fret, to cling to the terrible troubles of the world.

PUBLIC NOTICE

In response to the recent epidemic of influenza, the local Board of Health and Committee of Public Safety, in conjunction with the Buchanan medical community and Mayor Hoyt, has decreed that after October 12, 1918,

1. *Schools, churches, chapels, meeting halls, theaters, and moving picture houses shall be closed and remain closed until further notice.*
2. *Individuals caught spitting, coughing, and sneezing without a handkerchief in public shall be arrested and lectured on the dangers of influenza.*
3. *Public dancing and public funerals shall be prohibited.*
4. *Hospitals shall be closed to visitors.*
5. *The Board strongly advises against public assembly at any time.*

L. G. Carlisle
Medical Health Officer

Chapter 25

May had said so much at her kitchen table. She said so much and knew about all of our secret habits, and yet she seemed to remain as ignorant as I.

Some spirits get stuck in the places where they died, she had told me as she sat before her Ouija board with the love for her husband swimming in her eyes. *Some struggle to complete a task they didn't finish when they were alive. Others, they roam the earth, unsettled, restless, unsure what to do or where they belong. And then there are the lucky ones . . .*

Beneath the starry sky of that black and bitter-cold October night, I traversed downtown Buchanan via River Street, parallel to Willow Street. The jazz danced its way around the dark corners and leapt over the brick buildings with unbridled bursts of energy. It beckoned. It tempted. It pulled with all its musical might. The notes wiggled through my blood and pumped through my heart and told me that people still found the strength to pick up instruments and dance and drink as if the world hadn't cut off their lives in their prime of youth and health.

They accept their fate and just enjoy themselves.

Everything seemed so clear out there on the streets. Somehow, the music made it all make sense. If I just let everything go—if I abandoned my troubles and stopped worrying about the world collapsing into a pile of rubble if I wasn't there to save everyone—I could go to the party. And I could stay.

Because I could not stop for Death, wrote Emily Dickinson, long ago, *He kindly stopped for me . . .*

I passed a portion of town from which I could see the back side of the Hotel America and its little flag tower that shot toward the moon-streaked clouds. I thought of Mr. Greene, still working for people like Lucas and me, despite what he'd said: *I had that same illness myself. Knocked me clear off my feet right here at the front desk.* His son Charlie had swept the lobby floor, not paying Mr. Greene or me any mind, and we went about our business as if nothing had changed—as if none of us were stuck where we perished. Or wandering, waiting to be told what to do and where to go.

I WIPED MY EYES with the back of my sleeve and knocked on May's tapioca-colored door, which looked slate gray and almost stonelike in the unkind darkness of night. The three o'clock hour must not have arrived yet, for she opened the door, alone, in her red silk robe, and she smiled at me with a genuine look of hospitality that managed to warm my blood a tad.

"You're back." She reached out her hand and held fast to my fingers. "What a lovely surprise."

"Oh . . . May . . ." I wrapped my free arm around her and broke into tears against her shoulder.

"What's wrong?" She patted my back above my spine. "Oh, poor butterfly. Did you and your German quarrel?"

"You said that you had a sharp headache," I said into her perfumed silk below my lips, "and that you sat down for a spell. You said you thought God might have sent this flu to help all the Widow Street girls join their fallen husbands."

"Yes." She nodded, her head against mine. "That's what I did—and still do—believe."

"Oh, May . . ." I choked on the words that tried to push through my tears. My throat closed up, and I imagined Daniel with that rope squeezed around his windpipe until he couldn't manage another breath.

"What is it?" she asked. "What's wrong, Ivy?"

"It's not a haunting. Eddie's not coming back to visit the living."

Her fingers went still on my back, and I felt her entire body grow cold against me.

"What are you talking about?"

I swallowed. "You never got out of that chair."

She pulled away from me.

I took hold of both her hands before she could back out of reach. "We're both like Eddie, May. Both of us—the flu saw to that. My mother just told me. I saw our names in the newspaper. And my German . . . he's the one . . ." I nodded as if the gesture would fill in for my unspoken words, but May's brown eyes remained wide and utterly perplexed. Her irises darted back and forth, scanning my face. "Daniel is the one who was in the store when my father and brother attacked," I continued. "They killed him. They killed my Daniel—because of me. Because I had the flu, and they blamed the Germans."

"I don't . . ." She wrinkled her forehead. "What are you . . . ?"

"Ninety-seven people have died in Buchanan during these first two weeks of October. *Ninety-seven* . . . and counting."

"But . . . I don't . . ."

"It seems we're part of those ninety-seven, May." I swallowed. "This killer flu, it granted your wish. It did indeed help you to join your fallen husband."

"No." She breathed a small laugh. "That's not true. You're terribly confused, Ivy."

"My mother told me. She gave me those statistics. We're part of those statistics."

"Eddie wouldn't keep leaving me if I were like him. He'd take me with him."

"Come with me." Still holding her hands, I tugged her toward me and the open doorway, managing to move her two steps forward. "Please, come out of this house for a while and join me for some music and drinks. And when Eddie returns, you can tell him where you've been. Maybe you'll both become the lucky ones—the ones who accept their fate and just enjoy themselves."

"I can't leave."

"Yes you can." My own feet crossed the threshold to her porch. "There's a party every night, just down the street. Can't you hear the jazz?"

We both craned our heads in the eastward direction of the lodge, but only a soft bleat of the horns traveled the distance to May's residence.

"I'm not going anywhere without Eddie." She wrenched her hands out of mine. "He's coming back soon, and I'm going to be here. I'm going to be here and pretend like nothing is wrong." She turned and whisked toward her bedroom with her red silk swishing across her calves.

"No, don't pretend." I followed after her. "Daniel pretended, and it only made things so much worse for me."

"Eddie!" May tore inside her room and yanked down the covers of her empty bed. "Eddie, where are you? Where are you? I need you—now!" She dropped to her knees on the floor with her eyelet bedspread clutched in both hands. "Eddie!"

I knelt beside her, resting my knees against a fuzzy rug of black and gold. "It's all right."

"Eddie!" She bent over at the waist and cried into the fabric.

"It's all right." I rubbed her back, above the hard ridges of her curled spine and quaking shoulder blades. "He'll be here soon, and then you can speak to him about what you learned.

Both of you can free yourselves and accept your fate, and he'll likely stay with you for as long as you both want to be together." I brushed loose curls off the nape of her neck. "But don't pretend like Daniel and my mother did. It only makes the truth so much harder to swallow. It feels like poison and betrayal when you realize you've been sheltered like a child."

May eased her cheek against the floor, her chest still bent over her knees. Her lungs expanded and contracted with spasms that jerked her whole body. "We were supposed to have a baby," she said in a small voice I could just barely hear, "before he left. We kept trying and trying, but I just couldn't find myself . . . I couldn't get . . ."

"I'm so sorry, May."

"It's not fair at all. We had so many plans."

"I know." I nestled a hand over her right shoulder.

"What's the point of it all? Why were we born if we were all destined to be snatched away so soon?"

"I don't know." I shook my head. "But I think we're meant to make the best of it now that we are where we are. And maybe . . . just maybe"—I wound a strand of her black hair around my right pinky until the finger looked stained in ink— "those who survive will come to realize that too much time is spent on killing. They'll figure out that time is far too precious for all that hate and murder. Maybe, if we do our best to enjoy ourselves, they'll sense the force of our love and feel the emptiness of our absence, and they'll be sorry they ever whooped for joy over the idea of war."

May closed her eyes and sank her face farther against the snowy-white eyelet.

"Do you want me to leave, May?" I asked. "Or do you want me to stay until he arrives?"

She slowed her breathing. "Your father and brother gave him to you, then."

I sank back on my heels. "I beg your pardon?"

"They gave you the German . . . if he's the one they killed."

I swallowed down a dry patch as sharp as a razor blade. "That wasn't their intention, I can assure you of that."

"But it happened just the same. I like that." She smiled. "I like that love sprang out of murder. It makes me feel a little better." She closed her eyes again, and her lashes fluttered against her skin. "I've always enjoyed love stories. Men might call them silly and sentimental, but they all just want to be loved, too." She inhaled a long breath through her nostrils. "Tell me your whole story before you leave."

"What story? My life is so dull, May. I'm sure, compared to you—"

She took hold of my knee and tucked it beneath her right arm. "Tell me the story of you and your German. I want to hear about two people not meant to find each other who ended up tangled up in each other's lives and deaths. And give it a happy ending, even if you don't believe it will come true."

I pulled a stray piece of my hair away from my mouth. "I don't know if it will truly make you feel any better . . ."

"It will. Please . . . tell me."

With a sigh, I stretched my legs out in front of me and leaned back on the palms of my hands. As she wished, I sat with her for a spell, and I told her a war-torn love story about an American recluse and a German deserter who had never once crossed paths in life.

Chapter 26

*A*nother love story required completion.

It involved two young women compelled to save as many lives as they possibly could, even though they lost their own lives on a pair of lonely railroad tracks the week before.

> *Some struggle to complete a task they didn't finish*
> *when they were alive.*

I roamed a Southside neighborhood of crowded clapboard houses that all looked like duplicates of one another, all painted the same dung shade of brown, with identical square windows and tired front porches that sagged from time and wear. The waxing moon graced the rooftops with a weak and ethereal light that appeared almost violet.

I strained my ears, in search of the rumble of the ambulance's engine, and I pressed my lips together and forced myself to re frain from shouting out Nela and Addie's names, out of fear of frightening children or anyone else who might awake from the sound. To certain ears, my voice might resemble the keening of the wind or the desperate cry of a train charging down the tracks.

Back on Lincoln Street, I gave up and perched myself on the edge of a curb. A light shone in a top-story window of one of the shadowy textile mills that reigned over Southside with hawklike vigilance. A small part of me longed to creep inside the structure to see if some late-night mill worker hunched over his desk or his loom, struggling to complete a task he hadn't finished while he lived. I wondered if he hated Germans and wished men like Daniel dead. I imagined him as a round fellow with a cigar jammed between his lips, who overworked and underpaid the immigrants subordinate to him—and caused strife to Nela and Addie's families. Or maybe he possessed compassionate eyes and a worried brow. Maybe he mourned a son struck down overseas or fretted over his wife and children, who shivered in bed from the flu. Perhaps he was peeking out of his fourth-story window at that very moment, spotting me staring up at him, just as I often saw Billy and Lucas watching from the shadows.

I stood up and headed north, toward the tracks, while an eastbound train whistled across the fields a mile or two to the west. A Model T of some sort traveled up one of the nearby streets. The echo of the motor bounced across the houses and rumbled in my bones, and I thought of both the APL men and the Red Cross ambulance sneaking through the nighttime roads of Buchanan.

I stopped and turned, squinting to see through the darkness, hoping for the latter possibility.

A large vehicle peeled around a corner. Headlights blinded my eyes, coming closer at too fast a speed, swelling as large as two bright suns. I put up my hands and shrieked, and the vehicle screeched to a halting stop a mere four feet away from where I stood, quaking, my arms frozen in the air in front of my face.

"Ivy?" Nela turned off the engine and, with it, the headlights. She leapt out of the driver's side in her usual gray uniform and wiggled her mask down below her chin. "What are you doing in the middle of the street down here?"

I lowered my hands to my hips, bent forward at my waist, and blew a relieved gust of air through my lips—although I wondered, *Would I have truly gotten hurt if that ambulance had struck me down? Could I have stood there and let it pass straight through me?*

"I was . . . looking for you," I said, gasping to catch my breath as I spoke. "I'd just . . . given up."

The eastbound train clacked closer, the whistle screaming and hollering at us to stay off the tracks. Nela covered her ears and sank to her knees, and beyond the windshield, Addie did the same, disappearing from my sight. I crouched down next to Nela and braced my arm around her back, feeling the fear inside her hammer across my body. A squall of wind and the force of the locomotive's power tore straight through us—I tasted the sting of death in its fury of metal and steam. The whistle blew directly next to us, the cries blaring across my brain, making my eyes water, warning of broken glass and twisted metal and bodies tossed through the air.

The train passed. It wreaked its havoc and sped off to the eastern farms of Buchanan, chugging, whistling, clacking-clacking-clacking.

"Addie . . ." I kept hold of Nela, but I lifted my face toward the passenger who hid inside the ambulance. "Please come out here. The train is gone. I need to talk to you both."

The whistle faded into the pitch-black distance, and Addie slipped out of the truck, her hands still clamped over her ears. Nela rose to a standing position and removed her flu mask. I backed up to properly face them both, and Addie lowered her mask and cleared her throat.

"Tell me," I said, a tremor in my voice, "that night I first found you stalled on the tracks, how long had you actually been there?"

Addie and Nela glanced at each other with their lips half open. I heard the nervous beating of their breaths, but they did not answer.

"Do you remember what day it was when you first tried driving across those tracks?" I asked. "Was it Saturday, October 5?"

"I think . . ." Addie gulped and winced. "I think it was a Wednesday . . . or a Thursday. The flu was just getting bad."

"It was Wednesday, October 2," said Nela without hesitation. "That's when we tried driving Liliana to the emergency hospital and stalled."

"You . . ." I clutched the buttons of my blouse above my chest. "You stalled on the tracks on October 2?"

"Yes." Nela averted her gaze to her Red Cross boots down below the thick hem of her skirt.

"And a train came?" I asked.

Nela's chin shook. She wiped at her right eye with a knuckle. "Yes, a train came."

"Did it—"

"Yes." Nela looked me straight in the eye. "It hit us. I tried and tried to crank the engine back to life, and I jumped back in, while Addie was just about to jump out—and it hit us."

I turned toward Addie, whose lips shivered. She hardened her jaw and blinked back tears brewing in her eyes.

"Do you both know what happened to you, then?" I asked. "Have you known all along?"

"We don't talk about it," said Nela, bracing her hands on her hips. "After you leapt into the ambulance and helped it off the tracks, there seemed no point questioning what had happened. We just wanted to keep going. To keep fetching and helping."

"The people you're helping"—I swallowed—"do you know . . . ?"

Both of them turned their eyes away from me, peering instead at the dark patches of weeds that filled the land between the tracks and the houses.

"They already lost their lives," I said, my arms hanging by my sides like two bars of iron. "Do you know that?"

Both of them kept their eyes averted. The moon kissed their cheeks, and a silent wind plucked at their skirts and their sleeves.

"Their souls got stuck in their houses," I said. "Or else they didn't want to leave—that's why some of them yelled at us to go away with so much passion." I trekked over the pebbles in the road and wrapped my right arm around Addie's thin shoulders. "You don't need to keep fetching them unless you truly believe some of them are trying to get out."

"I don't know . . ." Addie covered her eyes and quaked against me. "If this is true, then why haven't I found my sister?"

"Didn't you say she succumbed to the influenza?" I asked.

"Yes." Addie nodded with her lips pressed together. "Our Florence. I can't find her anywhere here in Southside."

I squeezed her against my side. "Does she like to dance?"

Addie sniffed, and, out of the corner of my eye, I caught Nela cocking her head at me.

"Does she?" I asked. "Could you imagine her dancing to jazz?"

Addie nodded.

"Come along." I steered the girl back to the passenger side of the ambulance, my arm still tight around her. "Both of you. I'm going to show you another place where you can potentially take your transports. I have a strong suspicion Florence might already be there, discovering what happens when people bid good-bye to earthly troubles."

I swear, that Masonic Lodge ballroom had ballooned to twice its previous size in just a matter of hours. A saloon-style bar, topped with polished wood and rows of bright-colored bottles, now stretched the entire right side of the room at the far end. Three well-groomed men in white coats and bow ties served drinks to a line of Guests bellied up to the marble countertop, their feet resting on a brass foot rail.

I had to laugh a little, for in the middle of the bar stood a pyramid of crystal glasses, which Ruth Sellman turned into a fountain of champagne by standing on the counter in her blue fringed dress and pouring a bottle into the topmost glass. Golden liquid splashed and bubbled, and a small crowd of men and women, army boys included, cheered her on in a variety of languages, from English to Polish, Russian, and Norwegian. The more she poured, the more the music gathered speed.

The five windows that watched over the street and Daniel's store seemed to stretch twenty feet farther across the room, the exterior wall no longer made of bricks, but of glimmering golden paper with flecks of silver and swirls of crimson that resembled bodies intertwined. The Guests danced in their jewels and bandeaus and pinstriped suits with long tails, and some of them kissed and caressed each other.

I noticed that a freckle-faced redhead had joined the band, and his enormous brass tuba belched a vigorous bass line to "Livery Stable Blues," which inspired a whole slew of popular animal dances among the crowd: the fox-trot, the grizzly bear, the turkey trot, the bunny hug. Everyone wiggled and waddled and clasped one another and beamed bright-wattage smiles that made the crystal chandeliers burn even brighter. All the bedazzling colors of the place—the gilded coating of the walls, the deep red of the velvet curtains, the blues and the blacks and the greens of the gowns—gleamed with the warm hues of a Renoir painting.

I stepped farther into the room on the sweet bubbles of champagne, flanked by Addie and Nela, and I gaped at all the familiar faces I hadn't seen in the place before. Sigrid—dressed in white silk, a pearl comb shining in her pinned blond locks—now danced with her Wyatt. The synchronization of their feet in their polished black shoes, the gaze they shared as they stepped and turned across the floor, made my heart beat with a contented patter. I didn't see their children anywhere, as hard as I looked among all the faces gathered together in that room, and I hoped the absence of the little ones meant they had lived. Perhaps the abandoned rag doll in their house would be reunited with its tiny owner.

Mr. Greene from the Hotel America leaned against the bar with a flute of champagne in one hand and the other hand tucked in one of his trouser pockets, his position awkward, slightly tilted backward, as if he hadn't yet decided whether he belonged within those walls.

Addie looped her arm around my elbow and pulled me close. "I see our Florence."

"Where?"

"Over there." She pointed toward one of the windows. A pretty dark-skinned girl in a lime-sherbet-green dress turkey trotted with Benjie.

"Go." I patted Addie's hand. "See her."

Addie stiffened.

"Don't be afraid," I said. "She'll be so happy you've found her. Go to her."

"I don't know . . ." She untangled her arm from mine and inched toward the door. "I'd rather just get back into the ambulance and keep going."

"As would I," said Nela, also making an abrupt turn for the exit. "We've got work to do. People to help. This party here has nothing to do with us."

"Nela," called a fellow coming our way from the crowd around Ruth—a uniformed soldier, a tall one with pale-blond hair and hazel eyes that obviously recognized my friend. He removed a cloth army hat from his head and tucked it beneath one arm.

Nela stopped and pivoted on her heel toward him. A whispered Polish phrase slipped from her lips, along with a gasp of shock.

Without missing a beat, "Livery Stable Blues" slammed into "Jelly Roll Blues," and in the same amount of time, Nela and the soldier clamped each other in a firm embrace that warmed our side of the room with an unexpected blaze of heat. Nela squeezed her eyes shut and murmured the name "Freddie," and the soldier cradled the back of her head with his fingers embedded in her strands of fair hair.

Addie bolted from my side and left the room.

"Addie?" I followed after her, but by the time I exited the double doors, she had made it halfway down the hallway.

"Addie, where are you going?" I called after her.

"I'm not ready for this. I don't want to be here." She turned the corner in a streak of Red Cross gray, and the soles of her boots clomped down the steps of the lodge's side staircase.

"Addie!" I swung around the bend and chased after her, clinging tight to the slick rail. "Don't be frightened, please!" I rounded the bend in the staircase, not seeing her anymore.

The glass-paneled door of the lodge swung shut before I even reached the middle steps. I pushed the door open and found Addie in the driver's seat of the ambulance, the engine already rumbling, ready to go.

"Addie." I grabbed hold of the bar running up the right side of the passenger entrance. "I'm sorry. I should have spoken more delicately about what happened."

"I've got to go." She shifted the clutch lever into neutral, exactly as I'd instructed. "Please stop hanging on to the ambulance."

"It's not fair—I know. I feel too young for this, too. But it happened, and we might as well enjoy ourselves in the ways we still can. Don't you think?"

She peered out from the vehicle with wide, dark eyes. "We're just going to be numbers in the newspaper. 'Statistics,' my daddy called it whenever he read about the war over the breakfast table."

"Addie, no, that's not—"

"On the day Florence died, the *Sentinel* said six Buchanan residents lost their lives. They didn't even print her name. Just a number."

"But—"

"Have you heard about any motion picture stars or world leaders dying from this disease?" she asked, her left eyebrow cocked.

"Well . . . I-I-I've only read two newspaper articles in the past week . . ."

"Have you heard about any of those fancy, famous people dying in the war either?"

I shook my head, my mouth pressed shut. "No, I suppose not."

"The only famous dead person in all of this has been Archduke Ferdinand, who went and got himself shot and set all these troubles into motion. Everyone else is ordinary people. We're just numbers, and when I was a little girl, I sure as hell didn't dream of growing up and turning into a damned statistic."

"But people won't forget us." I dropped down to the seat beside her with a squeak of the springs beneath the leatherette upholstery. "I think, even years from now, they'll figure out that music like this . . ." I tilted my ear toward the lodge. "Cripes, just listen to that desperation mixed with a wild joie de vivre. That doesn't come out of nothing. They'll be able to hear that a massive eruption once rocked the world and scattered pain and passion in its wake."

She slid her hands down the steering wheel until the tops of her fingers and thumbs hung from the bottom. "I hope you're right."

"They won't forget." I scooted across the seat to her. "And I'm sure they'll learn from all of our mistakes."

She popped her bottom lip in and out of her mouth and seemed to waver over what to do next.

I rested my hand on the crook of her right arm. "Do you want to go back up there and see your sister?" I asked. "Or would you genuinely feel better driving around?"

"What are *you* going to do, Ivy?"

I sighed from deep in my belly and glanced past her head at the closed door of Liberty Brothers Furniture standing there, motionless, in the steady electric lamplight shining across the street. "I'm going to talk to my German for a bit. But . . . after that . . ."

She knitted her brow. "After that, what?"

"That's a very good question." I climbed out of the ambulance and smoothed down my skirt. "I spent so much of my life hiding and protecting myself from fear. I'm not quite sure what to do with this new taste of liberation."

"Well, I think I'm gonna drive around a bit." She pulled her gauze mask back up over her nose.

"Addie . . ." I leaned back down with my hands on my knees. "If you see a young doughboy with hair my color—someone who looks a little lost—will you ask him if his name is Billy Rowan?"

She nodded. "All right, I suppose I could."

"And if it is Billy, will you tell him that Wendy Darling said to go to the Masonic Lodge, which is a little bit like Neverland? If you mention that Ruth Sellman is there, showing off her gams, that would probably help."

"Your brother, right?"

"Yes, my brother. The one we lost in France." I cast my eyes down the sidewalk to the nearest streetlamp to see if he happened to be standing right there. A golden haze hovered beneath the bright bulbous casings, but I didn't see Billy—although a pair of thick lenses glowed in the darkness beyond.

"I'll tell him," said Addie.

"Thank you."

I stepped back from the ambulance and watched her adjust the levers for the throttle and the spark advance. With the skill of an expert driver that made my instructor's heart proud, she maneuvered the vehicle around into the opposite direction and puttered off to the westward junction to Southside.

I put my hands on my hips and braced myself against a stark chill left in her wake.

"Go upstairs to the music, Lucas," I called down the street without actually looking in the direction of the dark patch where I'd seen his spectacles. "Take off your badge and stop spying on me. You can retire now."

No sounds emerged from his unlit corner. I puffed a sigh through my lips and turned my head toward him.

"You got sick from this flu, didn't you?" I asked.

He didn't answer, but I heard him kick a pebble into the street. The stone rolled around in the blackness of night and spun to a stop somewhere in the middle of the road.

"Did it turn into pneumonia or some other complication?" I asked.

"Yes," he answered from down in the darkness. "Meningitis."

"Do you know what happened to you? After the complication set in?"

Another pebble hurled into the street and clanked against the curb on the opposite side of the road, in front of Daniel's store.

"Did you ever read any of Emily Dickinson's poems?" I asked.

"Oh, Jesus," said Lucas, still not stepping forward and showing himself in the light. "Billy said you read those things all the time. He worried you admired her so much, you wanted to *be* her, hiding away inside your father's house like that. You turned so strange and ghostly." He sighed. "You really bothered him with your oddness."

Instead of responding, I quoted one of her poems.

> *"Death is a dialogue between*
> *The spirit and the dust.*
> *'Dissolve,' says Death. The spirit, 'Sir,*
> *I have another trust.'*
>
> *"Death doubts it, argues from the ground.*
> *The Spirit turns away.*
> *Just laying off, for evidence,*
> *An overcoat of clay."*

Neither of us spoke after my voice finished echoing across Daniel's store and the limestone bank building beside it. I thought I heard the muffled pounding of a hammer beyond the boarded-up windows and the paint-spattered walls of Liberty Brothers, and I longed to be done with Lucas.

"Don't let Death and the APL keep you trapped in the shadows, Lucas." I sucked a deep breath of air through my nose and felt it settle inside my lungs. "Remove your badge, and go up and join the party in the lodge."

A pair of hesitant footsteps shuffled toward me across the sidewalk. Lucas, still in his charcoal-gray businessman suit, wandered into view from beneath the lamplight with his arms wrapped around himself. Another wanderer, just like me.

"Remove your badge," I said with a nod. "And go have some fun. All right?"

His dark coat quivered with the nervousness of his arms shaking against the fabric. He didn't speak or move until the jazz band switched to an old childhood favorite that all of us kids who grew up in the early years of the century adored: "Bill Bailey." Lucas lifted his face to the windows of the lodge with an expression of wonder in his bottle-cap eyes. Laughter and music and beautiful whiffs of booze streamed out with the glorious golden light of the chandeliers within.

He removed his badge and shoved it down into his right trouser pocket.

He passed me by on the sidewalk and hustled inside the humming and shimmying Masonic Lodge, which seemed ready to launch to the stars.

I heard his feet gallop up the staircase beyond the closed door.

Another soul had escaped the darkness.

Chapter 27

I blew inside Liberty Brothers Furniture as if carried on a breeze—which, perhaps, indeed I was. The little brass shop bell tinkled above my head with the flutter of an object unsettled by a shiver of wind, and all the ceiling lamps swayed.

Daniel sat across the room, hammering away at a piece of furniture with his back toward me, and my presence seemed to ripple through him as well. He shuddered, lifted his head, and turned halfway around on his spindle-back work chair with the same troubled eyes and pursed lips I had viewed on the night I first drifted past his store with my bags in hand. The band across the street played a cornet-heavy rendition of "Bill Bailey" that threatened to set me crying for the past. I balled my hands into fists with my nails digging into my flesh, determined not to shed a tear until I said what needed to be spoken.

"Why didn't you tell me?" I asked.

Daniel sat up straight in his chair. "How much do you know?"

"I know about the flu. What it did to me. I know"—I folded my arms across my chest and glanced at the faded pink patches on the scrubbed and bleached floorboards—"whose blood that is and why it was shed. I know that Frank and Peter Rowan burst into here . . ." I gritted my teeth and blinked back the sting of tears. "They burst into here, not just because of Billy. They came in here to kill"—I nodded to make the words shake free—"because of me."

Daniel lowered the hammer and wood, rose to his feet, and reached for the back of his chair, grabbing the empty air twice before taking hold of the furniture. "How did you—"

"My mother is able to talk to me. For some peculiar reason, we Rowan women have always been able to see . . ." I filled in the unsaid word with another nod, and he squeezed his lips together.

"I know about our poor town," I continued, "and my friends who drive the ambulance with me. I know about you and why you looked so lost when I wandered by that first night . . . why you have that rope burn scarring your neck, and why you can't ever . . ." My voice broke. "Why you can't ever father a child." I tucked my chin into the warm collar of my blouse and cried soundless tears with gentle shakes of my shoulders. I closed my eyes and tasted the sea on my wet lips—or at least what I'd always imagined as the flavor of the faraway oceans, miles and miles away from Buchanan, Illinois.

Daniel cleared his throat and shifted his weight. "Your father and brother called out your name when they were here. That's how I knew who you were that night you introduced yourself to me. The first thing they said when your brother pulled my arms behind me and your father socked me in the stomach was 'This is for Ivy. Your people k—' "

I opened my eyes when he didn't continue, and I watched him rub his hands across the sides of his legs while his lips sputtered and his eyes moistened.

"They said"—he wiped his cheeks with the back of a hand—" 'Your people killed her.' And for a moment, I thought someone found out about Belgium. But then they beat me and kicked me and shouted about Germans dumping the flu into theaters, and I realized I was going to die because of ignorance and this damned anti-immigrant paranoia, not because of the real reasons someone should kill me."

I inched toward him, my hands tucked beneath my arms, my fingers trembling against my ribs. "No one should have killed you, Daniel."

"You heard what I did over there. I saw the look of horror in your eyes after I confessed my sins."

"No matter how shocked and appalled I might have been when you first told me"—I stopped three feet away from him, feeling the firm pull of him within my chest—"I know others ordered you to kill. That wasn't you deciding to take lives."

"I took them just the same." He leaned forward against the back of the chair. "I still see them sometimes. I'll always see them."

"My father and brother made you pay dearly for the ills of your native country. Don't keep punishing yourself. I'm sorry I only made things worse with the things I said."

He swallowed and gripped the chair with whitening fingers.

My eyes strayed down to the pink marks on the floor below my black shoes, and my mind once again envisioned the brutality of the night of Friday, October 4, 1918, now envisioning Daniel as the victim bleeding and hurting down on the floorboards.

"Did they make you suffer long . . . before they . . . ?" I closed my eyes to squeeze away the image of my father tugging a rope around Daniel's neck. "Did they hang you in here like the mob that killed Robert Prager?"

"No." Daniel sniffed. "They held me down there on the ground—someone's knee pushed against my spine—and they yanked the rope around my neck until I blacked out. They garroted me."

My balance wavered. I raised my arms out to my sides to steady myself and planted both feet solidly against the floor. "And . . . Albrecht was never here?"

"No. Only me. I heard them break the glass from upstairs and immediately ran down, but they grabbed me before I could get to the drawer and fetch the gun."

I raised my eyes to his. "You've known what happened to us all along, haven't you? Even that night I first came here and spoke to you, you knew."

He nodded.

"How?" I asked. "How did you know when most of the rest of us didn't?"

"I'd seen enough of death. I recognized the scent of its arrival—the strange feel of it in the air—to understand precisely what was happening to me."

"Why didn't you tell me any of this before? Why did you let me believe you were a grieving brother and I was alive and healthy?"

"I'm sorry."

"Why?"

"I don't—" He lowered himself to the chair with a clumsiness that made the wood slide with a squeak against the floor. "You just showed up in the dark of night . . . and you made me feel"—he rubbed his right hand across his chin—"as if the entire world hadn't conspired against me. I didn't want to frighten you away. You were always flitting off so quickly as it was."

I wrapped my fingers around the back of his chair, close enough to touch the side of his warm hand.

"I'm sorry," he said again. "I wanted this to become our Eden."

"You wanted to keep me free of knowledge, you mean."

"No." He swallowed. "Just free."

I reached up to the rope burn beneath his collar and traced my thumb across the smooth red line. His unsteady breaths tickled the back of my wrist.

"Why is this mark still here if your other wounds healed?" I asked.

"I don't know."

"Is it like the pain in my stomach, waiting to be freed?"

He shook his head and again said, "I don't know."

"What would free you?" I cupped my hand around his cheek and his chin and stroked his soft skin that, now that I thought about it, never seemed to grow much in the way of whiskers, beyond a thin and bristly layer of stubble that never, ever changed. "What would allow you to leave this place?"

He turned his face in the direction of the front-counter drawer that hid the *Sentinel* article about the murder.

"What is it?" I asked.

He drew my hand into his and peered up at me with glossy blue eyes. "I want to know that Albrecht and this store will be safe."

I sank my teeth into my bottom lip, and the wood-paneled walls of Liberty Brothers seemed to squeeze against my chest, pressing all traces of hope for his well-being out of me.

"Oh, Daniel. You might be asking for the impossible."

"I know." He shifted his position in the chair with another dull squeak. "But my brother, he's lived in this country since 1912. He's never hurt a soul or betrayed America. And yet he'll have a struggle to reopen the store and marry Nora because of slanderous attacks like the ones—" He darted another sharp glance at the closed drawer.

I pressed my hand over his, molding my palm around his knuckles, which somehow grew colder beneath me. "What can I do to help?" I asked. "What can I ask my mother to do?"

He shook his head. "Nothing. The war has to end first. People need to change their way of looking at other people to set things right for Albrecht."

"And you believe you'll remain trapped inside this building until that happens?"

He closed his eyes and nodded.

"That doesn't seem right at all. Try to come with me."

"I keep telling you"—he peeked back up at me with the same haunted look I remembered from the day I first walked in on him cleaning up the blood, his pupils wide and dark—"I can't."

"Just . . . come to the music and the dancing across the street . . ."

"Ivy . . ." Daniel brought me down to his lap with a soft pull of my elbow. "I'm not ready to go. If you need to keep moving and find whatever it is you're searching for, I won't stop you. But I'm not going. I'm staying right here until I'm certain it's safe."

A tenor with a lush vibrato—perhaps the slick-haired piano player—burst out in song across the street and gave us both a start. His melancholy words and dreamlike melody caused my soul to tire inside me. The lights dimmed. The world withered. I lowered my head against Daniel's shoulder and said, "I can't stay here with you. This store reminds me of my father and my brother, and what they did."

"I know." He leaned his head against mine, and we trembled and fought against allowing the music to chip away at our hearts until nothing of us remained. We stayed tethered to the earth, for better or worse, and absorbed the sorrow of the tenor's voice.

Daniel swallowed next to my ear. "Last night was the end of the world."

I collapsed farther against him. "I know. I feel the same way."

"No, I mean"—he brushed his cheek against mine—"that is the name of the song. 'Last Night Was the End of the World,' by Henry Burr."

I emitted a sound that wavered between a whimper and a laugh and locked my arms around his shoulders. My eyes turned to the copper lamp dangling above us, and I stared at the unsteady bulb that hummed and flickered inside, fearful it would soon blink out and abandon me in a darkness where nothing ended or began. Just darkness and cold. And me.

The singer across the street reached his final crescendo; his voice shook throughout the store and volleyed across my legs and my head and my bones—or what I thought to be my bones.

And then the world fell silent.

I held my breath, clung to Daniel, and kept my face fixed on that teasing bulb above, willing it not to burn out just yet.

Friday night a band of vagrants broke into Liberty Brothers Furniture Store and attacked and killed Wilhelm Daniel Schendel, aged 24, a German enemy of the U.S. who resided in downtown Buchanan. A neighbor down the street from the scene of the crime telephoned the police after hearing the intruders break the glass windows and door. Officers found Mr. Schendel lying facedown on the floor inside the establishment. The coroner pronounced him dead at the scene.

Mr. Schendel's injuries included multiple bruises and lacerations, missing teeth, a broken nose, a ruptured spleen, and fractured ribs. Officers discovered him with a rope wrapped around his neck and speculate that the intruders strangled him to death.

Wilhelm Schendel entered the country directly from Germany in 1915 and has been on the American Protective League's watch list ever since he registered as an enemy alien in February of this year. Records show that he does not posses a draft registration card and that he and his surviving bother, Albrecht Schendel, aged 29, did not purchase Liberty Bonds during any of the drives. Albrecht Schendel also failed to produce a draft registration card when questioned.

Police assure the public that the incident was an isolated event committed by migratory ruffians passing swiftly through town. "Mr. Wilhelm Schendel likely perpetrated the violence

*by preaching his disloyal sentiments to the va-
grants," said Police Chief Clyde Madison. "The
anonymous men attacked an individual who posed
a tremendous threat to our country's safety and
then moved onward as quickly as they arrived."*

*Despite the victim's heritage and disloyal
tendencies, Madison emphasized that Mr. Schendel's death does not represent another Robert
Prager-style act of mob justice and should not
be treated as such.*

—BUCHANAN SENTINEL, *October 6, 1918*

Chapter 28

The shop bell down below stirred me from my rest. I awoke next to Daniel in his bed, still clothed in my blouse, skirt, and stockings from the night before, out of fear that I would need to spring out of bed at some point and run.

From what, I did not know.

I heard footsteps down in the store and assumed at first that they might be Albrecht's again. If he had seen our wreckage from our unhinged night of boozing—the broken lamps, the bullet holes, the shattered bottles—he surely must have assumed more "vagrants" had entered the store and inflicted additional anti-German damage.

Poor Albrecht. I wondered if he knew we haunted him.

The visitor down below sounded as if he were pacing in a pattern that struck me as familiar. I propped myself on my elbows and cocked my ear toward the bedroom door to better listen to the rhythm.

Step-step-step-STEP, step-step-step-TURN,

Step-step-step-STEP, step-step-step-TURN . . .

Yes, I had most certainly heard that particular style of pacing before—in my own house, on evenings when Father didn't receive fair payments for our crops. And during the night after he injured Billy with the shovel, when the doctor had warned us that my brother could slip out of consciousness without a moment's notice.

I slid out of bed without a sound, careful not to disturb Daniel and his gentle breathing, and crept downstairs to the store that glowed with morning sunlight stealing between the boards of the windows.

My father stood over the bloodstains with his hands on his hips—the same stance in which I had found Daniel on the night of the murder. Father's back was turned to me, so I could only see the curve of his spine beneath his tan work shirt, the rigidness of his hunched shoulders, the thin, combed-over hair that shared my same golden-brown color—and Billy's color. I doubted Father would see me, so I snuck farther inside the store from the workroom and leaned my shoulder blades against the nearest wall, in the comfort of shadows.

Father sighed with a deep grumble that rumbled up from his belly, and he just stood there, looking at the faded blood he himself had pounded out of Daniel.

"What do you want, Father?" I asked.

He raised his head and glimpsed over his shoulder in my direction, and for a moment I feared that he had drunk himself to death or keeled over from the flu—and that he could hear me. That he had come to spoil my newfound independence.

His eyes didn't focus on me, however, even though he kept his face directed my way, as if he felt but didn't see me.

He still lived and breathed.

A living man. A free man.

"What do you want?" I asked again, and he turned away and rubbed his hand across the back of his neck. Perhaps my presence resembled a fly creeping across his skin.

I heard a creak in a workroom floorboard.

Daniel appeared in the back doorway and immediately stiffened. He braced his hand against the doorframe and, with a sting to his voice, he asked, "Who is that?"

Father left the stains and wandered over to the maple cabinet Daniel had been trying with all his might to fix the first night I spoke to him. He ran his calloused left hand over the cracked and splintered trim, and I saw the shine of his gold wedding band.

Recognition registered in Daniel's eyes. He bent his legs like a coiled spring about to shoot forward.

"Don't hurt him." I lunged out of the shadows with my arms spread wide, for I imagined my poor mother, forced to nurse an injured husband in the midst of all her other worries. "I know you might be tempted—"

"I wasn't going to hurt him," said Daniel, but he kept his

gaze on his intruder with a hard stare and a taut mouth. He puckered his brow and watched Father tinker with the loose leg of an oak desk chair. "What is he doing?" he asked in the harsher tones of his accent that made him sound as though he were speaking German, even though he had uttered the words in English.

I shook my head. "I don't know. I heard a noise downstairs and just found him standing here. He sort of . . ."

Father bent down and screwed the wobbly chair leg back into place.

"He looks as if . . ." I paused and watched some more, astounded at Father's tender actions—the gentle twist he employed to mend that chair. "As if he's trying to fix his mess."

Intrigued, I crossed to the front counter and rested my right hand on top of the smooth grains of wood. I felt compelled to shift my attention back and forth between the two men, ensuring that Daniel wouldn't pounce forward and slam a chair over Father's head . . . and that Father wouldn't violate the store any further.

Daniel stayed frozen in place, his hand still gripping the doorframe.

"Is there anything that you want to say to him?" I asked.

Daniel's lips parted, but he said nothing. He seemed to lose his balance for a moment, his hand slipping off the frame, but he quickly straightened his legs and grabbed the wood with more force. His knuckles whitened. His brow bubbled with sweat.

"He won't hear you," I said, "but it might feel nice to release some of the anger. Is there anything you wish he could know?"

"Yes, there is." Daniel dropped his hand to his side with a soft brush of his fingers against his trousers. "I want to say . . ." He swallowed and stepped forward. "I want to say to him . . . 'I understand.'"

I wrinkled my forehead. "You . . . you understand? That's all you'd want him to hear?"

He nodded and squeezed his right hand around his left thumb, and he said again, "I understand." His eyes veered to me. "He's more yours to scold . . . and to forgive. You bear a far deeper grudge against him than I do. He was just doing what his country instructed him to do."

"But . . ."

Daniel retreated back toward the workroom before I could say another word, but we both stopped and turned when the front door clanged open.

Two mustached workmen in nut-brown caps and coats entered the store and surveyed the half-repaired tangle of furniture, as well as the floorboards lying there in the dim streaks of light, bleached and ugly and stained in that pink phantom blood.

"We're here to replace a window," said the taller man to Father. He was a burly fellow who sounded as if he were asking a question instead of making a statement. *We're here to replace a window in this godforsaken mess of a murder scene? Is that right?*

Daniel and I exchanged a glance of mutual befuddlement.

"It's just"—the worker pointed his thumb toward the boarded-up glass over his left shoulder—"an order for one window, according to the paperwork."

"Yes, that's right." Father got to his feet. "I could only afford to pay for one of the windows, but . . . well . . ." He slapped his hand against the back of his neck, perhaps feeling me there again, smacking the pesky-fly sensation away.

"What happened in here?" asked the shorter man with a smile, his eyes bright and eager for a tale of blood and gore.

"Vagrants," said Father. "They attacked this place pretty badly. Killed one of the store's owners."

"It's not *your* store, then?" asked the tall fellow.

"No, the window's just a gift." Father tucked his hands in his pockets. "That's why I requested you to come early in the morning. I arranged everything with your boss, so there's nothing to worry over. I paid for everything, fair and square."

"Well"—the shorter one shrugged—"if everything's paid for and arranged . . ."

"All right." The tall one nodded. "We'll get to work, then. We won't be any trouble to you, so you can go about your business."

"I'm heading back on home, as a matter of fact." Father rubbed at his neck so hard that his skin turned as red and scaly as a sunburn. "But you fellas do what you can to get the job done as quickly as possible. It's a . . . a sort of a . . . surprise, for the owner."

I peeked back at Daniel again and found his mouth agape.

The workers trooped back out for their supplies, and Father moseyed toward the door with the soles of his shoes swooshing against the floor.

I stepped forward and called out, "Father."

He stopped and straightened his neck.

"I don't know if you can actually hear me"—I slid my hand off the countertop and took two more steps toward him—"but I want you to know that *I* don't understand. I know the newspapers tell us to take patriotism into our own hands. I know our government isn't punishing violence against foreigners and Socialists. But I do not understand how a man could beat and strangle the life out of another man. I forgive you because Daniel forgives you. But I will never comprehend that poisonous drop of darkness that has always dwelled inside you—not when you've been surrounded by love and devotion all your life. I'm truly sorry my passing caused that darkness to get the best of you, but I swear, I will never understand."

He swiveled around and scanned the store, his eyes darting about. I didn't move—not because I believed standing still would conceal me from him, but because rising up tall and strong against him lightened the guilt on my shoulders. My stomach unclenched, and the pain seeped away. My hands felt light enough to drift away from my sides and into the air with the ease of a hot-air balloon ascending from the open fields of grass beyond the curve of the Minter River.

"Go," I said. "And be kind to Mama. Make yourself deserving of her unconditional love."

Father turned and left the building just as the workers pried the first boards off the rightmost windows and flooded Liberty Brothers Furniture with daylight.

Chapter 29

*T*hat night, after dark, just as the band awakened in its full hot-jazz splendor across the street, I disappeared into Daniel's bathroom and dressed myself in an evening gown the golden-red shade of the autumn leaves that scattered down the streets of Buchanan. Sheer sleeves graced my shoulders and upper arms; the squared-off neckline hung low enough to expose the white of my throat and upper chest. Five silken flowers hung off the folds of the bodice, adding a pinch of sweetness to the sin. The full skirt hung down to my calves, giving way to my black patent leather dress shoes down below.

I pulled up my hair in the back, let it pouf on the top, and allowed the shorter curls in front to frame my face. I rouged my lips and cheeks, strung pearls around my neck and wrists, and stepped out into Daniel's front room as a woman ready to soar.

Daniel sat on his sofa by the fireplace, whittling the same flat piece of wood with which I kept seeing him tinker.

I walked toward him with my skirt rustling against my smooth stockings. "What is it that you're making?"

He looked up at me, and his face fell. "Why are you dressed like that?"

I straightened the sash tied around the middle of the gown and fussed with tiny wrinkles far more than necessary.

"Ivy?"

"I'm going." I swallowed and looked him in the eye. "And I think you should, too, despite your worries. I think you should grab your guitar, put on a dress coat, and come have a bit of fun."

He lowered his shoulders and balanced the carving across his legs. "I already told you why I'm not leaving."

"Daniel"—I sank down next to him on the sofa—"you said that the greatest fears you and other Germans possessed over here were those of detainment and death by a lynching."

"What does that have to—?"

"Both of those appalling experiences, in some form, already happened to you." I pressed my hand over his hand upon the small slice of wood. "This country has trapped you in this building by planting fear for your brother's safety deep inside you. If you let them keep you here, then they've succeeded in controlling you—both in life *and* in death. The German and U.S. governments will have successfully squashed Wilhelm Daniel Schendel and stolen every single piece of his soul."

He removed his hand from mine and shifted his knees away. "It'll be two guitar picks."

I pinched my eyebrows together. "I beg your pardon?"

"That's what I'm whittling." He laid his knife on the round end table beside him. "I had one in my pocket that night, but it must have gotten knocked out and taken away."

"Daniel, were you even listening to what I said?"

"I'm not leaving, Ivy. I don't know how many times I'll need to say it before you understand, but you will have to go without me. I'm not going anywhere until this war and this scourge of violence and disease ends and I'm certain Albrecht is safe."

"All right." I stood up with a soft whisper of satin. "Then I'll stop asking, and I'll stop coming and going from here. This has gone on long enough, hasn't it?"

He raised his face to mine, rubbing his thumb over the smoothed-down piece of wood, and his eyes seemed to tell me, *No, you're wrong. It hasn't gone on long enough.*

His mouth, however, uttered nothing. I slid the cold clasp of my pearls better in place on the back of my neck, above my top vertebrae, and I walked away from him, toward the staircase.

"I'll at least go down with you and see you off," he said behind me, getting to his feet.

"Very well." I stopped and allowed him to join me by my side. "That would . . ." I pressed my chin against my chest to cut off an ache in my throat. "That would be nice."

He gestured with his left hand for me to descend the stairs in front of him, and we wandered down to the dark workroom below. I remembered the night we first trekked up that staircase together, his footsteps hurried, mine hesitant yet curious, after he asked me to join him in his bed. The night seemed to have occurred a thousand years before, even though I understood that time still passed at a normal pace for us. The war and the flu of 1918 still terrorized the world outside that newly replaced storefront window.

We passed through the unlit shop, our soles stepping across the pink stains as if they weren't there, and we stopped in front of the door, next to the new, unblemished glass, which allowed the streetlamp from outside to illuminate our cheeks and hair. We faced each other, not more than two feet away from one another, while the band played on. Daniel's thumbs fidgeted with the pockets of his trousers. I fussed again with my sash. The world beyond that clear windowpane tugged me toward it, as if magnets, not blood, traveled through my veins. The electricity of the jazz tingled up my arms and buzzed through the roots of my hair until my skin crackled and sparked.

"Oh, God, Daniel." I pressed a hand against my forehead. "This is so hard, letting you go."

"I know." He nodded and stepped closer, his thumbs still in his pockets, his head bent toward mine. "It's not that I don't wish to go."

"But you can. You have a choice. Don't let them take away your freedom to make your own decisions." I reached up and wrapped my fingers around his warm neck, and I almost pressed my lips against his, forgetting for a moment his personal punishment and the Belgian girl. "Daniel . . ." I closed my eyes and let my mouth linger a mere inch from his, feeling his breath brush like butterfly wings against my face.

"What?" His breathing quickened, and I could have sworn I heard both of our hearts pounding over the pulse of the band's beating drums.

"I love you." I lifted my lashes and saw the dampness in his eyes. "I love you. And your brother loves you, too—so much that I'm sure he would loathe the idea of your being trapped inside this place for all eternity. I'm willing to bet anything that right now he's saying to Nora, 'I will be fine, as long as I know that Wilhelm's soul is free.'" I stroked the smooth skin above his collar. "Wouldn't you want the same for him?" I swallowed. "If he had died first, wouldn't you be unable to move on with your life if you knew he wasn't at peace?"

Daniel's lips and lower jaw quivered. Tears brimmed in his eyes to the point of spilling over, and yet I knew he still would not join me in the outside world.

"How do you say 'I love you' in German?" I asked in a whisper, while the band filled the store with the type of rag meant for dancing, not departures.

Daniel cleared his throat and whispered back, "*Ich liebe dich.*"

I kissed his left cheek and said into his ear in my softest voice, "*Ich liebe dich,* Wilhelm."

And without another word, I slipped out the door.

THE RED CROSS AMBULANCE sat in front of the curb across the street again. Two figures standing on the sidewalk beyond—a gray one and an olive-green one—caught my eye through the vehicle's driving compartment, and when they moved farther to the left, toward the front door of the lodge, I slapped my hand over my mouth and squeezed my fingers into the skin against my teeth.

Addie escorted Billy to the Masonic Lodge door. I only saw the backs of them, the crisp lines of their uniforms and hats, but I recognized Addie's pinned-back loops of black hair and Billy's bowlegged walk that looked as though he were strolling inside our farmhouse for Sunday dinner.

I just stood at the edge of the opposite sidewalk and watched them, understanding Addie's hesitancy to run straightaway to her sister. There's simply no adequate way to describe the knocked-over-sideways feeling of viewing someone you were never meant to see again.

Billy opened the door for Addie, and they entered the first floor of the lodge.

All traces of my old headaches disappeared. My skull mended back into one solid piece, stitched up and smoothed over, never to split apart again. Pain had become the Uninvited Guest.

I thought one last time of Emily Dickinson, and her brightest, most optimistic of poems:

> *Hope is the thing with feathers*
> *That perches in the soul,*

And sings the tune without the words,
And never stops at all . . .

The band switched to a song that reminded me of the raucous
style of the Original Dixieland Jass Band, but I didn't recognize
the number, and I didn't know the name, which made me long to
turn around, knock on Daniel's door, and ask him what the song
was called. *Just one more song name,* I thought with my back to
his store. *That's all I'll ask of him. Just one more song.*

Instead, I crossed the street and pushed Daniel into the past,
along with my home and the war and my days of suffering from
the flu. The murder. My former reclusive self. Mama. Father.
Peter. Wyatt professing his love by the lake. Lucas bounding
toward our house in his untied shoes. Eddie Dover's broad smile.
May stretched out on a checkered blanket at a summer picnic.
Helen, Sigrid, and I, clustered around the display counters of
Weiss's Bakery. Buchanan, Illinois, on a starlit childhood night,
when its dark secrets hid so well. I left it all behind and strolled
over to the glass-paneled door waiting just beyond the ambulance. The music's potent allure caused my hands to shake and
sweat, and my fingers trembled so much that they looked like
blurs when I reached out to the cold brass knob. My heart shattered to a thousand pieces, but I knew I had to enter. It would be
for the best to just lose myself and forget everything, especially
him. *Just forget him. Forget it all.*

"Ivy."

I spun around.

Daniel exited his store, carrying his guitar in a black leather case by his side. He wore a dark dress coat over a pair of gray-striped trousers, and he had slicked down his hair and parted it on his left until it looked almost as painted on as the piano player's. He walked toward me across the street, the case swinging in his left hand, the moon brightening his skin, showing me a clear neck without a single vicious sign of rope burn. His eyes shone in a bewitching shade of blue, and I imagined pools of Rhineland waters gleaming in that same color on a German summer night, back when he lived wild and free.

He stopped in front of me, and for a moment I couldn't think what the devil I should say.

"The moonlight suits you, Mr. Schendel," I said when no other words seemed quite right.

"We're old friends." He cracked a small smile that crinkled the skin near his eyes. "He watched over me many a night, years ago."

"I don't . . ." I shifted my weight between my feet. "I don't quite know what to say. It seems so strange to see you out here. A minute ago, I almost ran back to ask you the name of this song."

" 'At the Jass Band Ball.' "

"By the Original Dixieland Jass Band?"

He nodded. "They're not even the best band, to be honest. They just recorded their music first, before everyone else got the same brilliant idea this past year."

"Well . . ." I scanned him from head to toe to make sure my eyes weren't deceiving me. "I still can't believe you're out here.

I just"—I wiped a damp spot from the inner corner of my right eye—"I honestly don't know what to say."

He peeked up at the windows of the lodge and tightened his grip on the handle of the guitar case. "Are you sure I'll be invited here?"

"I'm absolutely positive. These are the same folks who played Beethoven for you, remember?"

"And what if we don't like it here? What if we get tired of all the dancing and the music?"

"Then we'll go somewhere else and let the rays of the moon swallow us up. Or else we'll simply disappear into the notes of the music and drift through the streets of Buchanan, until we find somewhere else that better suits us." I wiped another stray tear and sputtered up a laugh. "I honestly don't care where we go. Let's just have some fun."

His eyes left the windows and returned to me. "Why do you want to be with me so badly, Ivy? Why did you always come back?"

"I don't think that's the sort of answer that can be properly explained with mere words." I took his hand and stepped backward, coaxing him toward the door of the lodge, which buzzed and rattled from the music and dancing within. "The head makes war, but the heart makes peace. And, thankfully, the heart ends up ruling more than not."

I moved to open the door, but he called out, "Wait."

He scooted closer to me with soft footsteps that brushed against the sidewalk, and he cupped his left hand around the back of my head. Before I could even wonder at his actions, he bent forward, and he kissed me on the lips.

I could describe that first real kiss in terms of piano crescendos or a blaze of fireworks or the brisk rushing of my blood through my veins, but I'm going to leave that particular moment as a gift for just him and me. It belonged to us, and nothing could take it away—even though those cruel years of war and disease seemed to have stolen everything else that once was ours. We lifted our heads and caught our breaths, and I opened the door and led him inside, where we joined the other members of the lost. We joined them in the sweet strains of music that lifted into the air and carried across all of Buchanan and out to the world beyond.

Acknowledgments

Thank you to my amazing Fairy Godmother of an editor, Lucia Macro, for getting this whole thing started. If she hadn't called up my agent and asked if I, a young-adult novelist, would be interested in writing a novel for adults set in 1918 (a dream call for any author!), this book would not be here today. Thank you from the bottom of my heart, Lucia. Thank you also to Nicole Fischer and the rest of the HarperCollins team who helped bring this novel to life.

Thank you to my indefatigable agent, Barbara Poelle, who stuck by me for four long years before I even started selling books to publishers. Barbara always champions my work with such passion and care, and I'm so thankful to have her guiding my path in this surreal and wonderful world of publishing.

Thanks to my husband, Adam, and our two kids, for putting up with all the times I've run upstairs to our home office or out

ACKNOWLEDGMENTS

to coffeehouses so I could disappear into my fictional worlds with my laptop. Their love and support mean the world to me. Thank you also to Adam for naming Buchanan, Illinois.

Thanks to my sister, Carrie Raleigh, for always being one of my first readers, ever since my childhood attempts at writing novels. Her help with this particular manuscript greatly boosted my confidence in the book's ability to work the way I wanted it to work, and I'm utterly grateful.

Thank you to my parents, Richard and Jennifer Proeschel, for sharing their love of history with me via classic movies, TV series, books, music, and trips to historical sites throughout my childhood. I suppose I should also thank my mom for being born in Illinois and for taking me to visit relatives and small towns in the "Land of Lincoln" years ago. Those visits most certainly helped me create my fictional town in this book and educated me in the way sweet corn "tastes like candy."

I'm extremely appreciative of historical societies, universities, and government agencies that have meticulously scanned documents from the past, including newspaper clippings about the Spanish influenza, letters and diaries from World War I, 1918 Alien Registration cards, photographs, and sheet music covers. Of particular help were the U.S. National Library of Medicine, the University of Michigan's online *Influenza Encyclopedia* (influenzaarchive.org), and the Library of Congress. Thank you also to archive.org and collectors of vintage music who have made recordings of songs from the 1910s available for all to hear in this modern age.

ACKNOWLEDGMENTS

Thank you to my team of supportive writer friends: Kim Murphy, Francesca Miller, Ara Burklund, Teri Brown, Miriam Forster, Kelly Garrett, Heidi Schulz, Amber J. Keyser, Lauren DeStefano, and members of SCBWI Oregon, The Lucky 13s, and Corsets, Cutlasses, & Candlesticks. My fellow writers never cease to cheer me on in all of my writing endeavors, and I'm grateful for their presence in my life, both in person and online.

Last but not least, I must give a special nod to Iggy, my dog of sixteen and a half years. He passed away on the same day that I turned in the first draft of this book, but he was by my side while I worked until the end. Here's to Iggy and his patience, and to our puppy, Wilbur, my newest writing companion.

About the author

About the book

Read on

Insights,
Interviews
& More . . .

Meet Cat Winters

CAT WINTERS was born and raised in Southern California, near Disneyland, which may explain her love of haunted mansions, bygone eras, and fantasylands. She received degrees in drama and English from the University of California, Irvine, and formerly worked in publishing.

Her debut novel, *In the Shadow of Blackbirds*, was released to widespread critical acclaim, including starred reviews in *Publishers Weekly, Booklist,* and *School Library Journal.* The novel has been named a 2014 Morris Award Finalist, a 2013 Bram Stoker Award Nominee, a *School Library Journal* Best Book of 2013, a *Booklist* 2013 Top Ten Best Horror Fiction for Youth, and one of *Booklist*'s 2013 Top Ten First Novels for Youth. She lives in Portland, Oregon, with her husband and two kids.

Visit her online at catwinters.com.

Tara Kelly

The Story Behind
The Uninvited

SOME BOOKS START with a single spark
of inspiration. Others evolve after a
series of ideas plant themselves inside
an author's head and germinate over
time. *The Uninvited* is one of the latter
types of novels. The basic plotline grew
out of various key moments in my recent
past: a phone call from an editor, the
deletion of a subplot about German-
Americans from another one of my
novels, a lighthearted tweet about
sending deceased characters from
my favorite historical TV series to
an afterlife version of a speakeasy.

Several nonfiction books played
a tremendous role in turning these
little seedlings of ideas into a full-
fledged novel. *The Uninvited* opens
with a murder. Although the victim,
Mr. Schendel, is fictional, his death
and the anti-German activity portrayed
throughout the novel stem directly from
information I gleaned from two books:
*The Last Days of Innocence: America at
War, 1917–1918*, by Meirion and Susie
Harries (Vintage Books, 1998), and
*Bonds of Loyalty: German-Americans
and World War I*, by Frederick C. Luebke
(Northern Illinois University Press,
1974). The texts introduced me to the
real-life murder of Robert Prager, a
German-born coalminer lynched by a
mob of 300 men and boys outside of
Collinsville, Illinois, on April 5, 1918.
The books also opened my eyes to other
startling events from World War I–era ▶

America: the passage of the Espionage and Sedition Acts to weed out disloyalty, the creation of the American Protective League, the disposal of German names and culture, the use of government detainment camps for German-Americans, and the various acts of violence committed against German-Americans. The more I researched, the more the element of "superpatriotism" in 1917 and 1918 America reared its head and begged to be put into a novel.

On the other side of the coin lay the German war experience. While working on a short story, I researched the history of the occupation of France during World War I, and I came across a series of excerpts from German war diaries in the form of the book *Convicted out of Her Own Mouth: The Record of German Crimes*, by H. W. Wilson (George H. Doran Company, 1917). I dug a little further and found the anonymous *A German Deserter's War Experience*, translated by J. Koettgen (B. W. Huebsch, 1917). The experiences of German soldiers in Belgium and France, as well as one German soldier's harrowing escape to America in the coal bunker of a ship, led to the creation of Daniel Schendel. When I first started working on the character, I knew he possessed secrets, but it took the discovery of these gripping and often difficult-to-read firsthand accounts to learn what those secrets were. Daniel is not meant to be an exact portrayal of specific real-life German soldiers and deserters, but a fictional character inspired by history.

Another factor I needed to consider when portraying the world of 1918 America was the "Spanish influenza" pandemic. *The Uninvited* is not the first novel I've written about this lethal and terrifying strain of the flu, which killed millions of people around the globe in the span of less than a year. Seeking to portray a different side of the flu's devastating effects, I turned to *Influenza and Inequality: One Town's Tragic Response to the Great Epidemic of 1918*, by Patricia J. Fanning (University of Massachusetts Press, 2010). Fanning's book details life in 1918 Norwood, Massachusetts, a small, ethnically diverse community that allowed prejudice to rule its health care system during the massive spread of the Spanish flu. The struggles of immigrants to receive access to doctors and hospitals during the pandemic tied in with my findings about superpatriotism. Even in the case of the flu, the push for everyone to be "100 percent American" during the war years deeply affected ordinary lives and too often resulted in deaths.

I chose to set *The Uninvited* in the fictional city of Buchanan, Illinois. I did not want to cast blame on one specific community. The fear of infiltration by the enemy, hate crimes, and the Spanish influenza affected every single region of the United States, not just Collinsville, ▸

Illinois, and Norwood, Massachusetts. Mistakes were made and heroes emerged in both big cities and small rural communities. *The Uninvited* is a fable about a tragic moment in history, and Buchanan is simply the fictional "all-American" town in which that fable is set.

I'm deeply indebted to the individuals who left behind their personal accounts of the struggles that they experienced during the World War I and the Spanish influenza years. Their courage and honesty moved me deeply, and I sincerely hope I've played a small part in ensuring that this heartbreaking yet fascinating moment in time will not be forgotten. ᴄᴡ

Reading Group Guide

1. Fictional newspaper clippings appear throughout *The Uninvited*. To what extent do these journalistic accounts of life during October 1918 enhance Ivy's descriptions of the time period? How would the novel differ without the inclusion of the newspaper excerpts?

2. Talk of ghosts, specters, and spirits pervade the novel, but what most haunts Ivy? What (or who) is the most frightening aspect of the book?

3. When Mrs. Rowan asks her husband if he and their son killed a man, Mr. Rowan responds, "That wasn't a man. He was a German." What factors most contributed to their decision to kill? How do modern hate crimes compare to those of 1918 America?

4. Ivy, once a recluse, aims to spread her wings and soar. May, a Chicago girl who has already tasted quite a bit of life, has withdrawn into her home. How important is it that these two women cross paths? How would Ivy's experiences have been different if she hadn't chosen to live with May?

5. Why are Ivy and Daniel drawn to each other, despite her initial prejudices against Germans and his knowledge of her family's guilt? How do they influence each other?

6. Jazz music is present throughout all of Ivy and Daniel's encounters. ▶

During their first moment of intimacy, Ivy says, "We were music. We were jazz. We were alive." What does music mean to each of them? How does music affect their relationship?

7. What impact do Nela and Addie have on Ivy? What lessons do they teach Ivy?

8. Flashbacks to Ivy's childhood and high school years appear throughout *The Uninvited*. What is it about Ivy's past that seems to affect her the most? Does she seem eager to escape her past, or to understand it?

9. Initially, Ivy doesn't react well when Daniel describes his experiences in Belgium. Are her reactions justified? How did you react to his confessions?

10. Ivy first becomes aware that all is not as it seems when Daniel says, "I can't *ever* leave this goddamned building." At what point did you begin to suspect the central secret in the book? How would rereading the novel change your experience with the book?

11. In one of the final chapters, Addie tells Ivy, "We're just going to be numbers in the newspaper. 'Statistics,' as my daddy called it." How would the portrayal of flu deaths in *The Uninvited* have differed if the dead were simply

mentioned as statistics? What was
your initial response to the way the
author chose to portray the deaths?

12. How would we, in our modern era,
    react to a pandemic the size of the
    1918 influenza compared to the way
    in which people in 1918 reacted?

13. When encountering Frank Rowan,
    the only words Daniel chooses to
    say to him are "I understand." What
    does he mean by this statement?

14. Is the final scene a happy or a tragic
    one? Why?

15. To whom does the title *The
    Uninvited* most seem to refer? ༂

The Uninvited Playlist

F. SCOTT FITZGERALD may have called the 1920s the "Jazz Age," but jazz was already smoking hot by the time the United States entered the Great War in 1917. A distinctly American invention, jazz grew out of the melting pot of New Orleans, Louisiana, in the late 1800s and early 1900s. African drum rhythms, military marches, ragtime, blues, spirituals, and other creative influences merged together in a style of music that inspired people of all races and backgrounds to stand up and dance.

The following is a playlist of the songs—mainly 1910s jazz and ragtime numbers—mentioned in *The Uninvited*. Most of the music, including the original recordings, can still be heard today, thanks to websites such as archive.org. Visit www.CatWinters.com to find links to samples of the music.

1. "For Me and My Gal," Van and Schenck, 1917

2. "The 'Jelly Roll' Blues," Ferd "Jelly Roll" Morton, 1915

3. "Livery Stable Blues," Original Dixieland Jass Band, 1917

4. "Tiger Rag," Original Dixieland Jass Band, 1917

5. "Joe Turner Blues," Wilbur Sweatman, 1917

6. "Bull Frog Blues," Six Brown Brothers, 1916

7. "I'm Sorry I Made You Cry," Henry Burr, 1918

8. "Maple Leaf Rag," Scott Joplin, 1899

9. Piano Concerto No. 1 in C Major, Ludwig van Beethoven, 1798

10. "Alexander's Ragtime Band," Irving Berlin, 1911

11. "Slippery Hank," Earl Fuller's Famous Jazz Band, 1917

12. "Nightingale Rag," Joseph Lamb, 1915

13. "Gun-Cotton Rag," Merle von Hagen, 1916

14. "Over There," George M. Cohan, 1917

15. Symphony No. 9 in D Minor, Op. 125, Ludwig van Beethoven, 1824 (lyrics in the final movement adapted from Friedrich Schiller's 1785 poem "Ode to Joy")

16. "Bill Bailey, Won't You Please Come Home?" Hughie Cannon, 1902

17. "Last Night Was the End of the World," Henry Burr, 1913 ▶

18. "At the Jass Band Ball," Original
Dixieland Jass Band, 1917

Courtesy of Library of Congress, Prints and Photographs Division, Bain Collection

U.S. Army Jazz Band from the First World War

D iscover great authors,
exclusive offers, and more
at hc.com.